DEL RIO

DEL RIO

A NOVEL

JANE ROSENTHAL

SHE WRITES PRESS

Published 2021
Printed in the United States of America
Print ISBN: 978-1-64742-055-0
E-ISBN: 978-1-64742-056-7
Library of Congress Control Number: 2020922740

For information, address:
She Writes Press
1569 Solano Ave #546
Berkeley, CA 94707

She Writes Press is a division of SparkPoint Studio, LLC.

For David

PART
ONE

1

CALLIE

Fletcher wanted me to meet him at the Starlight Lounge, an old roadhouse set on a bluff above the San Joaquin River a few miles south of town. I knew the place, knew as well as any rancher girl, or *campesina*, for that matter, that the Starlight was as close to big-city glamour as we'd ever get down here in the dusty Central Valley. At night, when the bar's revolving neon star scattered light over the tumbleweed and drooping locusts, you could forget for a while where you were, forget the bad air and the heat, the crummy trailer parks lined up at the edges of the fields. Back in the broad daylight, though, under the brutal sun, when Fletcher said we needed to talk, the place would have lost its magic, would have become once again just a squat, stucco building at the dead end of Del Rio Avenue, the booths and barstools filled with pesticide reps anxious to make a sale or ag inspectors reaching under the table for a payoff just to look the other way. The mood inside would have turned as grim and back-to-business as the daytime patrons.

I'd been standing in line at the Flor de Morelia Bakery on a sweltering August morning, waiting for a *café con leche* and a *pan dulce*, when my phone chimed and a quick look told me it was a Sacramento prefix, one I didn't recognize. It could have been anybody up at the capitol, a robo-call or solicitor, so I let the call go to voice mail. "You have reached the office of District Attorney Callie McCall" said everything that needed to be said. I was Del Rio's boss lady now. You'd be amazed how many people change their minds and hang up when they hear that. A second look at my phone, and the number jogged my memory. The call was from State Senator Jim Fletcher, and he was not one to hang up without leaving a message. Just as well I hadn't taken his call. It gave me some time to think.

Not that there was much to consider, really. If I ignored him, I'd never hear the end of it from every judge around. Senator Fletcher, my brother-in-law, got his way. Always. There'd be hell to pay if he didn't.

"*Has oido?* Did you hear?" Juan Barajas, the Flor's proprietor interrupted my train of thought and handed me my to-go bag. "The gypsies are back. Been bothering everybody over at the Valero station."

I dropped my phone in my purse. "Oh yeah?" I'd worry about Fletcher later. The gypsies were a more pressing issue, traveling up and down the middle of California, begging, turning tricks at the gas stations and truck stops, stealing. The last thing Del Rio needed was one more set of problems, but it looked like we had them.

"The gypsies, they're over in Simonian's almond grove, the one that's half dead," Juan continued.

"Anybody get in touch with Old Man Simonian?" I asked.

"Can't." Maryann Lopez aimed the tongs she was using to pull sweet rolls from the shelves in my direction. "He's got old-timer's. His kids put him in a facility, and they live up there in San Jose. Don't care about the farm." She went back to piling up her tray for the St. Aloysius ladies' Bible study.

"Anybody call the cops?"

"Nah." Juan shrugged. "The cops don't listen to Mexicans."

"Juan, the cops *are* Mexican. Half of them, at least."

"Yeah, that's why they don't listen to us." He laughed at his own joke.

"I'll send someone from the church," Maryann said. "See if they need anything. Soap, clothes, canned goods."

Great, I thought. *Nothing like a well-meaning church lady. She'll do-good the gypsies out of town.* They didn't like the nontravelers, as they called people who weren't one of them, snooping around. "Thanks, Maryann." I looked in the paper bag at the pastries. Two warm scones. *Es-scones*, Juan called them. "Hey, Juan, how come you don't put any raisins in your scones?"

Juan motioned me back to the counter. "Señora Callie, I'll tell you why. Wouldn't say this to no other white people. My father, he picked those grapes his whole life. Wasn't treated no better than a mule. Every raisin, to me, is a drop of my father's blood. Anyway, I put chocolate chips in them, just like Starbucks." He grinned, flashing a gold tooth.

I could feel the warmth of the fresh pastries from the bag and imagined magnifying the heat until it reached over 100. I thought of the farmworkers in the fields where the raisin grapes were drying on cardboard under the vines, where the vines twisted from the end bars across the wires like a crown of thorns for the head of every Jesús who made it across the border just to have a better life, sometimes just to survive. *No, don't think about it now*, I told myself. I'd start drowning in sorrow and never climb out, never get anything done. I tapped my heart to let Juan know I understood. "I'll look into the gypsies, see what I can do." Which I would. Because I owed him and his father. I owed all of them, when I thought about it.

Once the door closed behind me and I was standing outside the Flor, I set my coffee and bag on the car hood and listened to Fletcher's message. "Callie, Jim here. I'm driving up from LA and need to talk something over with you. Why don't you let me buy you lunch?"

So, Fletcher wanted a favor. That was a no-brainer. I heard a little too much bluster, too much strained bonhomie, in his voice. Now, there were only two other things I needed to know: What did he want, and what would he offer? At least he was buying. I sent back a two-word text: "Sure. Noon-ish."

Here's the thing I did know: No one comes to Del Rio at the end of August unless they absolutely have to. This time of the year, the valley temps soar to 112 degrees and the dry wind offers zero relief. Even the migrant workers have all headed to Oregon to pick fruit or up to the foothills to grow pot. On any given day, just for some excitement, you might spot a bunch of kids following snake tracks through the turned-to-dust farm roads, hoping to throw stones at a rattler just to watch it coil and strike. Everyone else was hunkered down under swamp coolers, waiting for the end of summer.

Why would a man who spent most of August in his beach house in Carmel, as far from the sweaty constituents he represented as he could get, drive over the Grapevine and up the 99 through Bakersfield just to have lunch at the Starlight with me and a bunch of fertilizer salesmen wining and dining their big clients? The answer is, he wouldn't. That is, unless he wanted something.

I turned on the ignition, let the engine drown out my questions about Fletcher's surprise visit, headed down Dinuba Street, drove into the parking lot behind the courthouse, and pulled into my reserved spot. Maintenance, I saw, had been hard at work. They'd already replaced the vandalized plaque, the one where the word "bitch" had been spray-painted at an angle over my name. I'd told Berta in maintenance not to worry about it when she called, said it gave me a certain je ne sais quoi. I could almost hear the sound of her side-eye over the phone. Well, at least they hadn't written "hag" or "*abuela*." It could have been worse, and besides, "bitch" made me sound like the badass I was aiming to be.

Reaching into the glove compartment, I pulled out my weapons—a tube of Chanel red lipstick and the Tiffany silver jewelry I never wore when I was trying to blend in with the *gente* over at the Flor. Here at the courthouse, it was another ballgame, and I needed to suit up. The earrings flashed in the rearview mirror, cold and bright, shiny as knife blades, and I drew on the lipstick like war paint.

Kicking off my flats, I dropped them in the back and reached under the passenger seat for the final touch—three-inch Prada nude heels. In them I stood six feet one and could go eyeball to eyeball with any good old boy in court. *Lista*, I thought—ready to rumble. Not too bad for a fifty-year-old broad. Grabbing my black Armani jacket, I draped it over my matching shift, lifted my Gucci tote, locked the Benz with a little *ping*, and headed into battle.

"Looking good, Miz C." Padhma Sundhrani, my assistant DA, whistled as she passed me on the stairs. I always took the stairs—good for the quads, and I never trusted the building's elevators anyway. "You got company," she told me, lifting her chin to the third floor, Del Rio's idea of a high-rise.

"Who?"

"The chief, Deputy Sheriff Rodriguez, and an inmate. They didn't say why."

I reached my office, squared my shoulders, and charged in. "Howdy, boys." I dropped my tote on the desk. "What got you three sent to the principal's office?"

Sheriff Rodriguez lifted his chin and raised his eyebrows in a way that I knew meant we should talk later. Chief Karkanian, though, didn't budge. Fine with me. He was a heavyset man. The only thing on him resembling a six-pack was the beer now lodged in his gut. He liked to conserve his energy, especially in August, when the building's last gasp of an air-conditioning system threatened to go into cardiac arrest any minute. I hung my jacket on the coat rack—hey, I didn't work on my biceps and triceps for nothing—and leaned against my desk, my legs stretched out on front of me, the sharp toes of my Pradas ready to do some serious damage.

The chief nodded at the heavily tattooed inmate. "This here's Manny Garcia. He ain't what he looks like. He's undercover on the force."

Garcia lifted his chin and rattled his arm shackles in a greeting.

"You can't undo the hardware?" I asked.

"Nah," Karkanian said. "We're supposed to be doing an inmate transfer up to the con camp in Miramonte. Someone's using a neighboring property to drop contraband. Gotta look like the real deal."

"I'm figuring this isn't a social call. Am I right?"

I glanced over at Rodriguez. His family and my family went way back—and yeah, I thought, we should talk later.

"You are indeed." Karkanian crossed his arms over his impressive belly. "Manny, you want to tell the DA what you told us? We figured you should hear this from the horse's mouth, McCall."

"Well, here's the deal." The undercover cop clanked as he shifted in his seat. "My partner and I were staking out a location at 431 Orosi Street, corner of Avenue 346."

"Meth lab, big-time," Karkanian added.

Manny nodded. "We're there for a couple of days, and we start to notice something weird going on in the next house. Men were bringing kids there like it was daycare or something, but they never picked them up. We got nothing else to do, so we look the place up on the iPad. Not a registered daycare center or nothing. So, the next day, we show up in a fake Verizon truck like we're doing maintenance, and my partner, whose wife got him all worked up over this—not that he should have been talking—says he's going to check it out. Goes over to the house, knocks on the door, is gonna tell 'em their landlines may be down for about an hour, woodpeckers dropping acorns in the box. He comes back and says, 'Stash house, dude. Nothin' but a couple guys and air mattresses on the floor.' Shit." Manny rattled his chains again.

"Wait, wait." I lifted my hand. "You said Avenue 346, right?

Which side? Because the south side is Mandarina County. Not my jurisdiction."

Manny turned to Karkanian, waiting for him to weigh in on this. I sensed I was on shaky ground for some reason. Okay, I knew the reason. I'd left the valley thirty years earlier and had lived in liberal, latte-drinking, no-common-sense San Francisco long enough that, in spite of my family name, I was going to have to start over from zero. A couple of years back in town wasn't enough to make up for my lapse.

Walking to the window, I fiddled with the mini-blinds and turned around so the guys would have to squint into the light to talk, feel less comfortable. The chief looked not at me or the window, but straight ahead, at Rodriguez, like, *This is your job, man.* Karkanian knew Rodriguez's history with my father and was just lobbing this ball into his court.

Rodriguez coughed into his fist. Asthma, I knew, from when he was a kid. It was a big problem here in the valley. Then he said, "See the way it works down here is like this: You do whatever it is you do in the next county over from your personal residence. That way, you can't lose property in a forfeiture, not unless the feds get involved. This info could come in handy. Something could cross over here in Del Rio."

So, I was getting schooled on "the way it worked down here." And by Alberto Rodriguez, son of one of my father's pickers. The men let that fact linger for a while, reminding me of what I should have remembered: that my Guccis and Pradas were worth only so much "down here"—hell, I could outfit myself at Boot Barn, for all they cared—and that, see, I really didn't remember how it worked down here at all. I walked back to my desk, my heels clicking less like the round of bullets I'd hoped for and more like some kid's cap gun, and breezed past my juris doctor diploma, lest anyone forget who was top dog in this office, especially me. "Please continue."

Karkanian spoke up finally, a thin smile of victory on his face. "Like, that meth house? We got the cookers, but the owner? Can't touch him." He turned to Manny Garcia.

"Like I said, my partner's all agitated now," Manny continued. "So he gets Reggie—you know, Regina Vazquez, over in Zoning?—to do a title search. And damn." He looked at Karkanian.

Karkanian went on, "Turns out, McCall, that residence used to be in a trust. Then, last month, someone put it into an LLC owned by some nonprofit called Homeowners' Relief.

I nodded. We both knew where he was going. Money laundering, concealing assets, you name it, but down here, probably drugs, given everything else.

"So, I put Garcia here back on it, and he did a little more digging. Know what? Your sister's name came up. Turns out she's CFO of Homeowners' Relief, so, technically, it's in your family." He paused, and I could hear my ears ring, the room was that quiet. "This here's a little courtesy call. Thought you'd want to know." Karkanian stood, shook his leg. "Damn thing's gone to sleep again. Rodriguez, give the inmate a hand. We don't get a move on, he's gonna miss his bologna sandwich for lunch. You take care, McCall."

After the sound of their stomping and rattling down the hall died down, I waited at the window until I saw the squad car pull out of the parking lot and head east on Reed Avenue, toward the mountains, now shrouded in summer's smoggy air. A little courtesy call, the chief had said—and speaking of calls, there was Fletcher popping up out of the blue. All around me, bad omens had appeared suddenly, like a swarm of crows. CFO? My sister never even finished college. She was only interested in getting her MRS degree. So how drunk was she when Fletcher got her to sign the LLC docs? What was he protecting himself from by having a rental unit in a county he didn't live in, like Rodriguez had said? Guess it was my job to find out.

I stood at the window a few more minutes, trying to figure out which direction Simonian's almond grove and the gypsies were. I could see the Del Rio water tower and the roof of Metcalf's Feed and Hay. What was that Mexican expression? "Small town. Large hell." Something like that. Then I thought about Mia and Fletcher. Small family. Large hell. You could say that, too.

The rest of the morning was pretty much normal ops around here. I had a plea bargain with a public defender and a little old grandma who was running a bordello out of an RV parked in her back-yard. Clients were long-haul truckers, mostly. The girls were from Mandarina County, or so they told her. But after this morning's con-versation with the chief, that tidbit gave me some pause. Next was Dewis Lempke, an old rancher who'd finally been thrown in jail for his umpteenth unpaid citation for driving without a license. We had to go a few rounds because he wanted me to show him where in the Constitution it said he had to have a driver's license. Besides, he wanted a trial with a jury of his peers. "You don't have any peers, Dewis," I told him. "There's no one else like you in Del Rio County." He also didn't want to spend more time in a cell with a bunch of tatted-up Bulldog Gang members, so we came to an agreement even-tually. When I looked at my watch, it was almost noon, time for lunch with Fletcher. I headed to my car.

Past Minami Packing Warehouse, past the Del Rio City water tower and Fruit Growers Supply Company, I turned left on Avenue 245 and headed through the orange groves, down toward the river. They were my orange groves, miles of them. Sometimes it was hard to get my mind around it, really. I was not only the DA but also Citrus Queen of the Valley. Trust me, I knew jack about farming. Inherited wealth. My Armenian father, Sevag "Grit" Giritlian, patriarch of Del Rio, left it to me. There were conditions, of course. There always were.

At least my POS ex, Sam McCall, couldn't get his mitts on it, much as he'd love to.

What Grit, and now I, didn't own of Del Rio County, Fletcher Family Farms owned. I knew the Fletchers wanted my land with a passion. Well, not the land, so much—I was sitting on water rights the size of Tahoe. Orange juice made a profit, but water rights? Now, they were worth real money.

About those conditions. Small-town stuff. A Hatfields and McCoys–type feud, the origins of which remained murky, but my father never forgave my sister for marrying Jim Fletcher. Her loss, my gain—hence the will, according to the terms of which, I was never to sell to the Fletchers.

"Never" was not a word in Fletcher's vocabulary. He knew people who knew people who could make it happen. Right now, I had something he wanted; I was in the catbird seat, and I intended to stay there. When he ran for governor, endorsed me for his senate seat, and made sure I won, we could talk. Until then, nada.

I pulled into the Starlight's lot, parked in the shade of a pepper tree, and saw that the place, the only real watering hole for miles around, was already filling up. I counted a Lincoln Town Car with government plates, a white Caddy, a few beat-up Corollas, one with a *Yo Amo Colima* bumper sticker, and a new black Lexus. The Town Car? County supervisor, counsel, something like that. They got the official ride. The Caddy? Garabedian, the Starlight's eighty-year-old owner. The Corollas? The help. And blistering under the valley sun? Jim Fletcher's Lexus, black and shiny as hot tar, not a speck of dust. He sure hadn't been out shaking farmers' hands in the fields. This meeting was just between us.

Standing under the Starlight's green awning, I took a deep breath like a diver about to go under, twisted the brass doorknob, and stepped into the air-conditioned gloom. The bartender, polishing highball glasses, looked up, recognized me, and nodded over his left shoulder toward the dining room. Sure enough, there was Big Jim Fletcher, Stanford quarterback from back in the day, taking up much of the booth's red leather real estate. He lifted a martini glass to his lips, sipped, and closed his eyes. I walked to the booth, slid into the seat. "You needed to see me?"

"Callie, good of you to come. Even a small town can keep a prosecutor busy, but you gotta eat, right?" He dabbed his lips with his white linen napkin and raised an arm toward the bartender. "What's your poison?"

"Diet Coke. And it's district attorney. And yes, I'm busy."

"Moving up in the world, aren't you? Well, country life seems to suit you. You're looking tan and fit. Sure you don't want to join me? Best martini in the valley."

"Here's a shock: I don't drink on the job."

The waiter placed the Diet Coke can and a frosted glass in front of me, and I traced a line through the condensation on the glass, showing off my just-manicured nails, my talons, signaling that I hadn't lost my San Francisco edge. "You wanted to see me. *Por qué?* as we say down here."

He didn't answer right away, just stared. Sizing me up, I guessed.

I poured the Coke into the glass, stirred the ice cubes with the straw, and let the Spanish chatter you hear coming from restaurant kitchens all over California fill the silence. A law professor once said to me, "If you're talking, you're losing." I'd wait until he asked for what he wanted. I didn't like to lose.

I could see why my sister had fallen for Jim. Nothing wrong with his physical attributes: a full head of salt-and-pepper hair, chiseled features, all of this movie star–ness framed by a bespoke Oxford shirt and perfectly chosen silk tie. And my sister, who was a pretty well-preserved, middle-aged lush—what did he see in her? Well, besides their fondness for booze? It would have been the land, the Giritlian name, which meant a lot down here. Thought he could win over the old man. Didn't happen, so now he was working on me.

Fletcher swirled the olive around in his glass, lifted the toothpick, and waved it at me. "What? Why so glum? You carrying your father's torch against me? He's dead. Let it go."

"You were the one who said it was important. I don't have all day here, Jim. Crime never sleeps."

Fletcher plunged the olive back into his drink and took another sip, his eyes scanning the room. He nodded at someone by the bar, and I looked over my shoulder. I'd been right about the Town Car. Robert B. Freemark, Del Rio county counsel, just out of USC, daddy a big raisin grower, big enough to make old Amarkanian, the former counsel, decide to retire early. It hadn't been a pretty story, hadn't won Freemark any love on the board of supes, but he really wasn't too clear on the concept that he might want to work a little harder to win some. He slithered across the room toward our booth, staffer in tow.

"I'll be damned if it isn't our esteemed state senator." Freemark beamed. "Senator, good day. What brings you here, and what are you doing these days, McCall? Aren't you supposed to be over at the courthouse, prosecuting pot growers?"

Okay, so I couldn't help myself. This guy was so deep in the cartel growers' pockets, he could be lint. "Freemark, you know something? I'm after the big guys. . . ." I paused but never took my eyes off his. "You know, the ones in the county government who make it all possible." I waited to see if my dart hit the board, and when he turned red, I thought, *Yup. Score.*

Fletcher cut us off. "Family business. This is my sister-in-law. I gather you two have met."

Freemark's head jerked back ever so slightly; his gray eyes widened. Good. A little fear could be useful. I buried my face in the menu, deciding on the rib-eye, the priciest thing I could find. "Oh, by the way," I said, keeping my eyes on the list of entrées, "how long have you been reviewing that ordinance, Freemark—the one that's supposed to give me the big fines I can hold over the growers' heads? Nine months, eighteen months? I never could figure out how Kern County cracked down on the cartel so fast. Maybe Bakersfield's county counsel is just smarter than Del Rio's. What do you think?" I tossed the menu onto the table, a gambler throwing down a full house. No one in California ever wanted to be compared unfavorably to Bakersfield, not even in Del Rio.

Fletcher raised his empty glass at the waiter, indicating another was in order. "Now, no fighting, you two." He turned in his seat, faced Freemark. "You just might be looking at your next state senator." He winked my way, because, hey, that's just what you do with the little gals, right? "I'm thinking of talking her into running for my seat when I move on. I'd start kissing up to her if I were you."

Whoa. Hadn't seen that one coming. I'd thought I would have to ask, if not beg—do a little more horse trading. Of course, he'd known all along what I wanted, knew why I'd gone after this job. I was going to run for Fletcher's seat after he termed out. If no one came to Del Rio in August, no one stayed here, either, not in August or any other month—including me. If it weren't for the Mexicans, the valley would be full of ghost towns. Even the dollar stores would have shuttered their buildings long ago and moved on. I sipped my Coke, kept my eyes focused on Fletcher, tried not to give anything away.

He was sweating now, wiping his forehead with the napkin. You could, if you were suspicious, and boy howdy was I, figure the cause was more than middle age mixed with gin. He wanted something big in return. Well, he could forget the farm. The farm was my campaign launch pad. George W. had the Crawford Ranch; Callie McCall would have Del Rio Farms. Think of the visuals.

Freemark was mumbling something about working well with all branches of California government, when the waiter came to the table and interrupted the blah-blah. Freemark nodded and made a quick exit. *Adios, pendejo.*

"Rib-eye, rare." I told the waiter. Had it cooked just the way Vato, my golden retriever, liked it. Fletcher ordered a porterhouse and another martini, even though he hadn't finished the last one. That made *número tres.*

"I can make a call, Jim. The minute you pulled out of here, a cop would be on your tail. Drunk-driving arrest wouldn't look too good for a guy planning to run for governor, would it? Or are laws just for the little people?"

Fletcher glared. "Okay, let's cut the crapadoodle here. I've got a question for you. I'll give you credit for having enough brains to have already figured that out. Here's the deal." Fletcher lifted the martini glass, sipped. "Any idea where your do-gooding brother is?"

Not the question I expected, and I admit it caught me up. But actually, no, I didn't. If he wasn't at work in San Francisco at that *other* big law firm on Kearny, bigger than my former big law firm, I had no idea. Not that I'd tell Fletcher that.

The waiter came with dinner salads. I pushed the iceberg lettuce around on my plate, waited for Fletcher to continue.

"I guess not." He poured ranch dressing over his salad. "Well, let me bring you up to speed. He quit his job at Barker, Mason, and Jenkins. Ring a few bells?"

Nobody left BMJ. Wrong. Apparently they did, if they were my brother, Mike. Why was I just hearing about this?

"Do you know how many people would kill for that job? You two were always thick as thieves. What is it? The twin thing? First you go off the rez and wind up in Del Fucking Rio, and now Mike has flown the coop with that fag boyfriend of his, the French guy."

Listening to drunks was always so much fun. I'd forgotten.

"Oh, *pardonnez-moi*, I should have said 'husband.' Any idea where the happy couple is? Frenchie is AWOL, too."

Fletcher pushed an envelope my way, my name written on front in my sister's chardonnay-fueled cursive. The day was only getting worse.

The waiter removed the salads, put the steaks in front of us, large knives on the side. I started carving.

"Your sister went to his house in Twin Peaks, got the number of a neighbor who was watering the plants. Here's what Mia wants you to do." He aimed his steak knife in my direction.

The request was as follows: Go to Mike's house, find the neighbor, wave my credentials in her face to get the key and look around. But here's where it got interesting: If anything came up, I was to give Fletcher the information and let him deal with it. *"Comprende?"* Fletcher plunged the knife into his steak.

Was there more to this story? You bet there was, and I was certain that Fletcher was keeping it to himself. Mike's being gone for a few days was no big deal. So what was? I listened to Fletcher drone on. My poor sister, worried sick.

We were definitely veering off the truth-o-meter here, what with the worry, something I never associated with Mia. Alcohol has a way of taking care of worries, at least for a while. Not that the truth mattered so much. I knew all I needed to know. Fletcher was up to his eyeballs in something that my brother knew about. Fletcher wasn't sticking his neck out this far because my sister was worried about Mike. I figured it was in my best interest to find out exactly what he was worried about. Sitting here a little longer, listening to his lies, was nothing a long, hot shower wouldn't take care of if I felt totally slimy afterward, which was a definite possibility.

My rib-eye was half gone. The rest was US prime for the dog, courtesy of the California taxpayers. Probably one of the better ways Fletcher was spending their money. I let him wait a little longer and then nodded at the envelope. "Obstruction of justice, Jim—that's a big favor to ask. You want to run all this by me again?"

Liars can never tell the story the same way twice. You watch them drop one little stitch, and damn, if the whole knitting job doesn't go kerflooey. Let's see what he wouldn't get right this time. I looked around the restaurant like I couldn't care less about this conversation and noticed that Freemark had gone and Mandeep Singh and Ben Lawson now occupied his booth. Singh farmed walnuts, a very big export to China, and a very big water suck, too, while Lawson farmed the farm bill. How many acres had he fallowed this year, and what did the federal government he loathed pay him to grow nothing?

"Don't get on a legal high horse. This is family, Callie. Are you following me? That's why I drove up here this morning. You have any idea how many meetings I canceled?"

"Shit happens, Jim. What can I say?"

Fletcher, sighed, gave me the dead-eye, and started the story again. My brother, an attorney, like I was, and his husband, Francois—an analyst for a global private equity firm with holdings in Singapore real estate; African oil, gas, and minerals; Hong Kong restaurants and hotels; US medevac helicopter companies; Hollywood movie studios; and even donut chains—hadn't answered their phones since last week. Both voice mails were full and not accepting messages, and neither Mike nor Francois was responding to texts.

"It's probably nothing, other than that they're self-centered little pricks, but Mia is very upset, what with your brother's lifestyle choices and all. Thinks something's wrong." Fletcher fluttered his hands around his temples. "You know, female-intuition stuff."

A marimba cell phone tune rang from the seat somewhere. He reached for his jacket and pulled the phone from the inside pocket, glancing at the number. "Speak of the devil." He tapped his cell. "Hiya, doll. Yeah. I'm working on her." He shrugged at me.

The restaurant had filled up, and the diners' voices hummed along in a low roar as wine was poured and deals were made. Clearly, word had gotten around that Fletcher was here; I caught a few heads turning in our direction. Since they had no idea what we were talking about, being seen with him could be a good thing—I could let his star power rub off on me. As Fletcher himself always said, "It's not what you know, it's who you know."

Sliding out of the booth, I pointed to the ladies', figuring I'd leave Fletcher alone to talk my sister up from the depths of Lake Vino. Mike and Fran had no doubt taken a little vacay and, given conservative Senator and Mrs. Fletcher's feelings about their relationship—let's just say they wouldn't be invited for Thanksgiving— had not told them of their plans. Mike's quitting his job? Okay, I thought, clicking the bathroom stall lock, more of a problem. But, Mike *was* a do-gooder, like Fletcher said, a shy do-gooder. Corporate law had never been a good fit for him. He should have been over at 350.org in some closed office, figuring out how to sue the fossil fuel industry.

I stood at the sink, washing my hands, looking down to avoid the mirror, not that there was anything wrong with my looks. I knew I was a better-than-average-looking, silver-haired, fifty-year-old divorcee with a fat paycheck and a lot of power in a dead-broke county. I just didn't want to see the fierce expression I sometimes had; I was afraid I might try to tamp it down just when I needed it most. Ambition, it's called, and most people, I had discovered the hard way, find it really unattractive in members of the fairer sex. But you know what? It was time to let go of what other people—mostly dudes—thought. Time to let my menopausal bitch flag fly. I'd earned my right to some big-time attitude. I yanked the paper towels a little harder than necessary, tossed them into the bin, and pushed open the door.

Turning the corner into the dining room, I saw that Fletcher had ended his conversation with my sister and was down to brass tacks over at Singh and Larson's table, laying on the charm, glad-handing, promising favors. Nice work if you could get it—that, plus the Lexus and the beach house. I took my seat and pulled out my phone, just so I didn't look like Fletcher had dumped me.

Most of the messages were a Pandora's box I didn't want to open now, but one caught my eye: Sheriff Rodriguez giving me a heads-up about a bust—"2gs pot 12:15 hrs. Hmong melons Sanger. LO knows nada." Translation: "Two thousand pot plants just now located outside Sanger in a field of bitter melons. Hmong gangs. Big landowner claims he knows nothing."

Orale! I texted back.

And then I saw it. Fletcher's phone, just like mine. A split-second impulse surged from my brain, which was processing information in nanoseconds: *Fletcher is lying; his phone is a gold mine.* It pushed my hand to his phone and locked my fingers around it. Before I knew it, I'd switched mine for his and dropped Fletcher's in my purse. Time to beat a hasty retreat. I grabbed the boxed-up leftovers for Vato and headed for the door. Waving the envelope at Fletcher, I said, "I'll be in touch. You're paying, right?" I nodded toward the check on the table.

"Hey, not so fast," he called out. "I ran into your ex, Sam McCall, the other day."

McCall. The name hit like a blow, almost doubling me over. I forced my spine into the upright, operating position and turned in time to see a sadist's icy smile stretch across Jim Fletcher's face. "Yeah." He had his hand on Singh's shoulder, just one of the boys, all of them staring at me, enjoying the show. "He's helping Mia with her charity work. Says he's glad you found your niche."

Hoping to pull off a casual reaction, I waved the envelope just to remind Fletcher I still had the upper hand. "Oh, really? Sam McCall? Charity work? Hard to believe," I said. "He's a big lobbyist now, isn't he?" I let that sink in for Singh and Lawson before I continued. "Finance industry, right? Well, like they say, gotta dance with them that bring ya."

I waited for a minute, staring the men down, as all the while my inner bitch shouted, *Yeah, I've found my niche, all right. Tell Sam McCall that when I'm state attorney general—because that's my plan here, gentlemen—I'll squash his lying, corrupt ass like a bug.* "Have a nice day, everyone." I turned to the door with exactly one goal in mind: make it to my car before the impulse to flip off Fletcher took over whatever self-control I had left.

And then I remembered the phone, the letter, and the fact that he was three martinis to the wind.

I had this. No middle finger needed.

2

CALLIE

Even at nine o'clock at night, my parents' old farmhouse—grandparents', really—held the heat like it would fight to the death before giving it up. The first thing I'd done once I got home was open all the windows and turn on the fans, but the temperature had dropped only a couple of meager degrees. Those old Armenian farmers were tough. I mean, with the genocide and all, what was a little heat? Who needed central air? Toughness was coiled in my DNA, too, generations of it ready to double down at a moment's notice. A therapist once told me that was my problem. Really? Since when could you be too tough? Never in my world.

Sheriff Alberto Rodriguez and I sat on the back porch, drinking cold Coronas, rehashing the day's events, the chief's visit, and throwing the ball to Vato over and over again. I mentioned I'd had lunch with Fletcher, told him about Freemark, but that was it, nothing about the phone or Mike, the envelope, the mention of an endorsement. I wasn't one to blab. Guess I got that from El Patrón, as the workers used to call my dad.

I lifted the ball, aimed at the fence, and threw. Vato was off in a flash, and I went over in my mind the whole series of events that occurred after I'd left the Starlight. I'd driven over to River Vista Park, stopped the car, and—first things first—tried to remove the image of Sam's charity work, meaning he was doing something sleazy, from my consciousness by breathing through one nostril at a time until I almost bored myself into oblivion, which didn't take long.

A sandy beach stretched along the banks of the San Joaquin; some leafy sycamores shaded the picnic tables. I wandered over to a table, figuring I'd sit there for a while, try to lose the racing heartbeat I got when I was in a rage, which I was, before I plunged into Fletcher's voice mail, searching for the dirt.

Some Mexican kids splashed in the shallow water under the watchful eye of their mother. River Vista Park was hardly the Riviera, but when I saw it through their eyes—the shady trees, the green grass, the cool water, the remains of lunch on a blanket, and the leisure to enjoy it—this place was paradise. The woman wasn't cleaning toilets in some Mexican resort hotel; her kids weren't selling Chiclets on the street. My job was to keep it that way for them—a safe place to live a normal life. I remembered Fletcher's phone and pulled it out of my bag.

I was in luck—no password, so I could just swipe—and voilà! Messages. They were pretty much what you'd expect: stuff about committee meetings, the next farm bureau town hall, a few from my sister, and one from a hotel in Mexico. "Señor *Flaychair?* This is Concha at Ventana Azul. We have your reservation. All is confirmed. Please contact me for information about your arrangements. Gracias."

The next one was from Mike. "Fletcher? Mike here. What I said still holds. Francois can back that up." That stopped me right there in my tracks. What still holds? I remembered Fletcher's sneering *pardonnez-moi.* He was probably not too happy about having a gay brother-in-law. Wouldn't help with his base. Another message was from a guy named Bud with an outfit called Pescado de Oro, some fishing trip connected with the Mexican hotel.

Mexico? Fishing? Another junket on the taxpayers' dime—
Fletcher's MO. I went back to my car and, grabbing an almost
dried-up pen from the glove compartment, wrote down the messages
on the back of an old receipt. Maybe the Mexico thing could come in
handy. I could threaten to leak it to the press the next time Fletcher
claimed there was no money for alternate drug-rehab sentencing in
Del Rio. I listened to a few more, until I heard Sam McCall's voice.
"Jim, how about you stop by my office on your way out of town?
Something I want to run by you over a most excellent single-malt." I
must have played that message five times, but there was no nuance I
could discern, no undercurrent, which was too bad. Just Sam being
his übersuave self. Finally, I hit the keypad, tapped in my own phone
number, and waited for Fletcher to pick up.

"Shit!" Jim shouted. "What the hell? How did you do a dumbass
thing like that?"

"I'll be there in twenty minutes, Jim. Sorry. Get off at the Olive
exit and go to Carl's Junior—slum it a little, have a cup of coffee, see
how the real folks live. Oh, and learn how to talk to a lady. I'll be there
before you know it."

Now, throwing the ball to the dog, I wondered if I shouldn't be
thinking more about Mike, be worried about him, instead of moping
around about Sam. I'd texted my brother a couple of times, but no
response, which was a little weird. Hey, he and Fran could have taken
off for Napa and ditched the phones so they could relax. Still, I was
trying to figure out why Mia and Fletcher were so hot to get in touch
with him, fooling around with ideas. Maybe they just wanted to
court the gay community in San Francisco and were trying to pressure Mike to campaign for Jim. Good luck with that.

Rodriguez got up to get a couple more beers and called out from the
kitchen, "Your sink's clogged again. Didn't I just fix this damn thing?"

"I should get Lupe a garbage disposal." Lupe was Grit's house-
keeper, had been for years.

"She won't use it. She thinks the machine will pull her hand down there and chew it up." He shrugged. *"Suegras."* Mothers-in-law. "Rosie and I go through the same thing at our house. I'll bring a piece of screen to put over the drain. *No te preocupes."* Don't worry.

"Where is Rosie" I asked. He really shouldn't be here; he should get back to his wife and kids. He put in long enough hours as it was.

"Rosie wants me to keep you company. She says you shouldn't be all alone."

"I can shoot straight, B-Rod. Not to worry."

"That's what I told her. I said, you know how white girls are. They like their space."

"What'd she say to that?"

"She said, 'What's space?' Anyway, it's Kentucky Fried Chicken night tomorrow at my house. You game for dinner?"

"That's an actual event at your house?"

"Yeah, it's called my night to cook."

Then, against my natural proclivities and because I needed to bounce stuff off somebody, I told him a little about Fletcher's surprise visit. Nothing about the phone, though—I was just testing the waters.

"So, what do you think?" Rodriguez asked, looking over at the orchard, a deep, black sea of leaves.

"Next year, I'll plant mandarins over there." I pointed to the plowed field to the north. "They don't transport well, but restaurants in the Bay Area pay a fortune for them come December." Didn't hurt to be a real farmer if you wanted them to vote for you down the line.

"You work like a Mexican, Callie." Rodriguez laughed, took another swig.

"Hell, I work like an Armenian farmer who hires a whole lot of Mexicans, like El Patrón. You know that."

"What I do know is that my brother's kids think all Mexicans ever do is grow pot. Hard raising them here. Not like it used to be. Mine are little, but I'm dreading middle school, you want to know the truth. But I wasn't talking about *las naranjas*. I was asking about Fletcher. What do you think? Why'd he stop in Del Rio?"

"I don't know what to think, yet." I let it go at that.

Vato dropped the tennis ball he'd chased down at my feet. "Good dog," I told him, as he panted, waiting for the ball to fly into the air again. I picked it up, lifted my arm, and aimed at the chain link fence that separated the yard from the groves. "Jesus, that dog could do this forever." I turned to Rodriguez. He was staring at me. "What?"

"Anything you're not telling me?"

"Not really."

"Why am I not believing this?" Rodriguez stood, waved his empty Corona bottle. "You keep a lot of things close to the vest, Cal. You recycle, right?"

"Can in the laundry room. See you tomorrow. Another day, another deadbeat."

"You got that," Rodriguez said, opening the screen door. He'd let himself out like he always did. He'd been in and out of this house since he was a kid and his father was my father's foreman.

It was so quiet out here in the boons that I could track Rodriguez's progress by the fading drone of his engine, straight down Buttonwillow, right on Kings Canyon. Then, he was gone.

Nights were long here in Del Rio. A middle-aged lady DA's love life can sort of suck. Guys run the other way when they know you can send them to jail. Vato came back with the damp ball, dropped it on the ground again, and waited, his whole body vibrating. I took his pointed face in my hands and rubbed my forehead against his silky fur. "You're a good dog, Vato. Best damn dog ever."

Then I lifted the ball one more time and threw.

By eleven, the house thermometer read 78 degrees, cool enough to bring Vato in. I closed the screen door, slipping the lock's hook into the little eye, poured kibble into a large metal bowl, and filled another one with water. Without the sound of Vato's food snarfing or his collar rattling against the bowl, I might have thought I'd gone deaf. The place was that dead quiet. It was, as Mike had said many a time, in the damn middle of nowhere. Yeah, but it was beautiful, I told him, surrounded by orchards, majestic palms, and the snow-capped Sierras as a backdrop.

"And meth trailers and car boneyards," Mike replied.

"Yeah, that's why I'm in business."

I flopped down on the sofa and grabbed the remote. Bill Maher was going through his new rules, which kept my mind off things for a while, but after that, there wasn't much—just PBS droning on, a bazillion TV preachers, Univision soap operas, ESPN reruns. I hit the OFF button and tossed aside the remote. It landed next to the envelope Big Jim had shoved my way at lunch. I reached for my purse, pulled out my all-purpose Swiss Army knife, slit the envelope open, saw the check, and read the letter. Then I read it again with all my pistons firing. My sister was offering me a bribe. No, wait. Fletcher was offer-ing me a bribe to obtain and conceal information, and he was using my sister, a drunk who had no clue about legal peril—hers, mine, or his—to do it. But Fletcher knew, and this way, he'd be held blameless. I, on the other hand, would be under the bus, flat as roadkill, if some-thing was actually wrong and an investigation ever happened.

I walked into the kitchen, grabbed my phone, and carried it to my bedroom, punching in Mike's number as I climbed the stairs. "Mike, dude, call me now." I set the phone on the nightstand by my bed and stared for a good five minutes. Nothing. I left it on just in case, pulled on a T-shirt, and slipped into bed.

The phone rang at 5:30 a.m., dragging me out of one of those deep-sleep dreams. Not a good one. True that. But I was stuck in it like a horse in a muddy creek, struggling to get out. I kept hearing a bell ringing. When I finally hauled myself awake, I hit the alarm, only to realize it wasn't the damn alarm. I grabbed the phone, hoping Mike was calling from some other time zone. It wasn't Mike. The number was the dispatcher. I punched it in.

"Hey, Lorena. Callie here."

Lorena's voice came out scratchy with static. "Callie? Stand by."

The next voice was the chief's. Karkanian didn't speak, he barked. "Got an incident, McCall. You're right there. Fletcher Family Farms. You know it. You're only a mile away, gal."

Oh yeah, I knew it.

"Crew boss called in," Karkanian continued. "Worker found a body part in a grove. Get out there before the damn United Farm Workers lawyer comes and tells the hombres to clam up. I'm sending Rodriguez to calm the waters. You and him can *habla* the lingo. Tell that Farm Workers' lawyer not to get his panties in a bunch. Nobody's getting papers checked; nobody's calling Immigration. I've already got the chopper on its way in case anybody runs. Make sure the labor contractor, Lopez, knows we'll go after him, too, if somebody does. We'll figure he's hired illegals and is stealing their pay. I'm sick of these contractor assholes. Tell him I'll personally be up his nose."

"Roger that, Chief. I'm in my car as we speak."

"McCall? Another thing. Heads-up. All they found was an arm. A kid's arm, they tell me. Then pretty much all hell broke loose. A kid, for Christ's sake."

And with that, he was off the line.

By the time I got to the grove, the sun had just crested the tops of the distant, blue Sierras, the sky a bright, cloudless glare, and Rodriguez was talking to the crew boss while a few other men milled around a wikiup shade tent. I drove past, turned around at Dinuba Avenue, and headed back to the scene. Pulling onto a dirt spur on the opposite side of the road, I checked the rearview mirror. Some of the guys were leaning on trucks, some just standing like statues, their faces blank. It was going to be like pulling teeth. They weren't giving up anything. In fact, I was surprised anyone had even reported the body, which meant—it was slowly dawning on me—they hadn't. What had the chief told me? The crew boss had called it in. I could tell by the body language between him and Rodriguez that that was not the case. None of these guys would have called in squat. So who had, and why? Ah, that was the question, wasn't it?

I pushed open the door, swung my legs around, and stood by the car, listening to the sound of the circling chopper and watching the men's faces as they registered *procuradora, gringa,* trouble. Then, crossing the road and flashing my ID at a few of the guys, I asked, "*Jefe?*" and one of the men nodded in B-Rod's direction, to the man standing next to him. "He know anything?" I asked Berto. But the crew boss just shrugged and told me what I'd already figured out: He hadn't seen anything. He didn't know what the hell I was talking about.

"Just get a statement, Sheriff," I said to Rodriguez. "Contact numbers. You know the drill."

By now, word was out all over town. A big white truck with Fletcher Family Farms painted on the doors turned in to one of the grove roads, kicking up dust, followed almost immediately by Nick Lozada, the UFW lawyer. Nick got out of his car and headed my way, Steve Barnes, Fletcher's general manager, close behind. A regular powwow.

"You want to tell us what's going on here, Callie?" Steve shook my hand, nodded to Lozado.

"Homicide, Steve, Nick. That's all I'm saying. Don't go past the crime scene tape. Don't talk to the workers until Sheriff Rodriguez gives you the okeydoke."

"No one talks to the men without me," Nick said. "I'm their attorney. You tell Rodriguez to stop right there."

"Wait a minute, Nick," Steve chimed in. "None of these guys are union. You don't represent them. Not that I hear tell."

"Nick?" I waited for a fight.

"I got boilerplate contracts in the car. All they have to do is sign."

"Steve?"

"They go union, and they don't get hired."

"Oh, really?" Nick said, sneering. "Can I quote you on that?"

"Sure. And here's something else you can quote me on: The damn union can go to hell. We pay good wages. We don't need you riling everyone up."

I held up my hand. I'd heard enough. Barnes was pissed because Fletcher Farms had just lost a labor dispute in the higher court.

"Nick, I'll walk you over there. You can ask. But you, Barnes, and I know they aren't signing up, not with Steve breathing down everyone's neck. So, here's what we're going to do." I told Barnes I was sending everyone over to sit in the cool, comfortable office, where they could see what desk jobs looked like. Furthermore, he was paying them for a day's labor. This was met with a groan of protest.

"Hear me out, Steve. You're a smart man. Two reasons you're going to do this. *Numero uno*"—I held up my thumb—"the last thing Fletcher needs is an ICE raid. And right about now, the feds have got wind that we have a bunch of sitting ducks just waiting to be picked off. Hiring illegals? Not good for Big Jim, and I'll bet my last nickel that's what you've got. *Numero dos*"—I aimed my index finger toward the sky—"doesn't take much to spook the workers. This place gets known as *los árboles del muerto*, the trees of death, and next January all your oranges will rot on the limbs. So, out of the goodness of your heart, you're cutting them all checks, and the only thing they have to do is head to the office. We'll send a van. I want their names and fingerprints, or no check. Got it?"

Nick was hopping from one foot to the other. "I know. Nick. I know. You go over to the office, you video the whole damn thing. If it's not on the up-and-up, you send me the video. I'll let you ride in the van with the guys. The minute the van pulls off Fletcher property, you start passing around the cards and telling them why they should join up."

I turned to Barnes. "It's a free country, Barnes, last I heard. That's why these immigrants are here and not back in El Salvador, getting picked off by the MS-13. Once they're off your property, it's none of your howdy-do."

The grove was five acres by about the same, trees so close together you couldn't stand under them, leaves thick and difficult to maneuver around. Rodriguez and I walked along the ridge between the trees, I on the left side, Rodriguez on the right. Rodriguez aimed his flashlight, taking slow steps, careful to feel his way and not step on evidence.

"Rodriguez," I said, "take me through a worker's day, just like everything was *todo normal.*"

From his description, it didn't take a genius to realize that the only way a guy was going to find anything was if he stepped on it. He'd be too busy lopping off limbs, checking for cankers, disease, dead wood. He wouldn't have time to study the landscape, time being money and all.

The body part would have had to be in the ditches next to the mounds where the trees were planted. That was the only way a picker, working as fast as he could, would have found it if—and a big if it was—that worker had called it in and wasn't copping to the deed. He wouldn't have been looking around in the dark shadows under the trees. Still a needle in a haystack, still a job for the cadaver dogs, but it was a start.

We reached the trees by the river, and Rodriguez and I made our way down the bank. We'd pretty much given up at that point, were just waiting to hear the dogs. The river was still running, the flow from the Yellow Trout Dam coming down this way.

"What's your best guess, B-Rod? Someone planted this here, right?"

"Could be coyotes dragged it. Could be a shallow grave."

We'd find out soon enough; the detectives would have to start looking for more body parts, for a grave, and they had only so many resources at their disposal. They'd search the grove where the ground was softer for a day, maybe. Beyond the grove, there was no point, just hardpan, bone-dry dirt you'd have needed a jackhammer to dig up.

A heavy weight bore down on my chest. I straightened my back and rolled my neck just to break up the tension I was holding in and stared past the sycamores on the other side of the river, past a bare field, to a makeshift trailer park. Not legal, no hookups—I'd swear to it. I pointed to the trailers. Now that I thought about it, the property was Old Man Simonian's. These trailers were the gypsies'.

Rodriguez shrugged. "That's Code Enforcement's job. We got enough to do."

"Worth talking to them, don't you think?"

He shrugged again. "Gypsies. Romany people, we're supposed to call them now. It's PC. They've only been there a week. We'll have to see how old the evidence is. They'll lie anyway, but CYA is the name of the game. Cover your ass, right?"

"I thought it was protect and serve." I fist-bumped Rodriguez just as we heard the dogs barking. He got up and headed out to meet the K-9 team and the medical examiner. The dogs sounded so happy. If you didn't know the dark side of the valley, you'd be thinking, *How lovely—a peaceful day in the country.* You'd be conjuring up images of making orange marmalade, putting up the jam in old Ball jars. You'd be thinking about Martha Stewart and her designer chickens and espaliered fruit trees. And you would be so completely wrong.

Climbing up the riverbank, I saw the dog handler leading the

K-9s down another row and the ME, Tom Morven, kneeling, looking at something on the ground. Someone had thrown a pound of
bacon some distance away from the evidence, and a thick swarm of
meat bees buzzed around it, away from the deceased, or part of the
deceased. Tom stayed kneeling even as I approached.

"What do we have?"

"Stay back until we get the pictures, McCall. You know the pro-
cedure. Gotta keep it dry. Don't even want you breathing near this."

Tom never talked until all his ducks lined up, until he could tell
you something beyond a shadow of a doubt. So, the arm, reaching out,
rigid and black from livor mortis, could be male, female, Mexican
or anything, probably older than nine or ten, but maybe not. Odd
thing was, there was some kind of bracelet on the arm. I took out my
phone, snapped a picture, AirDropped it to Rodriguez.

"No *problema*, Tom. You're the man."

I would have to wait to ask if the arm looked like coyotes had
dragged it, or if humans had severed it, before or after the kid died. I
knew Tom wasn't chatty while he worked. I looked over at Rodriguez.
He was halfway down the row, on his cell. He clicked off as I got there.

"Hey, B-Rod, what kind of person leaves a bracelet on a murder
victim?"

"A stupid person."

"Or someone in a big hurry. Or . . ." It hit me. That arm was
planted. I was sure of it. Could have been the gypsies, if someone
had paid them enough and if the kid wasn't one of their own. Could
have been one of the workers. "I want that bracelet on that arm in
the morgue, B-Rod. Don't let it out of your sight. You tell the coroner
no one goes near it, or I'll charge everyone with tampering with evidence. Everyone."

Rodriguez raised his eyebrows, started to speak.

"Yeah, I'm talking about you, too. You tell them down at the
morgue that I don't play. Let the word get around. Things have a

way of walking out of that morgue, and this bracelet is not going anywhere. Another thing: fingerprints on everyone, and that means Lopez, too. He's a coyote if there ever was one." With that, I turned and waved. "See you tonight when I get my appetite back, Berto."

All through the rest of the workday, I kept seeing the child's arm stretched out, reaching for help. If someone had planted the arm there and left the bracelet as a clue, I didn't have a lot of faith that Del Rio's brilliant detectives, who were underpaid, overworked, and required to spend most of their time on ag theft, were going to put much effort into the case. Not without a lot of pressure, which I intended to apply. They'd figure it was just one less illegal they had to deal with. Brutal but true. If the child was reaching for help from beyond the grave, I was going to have to be the one to latch on.

I left the office early and headed home. All I wanted was a shower and a cold iced tea, which I found in a pitcher in the refrigerator. Sitting in the kitchen at the old Formica table my mother had never replaced, I could hear a distant tractor and, I was sure of it, the whooshing sound ghosts make, or memories, or whatever those noises were: someone coming down the hall; someone flipping on a fan; my parents, my grandparents, their souls moving through the warm, trapped air in the house, still with me, going about their spirit business, hovering, watching, whispering advice, admonitions. *Mind your own business. You let them keep to their own. Don't go looking for trouble. You never listen, do you, Callie?*

Around five in the evening, I drove to Berto and Rosie's home, and when I neared their subdivision, I turned right at the stop sign on Merced Drive, slowed down, and let the deep shade of the valley oaks wash over the car. If Del Rio had a country club, then this neighborhood would be its gated community, complete with a private swimming pool, leafy streets, and people jogging in the evening. It was a stretch financially for Berto, but the schools were good. Very yuppie, or Muppie, as the case was. Rosie even had the neighbors in for book clubs and wine. I, on the other hand, was lucky if I didn't fall asleep after two pages of a legal thriller. I know—go figure, right? I guess I liked seeing my own life tarted up in a book. Made me feel smart to see what the writer got wrong about my job.

Speaking of which, I could be wrong about a lot of things, like who had phoned in the body (well, the body part), whether the cops should talk to the gypsies, whether it was coyotes, who'd leave a tell-tale sign like a bracelet on the victim. It was going to be a long investigation, and since Del Rio had a shortage of detectives, I'd be doing double duty. We might never even get to trial. The chief was not going to send the dogs into every field. The growers were the ones who got us elected. They'd be up in arms, and B-Rod and I were going to be pressured to wrap this up. Fletcher would see to it.

Vato was riding shotgun. He recognized the Rodriguez house, had spotted it from the window, and was now going berserk, barking for joy. He knew that in about one minute we would be pulling into the driveway, where his buds, two of his litter mates, would come bounding out the front door. No sooner had I cut the engine than the dogs raced toward the car. Four paws slapped against my passenger windows and full-on pandemonium ensued. B-Rod followed, yelling, "Down, you guys, down!" as he grabbed Lula and Belle's collars and shook his head. I opened the door, Vato raced out, and Berto let the dogs go.

"Hey, girl." He gave me a big hug, like we hadn't just walked a homicide scene together, like it had been years. "I think my dogs flunked obedience school. Oh, wait—they never went."

"Don't feel bad. Vato's been cooped up all day. He needs the exercise." It was about twenty degrees cooler here under the big trees, though, expensive subdivisions in the valley being what they were, you could hear air-conditioners humming all around. I wondered how my grandparents had survived eighty years earlier. Maybe it was cooler then. No global warming. Or maybe if you were a farmer during the Depression, you could survive pretty much anything.

"Where's your better half, B-Rod?"

"She's with the kids, telling them that Mom and Dad have to talk grown-up talk with Tia Callie. They get to eat their KFC in the TV room and watch the new *Independence Day* sequel. It's a loud movie. That way, they can't hear us. My tactic would have been to tell them they had to eat with the grown-ups and make them beg for a movie. Now, they're interested. Oh well. Before I clocked out, I read the cops the riot act about the bracelet—doesn't leave the morgue, or heads roll."

"Good," I said, following him down the walkway. We knew there were dirty cops. Always had been, always would be. If someone screwed up leaving that bracelet on the victim, it would be worth a lot of money to them to have the problem go away, and ditto for the cop who solved the problem. "You think it's significant?"

"Everything could be significant, but it's usually not."

"So true. So true."

"Hey, kids." I stuck my head into the den, where Laura, Rodriguez's six-year-old cutie pie, and her more serious brother, Saul—a big man, now that he'd made it into the double digits—were sprawled on their stomachs in front of the TV. "Can I watch the movie in here with you? We'll let your parents have the grown-up talk."

Laura rolled over onto her back and giggled. "You're silly, Tia Callie. You have to be with the *gwoan-ups*. You're a *gwoan-up*, too."

"Well, if you say so." I tousled Saul's curly hair on the way out, and he shot me the look kids give when they know something's up.

"Not about you, kiddo, or your folks. Not to worry." He was, I knew, a worrier.

—

After the chicken bones and slaw cups had been pushed aside, the honey packets and napkins rolled into balls, I pulled out the letter my sister had supposedly written of her own accord, read it aloud, showed Berto and Rosie the accompanying check, and then placed both the letter and the check on the wooden farm table, where they lay like bright white warnings. Every now and then, Berto pushed the papers around with his index finger. He reminded me of someone searching for answers on a Ouija board. Just as effective, too.

The check was from my sister, the exact tax-free gift amount of $12,729. The letter promised more if I would help. Also included was a draft of a letter she swore Fletcher would write endorsing me for the Senate, even though I was not in the same party. Suddenly, I was all bipartisan in his eyes, capable of working across the aisle, et cetera, instead of some libtard progressive. The check and letter were written in my sister's hand, of course, so that Senator Fletcher could claim ignorance should any of this come to light. There would be no way ever to prove it and no point in even trying. I mean, you know how women are. And if the situation became desperate, my sister could be sent off to the Betty Ford clinic for treatment for her "disease."

"You cashing the check, Cal?" Berto asked, taking a swig of beer, his gaze almost daring me to say yes.

"Hell to the no. Does the word 'disbarred' mean anything to you?" I caught the look between Berto and Rosie. The couple look. The one quick glance that tied them together with a common secret. "What?"

Just then, Rosie nodded at Berto, who turned to see Saul standing in the doorway. "Hey, buddy. What's up?" Berto asked.

"I have a stomachache." Saul sat down on Berto's lap, his head on his father's shoulder. He reminded me of a big dog who still thinks he's a pup.

Rosie got up and motioned me out of the kitchen and into the living room. From the kitchen, I could hear Berto murmuring all the right things, offering Saul special ice cream that always, always helped a stomachache. Then Rosie pulled me by the hand into the hall, opened a door between the bedrooms, and nodded to me to follow. She flipped on a light to the stairway leading up to the attic.

"Command decision," Rosie said. "But I think you need to look at something Mama Lupe found under Mike's old bed about a month ago."

"Really?" My voice pierced the hot silence of the attic, right through the smell of dusty wood and insulation. "Found what? Why am I just hearing about this?"

Rosie walked between two ceiling trusses. "You know how my mother is a cleaning fanatic, and you don't really make enough work for her. So she got it in her head to vacuum the box springs, and she got my dad to help lift the mattresses." She reached behind the Mylar insulation and pulled out an old album cover, one of Mike's from around 1983. Four crimson faces of the Talking Heads stared out from a blue background. "They found this." Rosie handed the album cover to me and pulled over a suitcase, and I dumped on top what had been hidden there: an eight-by-eleven manila envelope with a logo on the back. American Transport Solutions.

I stared at two travel brochures from a Mexican resort called Ventana Azul; a business card from William Delano, proprietor of a deep-sea-fishing outfit called Pescado de Oro; and a couple of financial statements from American Transport Solutions, which appeared to be some kind of shipping company. Finally, an email to Fletcher from an Alain Chiu at an ATS office in Hong Kong. The email was written in French. Did Fletcher even speak French?

The resort, the fishing guide—all of it echoed. I'd heard those names on Fletcher's phone the day before.

"Was Mike planning any foreign travel with Jim Fletcher?" I waved the brochure.

Before she could answer, I heard Berto climbing the stairs. "I was the one who put them there, Callie," he said from the stairwell. "I didn't want Rosie's mother involved, so I brought all Mike's stuff here. I didn't think about it until now."

"Okay, guys." I could hear the irritation in my voice. "This is Keystone Cops stuff. Last I heard, the banks in San Francisco had safe deposit boxes. Hiding things under the mattress? This is a joke—"

Rosie interrupted me: "At first, Berto thought Mike might have been embezzling or something, because . . ."

"Please don't stop now. You had me at 'embezzling.'"

"He left his job."

The attic heat was getting to me. Mike wouldn't embezzle, and if he were to even consider it—which he wouldn't—it would be for some cause like saving the rain forest. I put the brochures, card, email, and papers in the envelope and handed them to Rosie. "Guys, not my county, not my case. And I don't speak French. Nothing I can do. Can we get out of this hot box?" I headed for the stairs.

"Wait," Rosie called out. "There's more."

I caught the look of surprise on Berto's face.

"More what?" he asked.

Rosie peeled back an old sheet of linoleum that must have been there since the late '80s, pulled out another envelope, and said, "You're not going to like this, but, given the check and the dead kid, I think you have to see it. I put it under the linoleum, thought it was safer from the children. I don't know." She shrugged.

Berto was standing behind me when I opened the envelope and pulled out some photographs. "Oh, Jesus," he said. "Oh, shit." He walked over to the railing and leaned on his arms for a minute, then raced down the stairs, slamming the attic door behind him.

Three glossy four-by-sixes floated in my hand, all of them about the size of my phone, but flat, slick and warm from the heat, weighing nothing. With every rapid breath I took, the smell of attic mouse droppings and dried-out insulation seeped into my nose and mouth, making me sick. Okay, I knew what I was holding: child pornography—as if those two words should ever go together. Every DA in the country had seen things like this, just not as part of her brother's personal belongings. This was not some souvenir. These things were worth money. They got traded around like baseball cards for lots of cash.

"Rosie, how old do you think this kid is? Twelve, thirteen?" He was skinny, and brown, and naked, his face twisted in pain, as far as I could tell from the angle. His mouth was duct-taped, his ankles tied tightly, while a hand and arm, visible in the shot, penetrated him with an ugly-looking dildo. I leaned against the wall, feeling as if my legs had given out under me, and studied the next picture. In the silence in the attic, I heard the giggles from the kids downstairs watching the movie, a dog barking down the street. A door slammed somewhere in the house, and Rosie put her face in her hands. She straightened up in a minute or so and fixed me with a hard glare. "Go on," she said. "Look at the others."

I lifted the next photo and found myself staring at a body I'd seen many times around the family swimming pool: the long, white jagged scar down his side from a bar fight that had become family lore, like a u-shaped piece of cord stretching from one brown nipple, down the rib cage, to the back. The same kid was kneeling in front of this torso, gripping a small black-and-white teddy bear tightly, as he fellated the huge white man, the man's hand on the kid's head, pushing.

The man was Jim Fletcher.

I shoved the pictures back in the envelope, but the image of Fletcher with that kid was seared into the insides of my eyelids. It couldn't be true, but somehow I knew it was. Besides, the same scar. What were the chances?

Rosie's voice pierced the silence around us. "Fletcher. It's Jim Fletcher."

I looked up. How could she have known? And then it slowly dawned on me. "Oh, God, Rosie, I'm so sorry."

At that, a harsh sound came from her throat, a bitter laugh. "Not me, Callie. Berto. He told me everything once, when he got drunk enough—everything down to the big white scar—like confession. He was fourteen when it happened. You have no idea the shame he carries."

This was not what I'd ever expected, and all my images of Berto— the invulnerable cop, the warrior, whatever I thought I had known or understood about him—shuffled and fell like a bad deck of cards. "Rosie, it's not his fault." Even to me, the words sounded lame, but I was grasping for something, some response, other than shock. There are things you don't get over, I knew, events, actions still assembled in your mind the way a child assembles them. Berto would always believe it was his fault, his weakness.

"That wasn't from some bar fight." She dragged her finger along her side in the shape of Fletcher's scar. "Berto's father almost killed him. She said he went to the union. There was some settlement, so it never became public. That's when Berto's father became ranch foreman, got a brand-new mobile home courtesy of Fletcher Family Farms. "They moved out of it a few years later, went to work for Grit. Couldn't live in it, knowing how they got it, which only made Berto feel worse."

Rosie waved her arm toward the photos and the brochures. "I don't know what Mike was doing with all this, but you need to find out." She said there was a cousin in Mexico, near Vallarta, who was a cop. He would know the resort, *todo*, and that planes left the Fresno airport once a day for Guadalajara. I got the sense she'd been planning this for a while. "From Guadalajara, you take a flight to the coast, and I will see to it that this cousin finds you. You need to stop Jim Fletcher. You're the only one around here who can." And with that, she turned and headed down the stairs, leaving me in the suffocating attic with the sordid pictures and the rising awareness of my family's guilt and, in a way, of my own.

3

NATHAN

Thursday. Garbage day. How did he know? Because every Thursday, his extremely fit and healthy neighbor—the radiologist, the one with the body like the statue of David, the neighbor with the young wife who was always ferrying their small kids to various lessons all around Berkeley in a bumper sticker–covered Subaru—pulled his trash and recycling bins out to the street before his morning run, banging and rattling all the way. Consequently, every Thursday morning for as long as Nathan lived in this house, as long as he stayed in the same room he had shared with Karen—and he couldn't imagine not staying in that room—he would wake every Thursday morning, and his first thought would be *Garbage*.

Every other morning, his first thought was of the *San Francisco Chronicle*. Okay, he recognized the comparison, but still, it was a ritual. And weren't rituals important to maintain after a spouse died? Or was it the other way around? Was he supposed to try new things, break out of the mold? Well, so much for therapy. He couldn't even remember what he'd been told to do.

He knew he was probably the last person in Berkeley who still had the *Chronicle* delivered, what with dead trees and all. Most likely, if Karen were still here, he would now be squinting at a screen just like every other person he saw at the French Café up on Shattuck. Karen had taken saving the world seriously—trees, people, whales, and even bees, for Christ's sake. And how had the world repaid her? She was dead, from some freak blood clot that felled her in a second. So, basically, fuck the world.

And that was generally his next thought on any day, Thursday or otherwise.

But today something was gnawing at him, something new. Oh, God, that trip to Mexico. The one that had seemed like a good idea at the time. His neighbor had clapped him on the back when he'd told him where he was going and asked him to bring in the mail. "Great idea, Nathan," he'd said, giving him one of the pitying smiles he'd seen on all his friends' faces so many times in the past year. "That's wonderful. Get away from everything."

The last thing he wanted to do was get away from everything. It was everything, and by that he meant Karen, that had gotten away from him, and no trip to a fancy resort in Mexico could change that.

Nathan swung a long, too-thin leg over the side of the bed and pulled on the boxer shorts and T-shirt he'd dropped on the floor. He reached for his bathrobe, the one Karen always said looked like the Shroud of Turin, also in a pile on the floor. Jesus, what had she seen in him, his lovely, dead wife? She was always having to fuss with his attire, pushing his shirttail into the back of his slacks where it had pulled up, spritzing stain remover on his khakis before she threw them in the wash because his felt-tipped pen had leaked. "If you needed a license to carry one of these, Nathan," she would say, waving the pen as evidence, "they would never give it to you."

And here was the kicker: The skinnier and more disheveled he became, the more his friends' wives seemed to want to fix him up. Maybe they were just at that empty-nest age and needed a new project, now that their kids were off in college. Well, he was that for sure: a project.

Thud. The newspaper hit the porch floor with that cartoon sound, which meant his neighbor had returned from his run and had, out of the goodness of his heart, thrown the widower next door's paper onto the porch for him, so the poor slob—and he was looking terrible, wasn't he?—didn't have to go to the sidewalk and get it.

Nathan lifted his phone from the bedside table and checked the time: 6:10 a.m. His flight from Oakland left in two hours—still time to change his mind; bail on the whole Ventana Azul resort thing; bail on his arrangement with *Birdwatcher* magazine to lead a tour with a group called, of all things, Birds of Paradise. But then the texts started pinging. One from a guy named Bud Delano, who was meeting his plane; another from the small hotel in San Benito, a nearby beach town, where he would be spending two nights before heading up the coast to the resort. They had received his FedEx. Little did they know what was in it, and he didn't have the energy to fight the momentum—karma, Karen would have called it. Via FedEx, Karen's ashes, some of them, at least, had gone on ahead of him, held in a little silk pouch he'd found in her jewelry drawer and placed in a Huichol medicine bag that some shaman she'd met at a conference on native healers had given her. When he'd checked with the TSA, they'd told him their agents might confiscate the cremains—that was the word they'd used—at the security check (hence the FedEx), and now, in her own way, she was already there, waiting for him to do what she wanted and give her back to the turquoise Pacific off Mexico, which she loved so much.

That was why Nathan had not fallen back into bed, his arm thrown over his eyes, the minute he'd heard the paper hit the porch, and was now, a mere six hours later, having filled out his customs form, having fastened his seat belt and turned off his computer, floating down from the sky as his plane descended through a few clouds, until the steep, verdant mountains appeared in his window around a bright, glassy bay. The wheels touched the tarmac, the palms trees sped by, and the plane was on the ground, taxiing to a stop. After the usual announcements, they were allowed to stand and scramble for the overhead bins. Then the doors opened and they were released to a rush of damp tropical heat.

Airport transport was included as a resort amenity, the secretary at Birds of Paradise had told him, and so Nathan had assumed a driver would be waiting in the crowd around the arrival gate with the others, all holding up last names like so many flash cards. It wasn't until the crowd had departed, everyone going his or her chattering way, that he'd spotted a sunburned, middle-aged gringo sitting in the waiting area. He was wearing a canvas cap that said JUNEAU KAYAKS on it, along with a Hawaiian shirt, and his arms and legs were man-spreading along a row of fiberglass seats. Unfolded thus, his driver's formerly athletic frame, now gone to seed, took up three chairs. No one could miss the slogan on the T-shirt he wore under the yellow orchids. Beneath a spray of cannabis, big letters proclaimed THIS BUD'S FOR YOU.

"You Nathan Bernstein?" The gringo didn't get up. "Bud Delano. Congo Bud. That's what they call me. Why don't you get your bags, and we'll boogie on outta here?"

Nathan was aware that roads down the west coast of Mexico were not exactly the safest spots in the world. So one could assume, as Nathan had assumed, that Birds of Paradise, the tour group that *Birdwatcher* magazine had connected him with, wanted its clients to come back alive, Nathan among them. The birders' happiness and comfort were the tour company's most important priorities, he'd been told. Now, on his art history PhD's stooped and narrow shoulders rested the responsibility not only for the birders' enjoyment but for the possibility of return customers whose five-figure fees permitted the existence of a San Francisco office, high-priced brochures, the tour company director's salary, and so on up the multinational corporate food chain to the conglomerate offshored in Hong Kong, no less, that had a controlling interest in the whole endeavor, including the airline charter company and the fancy spa, Ventana Azul, where they'd all be wined and dined after a day of staring through binoculars in the sweltering heat.

Anyway, a driver had seemed like a plus at the time. Now, its rewards seemed a bit dubious. He and Bud, or Congo, were going to be together for seven days, and if that had seemed like a long time back in PV, it was an absolute life sentence by the time Nathan was halfway to his first stop: a small fishing village called San Benito, a place he and Karen had been when they were younger, so overwhelmed with love and lust, the place was seared in his memory.

Once Congo Bud hit the coastal range of the Sierra Madre, he gunned the jeep and switchbacked up the hills. Nathan felt himself speeding down into thickets of green scrub and then up again onto hairpin clearings where the Pacific was just a daub of blue in his eye and a terrifying crash of surf way, way too far down the cliff. To add to his misery, Bud took advantage of the hot, winding drive to expound upon many of his deeply held spiritual beliefs. They were as follows: Fat chicks should not wear bikinis, man and nature were one, and drugs were powerful forces that had to be used only by those with highly developed psyches, like his. And how had he developed his into this sublime state? Wherever he went, he always made sure he lived among the people. He knew *los costenos* like the back of his hand, he told Nathan, lifting it in all its wise and age-spotted glory right in front of Nathan's face.

It was at moments like this that grief hit hardest, when there was no Karen sitting in the back, hearing all this, waiting to imitate it at the first opportunity. If she had been there, Congo Bud would have been another link on the chain that connected them. Later, holding hands, walking down Fourth Street in Berkeley, she would have waved her arm at all the well-heeled locals and laughed, saying, "We are living among the people, aren't we, Nathan?" He felt tears welling up. Good God, he should never have come here. He unzipped the plastic window flap just to get some air and let the noise put an end to Bud's unbearable palaver.

To reach San Benito and Melaque Bay, Bud turned west down a narrow road, macadam for about five minutes, then graded dirt, and then ruts. Nathan could smell the briny ocean before he could actually see it. As the air grew thicker and the fringed tops of palms appeared on the horizon, the road turned from dried, rutted mud to sand and shell. There was a Pemex gas station of sorts on the outskirts of San Benito, a few palm-thatched *palapas,* and then an unmarked and undistinguished intersection where an arrow pointed left into the town proper. Only a few more minutes, Nathan thought, and he would be free of Bud's surfer-dude pontificating for at least twenty-four blissful hours. Nathan caught a glimpse of a roadside arrow pointing toward town. SAN BENITO: 0.5 KILÓMETROS. Salvation was at hand.

Bud came to a full stop in front of a bright blue wall where an unlit neon sign read CABANAS DEL MAR. "Well, my friend, here we are," he said.

Nathan pushed open the jeep's door. "Thank you so much for the ride."

"Hey, your outfit pays me the *lana.*" Bud rubbed his thumb against his first two fingers—universal sign language for money. "I'm your dude." He yanked the wheel with his left hand and pulled a zero-to-sixty-in-two-seconds exit.

Nathan stepped into the street, watching Bud tear off in the proverbial cloud of dust, his KING OF THE ROAD bumper sticker fading into the sunset, as it were. He felt a little dazed, still carsick, until the sound of the muffler stopped ringing in his ears. Looking around as the damp afternoon heat settled on him, sticky and foreign-smelling, he thought the place seemed a little *too* deserted, but maybe it was just siesta. Up and down the street he saw evidence of construction—cement mixers, ugly half-built structures with iron rebar sprouting from the cinder blocks—but no noise, no people. The town had grown since he had traveled here with Karen years earlier.

Just then, an iron gate creaked behind him and a man nodded and chirped in English for his benefit. "Señor Garcia," he introduced himself, grabbing Nathan's suitcase. "At your orders."

They entered through the gate and passed a small, pristine pool on the left, bordered by cool grass. Garcia lugged the duffel past the reception desk, assuring Nathan they could settle accounts later, and led him through an open hallway to the back of the building. The cabanas were right on the beach, and from there he had a view of the whole green circle of the bay. Señor Garcia twisted the key in the latch of cabana number 9 and shoved open the door.

"*Aire*-condition." Garcia stood in the middle of the cabana and swung his hand back and forth, the promise of an air current coming from the open door. "*Aire*-condition," he repeated, grinning, this time cranking the aluminum hurricane shutters so their slats were parallel to the floor.

"*Si, comprendo*," Nathan told him. "*El cuarto tiene el aire natural.*"

Having reached that understanding, the proprietor continued around the room, displaying its many charms. "*Toallas*," he said, lifting two frayed terry-cloth postage stamps that had seen better days. "*Vaso*," he said, holding up a glass.

The room had been painted lime green sometime in the distant past, and the bed, covered with a clashing, bilious bedspread sprouting little pink pom-poms from its worn surface, took up most of the room. The color scheme was a real eye-catcher, but it was the FedEx envelope propped up on the pillows that drew Nathan's eye.

"For you." Garcia reached for the blue-and-orange cardboard and handed it to Nathan. "Fade-Aches," he said, giving the bedspread a slight tug to straighten it, pleased with Mexico's link to global communications.

And who was the FedEx driver? Señor Bud, of course, according to Garcia. This guy had quite a little scam going.

"Work. *Trabajo*," Nathan lied. He stuck his thumbnail under the wide strip of white cardboard on the back of the envelope. It gave easily—no need to pull the tabs. It had been opened once before. His chest clenched with fury. Bud. The bastard.

He had given Señor Garcia his exit line, and the man was polite enough to use it. "*Trabajo*," he said, excusing himself. "Work. For me also."

Nathan waited for the screen door to slam before he sat down on the bed and examined the FedEx envelope. He'd been right about its having been opened before and retaped. The thought of Bud anywhere near Karen—and he couldn't think of this quarter cup of grit and bone shards as anything else—stopped his breath. He lifted the little silk bag out of the Huichol beads and held it to his lips, whispering, "Karen, sweetheart." He closed his eyes, as if he could conjure her once more from the dark.

And when that exercise in futility was over, he opened his eyes and, from his perch on the bed's nest of pink pom-poms, looked up. Through the screen door's gray mesh, he watched Garcia walk down the swoop of white sand to the shoreline, where a man who looked to be drunk had passed out on the beach at low tide. Now, the water was lapping at his toes. Garcia dragged him a few feet out of harm's way, turned, and trudged back up the beach to the hotel, brushing his hands off on his trousers. A slight breeze was picking up. He could feel it circulating around his shoulders. Garcia had been right. *Aire acondicionado.* By night, it might actually be cool.

He got up from the bed, pushed open the screen door, and dragged a rusted aluminum chaise lounge in front of the cabana to the sand a few feet away. He had the creepy feeling that Bud, that self-inflated beach bum, was somewhere watching, keeping an eye on the new guy in town, and, if not Bud himself, then perhaps one of his minions: a shoeshine boy, a Chiclet seller. Nathan decided to bring up the opened FedEx envelope with Garcia just to hassle Bud, the two-bit wheeler-dealer.

Stretching his legs out in front of him, he lifted his iPhone from his pocket and shot a picture of his bare feet, the beach in the background. Then he tapped on the keyboard and sent the photo to his neighbors. "Gringo in paradise," he typed. He would play the part if only to stop being seen as such a loser, a burden. They'd like that. They'd be relieved, he imagined.

Eventually, blue twilight settled over San Benito, letting Nathan know it was time to rouse himself. One by one, lights began to sparkle around the curve of the beach. Over the sound of the surf and the hoarse rattle of palm fronds, Nathan heard music blasting from a beachside bar's jukebox. *Better move it if you want to eat,* he told himself. It was the off-season. Places probably closed early.

A shower and a beer, and he was one day down and six more to go with this tropical getaway. The day after tomorrow, he would be at the swank resort, but tonight and the next he could wallow in his memories of Karen. He padded through the sand to cabana *número* 9, where the shower turned out to be less than satisfactory. The pipes had rattled and clanged with promise, but in the end only a limp stream of water emerged; it was like trying to shower by pouring a glass of water over his head. It took forever for the sweat and grime of the trip to wash off. The bad vibes from Bud would take Clorox, acid rain. Who knew? Anyway, once he had accomplished the whole toilette, he donned a pair of khakis and a white T-shirt, caught a look at himself in the mirror. He'd gotten a little sun, looked a little more debonair—although for what, he had to wonder.

He chose a large, oceanfront restaurant—El Tropical, it was called—about a quarter-mile walk down the beach. From a distance, it seemed atmospheric like its name, with strings of colored lights and a live guitar trio inside. He could hear them playing *"Bésame Mucho,"* a song Karen loved, over the sound of the surf. But once he'd walked up the stairs from the sand, he saw that the *palapa*-covered terrace was closed and dinner was being served inside, under the cold, white glare of fluorescent lights. Too late to change his mind. The restaurant owner had seen him, was homing in, menu in hand. Nathan's feeling of doom only increased when the trio began packing up and hauling their instruments out the other exit, the one that opened onto the street. Even they had given up.

Determined to ring in another customer, the owner hawked the menu in English, reciting the litany. "We have fish. We have chicken. *Tenemos pescado blanco Huachinago. Tenemos pollo al mojo de ajo.*"

Nathan gave up and headed toward a table a few seats away from a silver-haired woman about his age, alone. Another lost soul, probably. Maybe he should steer clear. Anyway, she was looking at a map with little circles drawn in red marker, in between bites of her taco, and obviously had better things to do than pay any attention to him.

Now the evening was truly ruined. An empty chair loomed at the end of the table where his *paisanos*—Bud and two other stoner gringos— had already finished dinner. At least, Nathan assumed that was what the cigarette butts crushed into their plates meant. They were all well on their way into a bottle of mezcal. The restaurant owner wouldn't hear of the *Norteamericano* dining by himself and insisted Nathan sit down: "*Siéntate. Siéntate.*"

Bud seemed to realize it was a fait accompli as well, and shoved the chair in Nathan's direction with his foot. "Take a load off, Bernstein," he said, and began to make a few drunken introductions.

Down at the end of the table was Paul. The Pharmacist, they

called him. This got a big laugh from Bud—his own joke. What a riot. Nathan filed el Farmacéutico away in his head under the category Deadbeat Pot Grower from Humboldt County. Must be down here lining up investors, so to speak. Next to the pharmacist, a skinny girl was pouring mezcal carefully into a glass, drop by drop. "Trying to get the worm." She giggled. She was so stoned, even the giggle came out slowly. "My spirit name is Xochi." She paused for a long time, as if trying to figure out what to say next. It finally came to her. "You know Xóchitl—that's Aztec for 'Flower Princess.'"

Oh, dear God, Nathan thought. Flower Princess must have been under eighteen years old if she was a day. Turned out there was a reason her picture was not on the back of a milk carton with a caption under it that read, "Have you seen this child?" Her parents, she told him, were part of the Rainbow Family. She was down here on a vision quest. The Pharmacist was her spirit guide. She wrapped one of her skinny arms around him. It was covered with a filigree design, a kind of tattoo done in henna.

"That must have taken hours." Nathan strained to make small talk.

"Yeah," Xochitl eventually replied, before turning her gaze toward her arm and tracing the reddish pattern with her finger. She looked like she'd be doing that for quite a while.

Bud reached for the mezcal bottle, pulled it toward him, and filled his glass, leaving a puddle on the table underneath. "One big, happy family," he shouted, the life of a nonexistent party. He lifted his glass high in the air. "Here's to the *buena vida*, the *buena* fucking *vida*." Bud downed his drink and was in the middle of pouring himself another round when the owner's young son arrived, pencil and a strip of paper bag in hand, to take Nathan's order.

"Quiere ordenar?"

"Get the whitefish," the Pharmacist said. "It comes from the lagoon. Pollution's not too bad this time of year, they say."

That didn't sound particularly encouraging, but Nathan decided to go with the prevailing wisdom.

"*Pescado blanco*," the young waiter repeated, and was gone.

Fish and fishing. Apparently, they had touched on one of the subjects near and dear to Bud's heart. According to Bud, back in the good old days, when he'd first come to San Benito, men had really fished. He banged his fist hard on the table, just to let everyone feel his pain. Xochitl was still absorbed in her tattoo. Her head lolled back and forth a bit from the reverberation of Bud's fist, but her eyes were transfixed on one particular spot on her forearm. The Pharmacist, however, looked agitated, like it mattered if this got out of hand, which it appeared to be well on its way to doing.

"Fuckin' goddamn virtual-reality lures."

Nathan had absolutely no idea what Bud was talking about.

"Some asshole wants to play mind games with a fish. They computer-program these lures to mess with the fishes' natural instincts. You call that sport fishing? How sick is that?"

"Bud, I'm sure everyone at the table agrees with you." Nathan, even as he was adding his two cents, had to wonder why he bothered. "No need to inform the whole room."

Now, Bud was really ticked. "You don't know what you're talking about, Mister College-Professor Twerp. What? You read *Old Man and the Sea* in college, heard some windbag professor lecture on the significance, the veritable metaphor, of the damn fish, and you think you know everything? You don't know jackshit, you little turd." Bud poured another shot and downed it.

In the midst of Bud's diatribe, the owner showed up with Nathan's *pescado blanco* and set it down with a slight flourish. Maybe he thought this was the way gringos always had dinner, screaming and drinking and shouting. Nathan could only imagine what the map-reading woman of a certain age in the corner was thinking. He looked over and saw her staring at him. *God*, he thought, *I hope she doesn't think I'm one of these boors.* Although why should he care? Afraid he would embarrass his dead wife or her memory? But this moment of shame was interrupted by Bud's even louder tirade about real men and the spiritual nature of sport fishing, how it used to really mean something if you caught a marlin or a sailfish, how he was sick to death of these frat-boy banker types coming down here and pretending to fish.

"So, what do you do back in the States?" the Pharmacist asked.

Amazing. The stoner was going to try to have a civil conversation, and Nathan wondered, spooning beans onto a tortilla, how long the Old Man and the Sea on the other side of the table would let that go on. "I'm a professor. Art history."

Paul, the Pharmacist, stared into his shot glass. "My art teacher in high school was totally cool," he said. "He had a profound impact on my life."

"Really?" Nathan hoped he didn't sound too snobby, as if he couldn't equate his lofty stature with that of a mere high school teacher, because Karen would have hated that. "Yes, teachers can make a real difference." Did that sound tepid? Oh, God, he was asking Karen again. If it did sound tepid, as it were, Paul didn't seem to notice.

"Yeah, he gave me my first joint. Blew my mind."

Nathan raised his eyebrows, for Karen's benefit, really, as if to say, *See? I'm not being snobby. I'm being realistic.*

Bud added his two cents: "My history teacher was a bitch from hell. Mrs. Hooger. We used to call her Mrs. Booger. She got me suspended three times. You know what that meant in Oklahoma back then, you wusses? Reform school or the army. The army was all the education I ever needed." Bud reached for the bottle. "A regular boat-load of education, *amigos.*"

"Well, you survived, Bud," Paul said.

Big mistake. Bud looked pissed.

Nathan figured he knew where this was going—downhill. He placed some pesos on the table, and, waving to the waiter, he fled, actually fled, something he had never imagined himself ever being in a position to have to do. He hastened through the unused terrace and down the stairs, choosing the beach route for a quick getaway. No need to get in the middle of a drunken brawl on day one. He was practically jogging down the beach, and by the time he was out of sight of the Tropical, he leaned over, pushed his palms into his knees, and gulped air like a diver who had just breast-stroked several meters. Once he caught his breath, he straightened up and trudged on. *This is the part they never show you in the Corona ads*, he thought: the stoners and lifers on Mexican beaches, the guys who'd pretty much landed here with a copy of *The People's Guide to Mexico* in their hands sometime in the '70s and never left.

The sky was black, no moon, just the stretch of sand, gray from the light of the beachside hotels. Every now and then, a wave rushed up and left a soapy lip of foam near his feet, and the humid wind whipped across his cheek, leaving it sticky with salt. It would have been easier to walk on the wet part of the sand where the pounding surf had hardened it, but the drop-off was too steep. His travel app had warned him to watch out for rogue waves, riptides, ones that swept in waist high. People had lost their footing that way and been pulled out. There was something about the shape of the bay and how the swells from the Pacific affected the water level. He didn't really understand it, just that it wasn't all that safe. Not, of course, that there were any signs warning you around here. *Viva México*, he thought, wondering if Karen were watching him be such a chicken, something she never had been.

Nathan sat down on the sand far enough away from the white lip of surf to feel safe, then stretched out and stared up at the vast, dark sky until the stars' chaotic swirl began to make some sense, the blur of the Milky Way running from Sagittarius through the Southern

Triangle. He thought of all those stupid sayings about stars being the spirits of dead loved ones. Would that it were true.

"Karen," he said out loud, now that the drone of the ocean would cover his voice. He said it for the pleasure of feeling her name in his mouth again, in the back of his throat, and on his lips. It was one of the many words he never got to say anymore, words like "sweetheart" and "hon"—all the lighthearted names that use to flit about his now silent house.

He looked at the motel behind him, its yellow, bug-luring porch lights casting half circles on the sand. Nathan stood, brushed himself off, and headed toward his room. In retrospect, he couldn't remember whether he'd been aware of footsteps behind him or not. Probably the surf was too loud and he wasn't looking behind him. He had just turned up the little sand dune to the cabanas when he felt an arm around his chest and a large hand covering his mouth and nose. He couldn't scream. He couldn't breathe.

"Gotcha." Bud breathed hard in his ear and then released him.

He flew like a top from Bud's grip, but his scream, not quite in sync, came later. He sat down hard in the sand, his whole body shaking. "*Pendejo!* Asshole!" he shouted.

"What's the matter? Can't take a little fun?" was all Bud said.

"Fuck you." Nathan jumped up and lunged at Bud, remembering, in a white-hot rage, that Bud had opened the FedEx containing Karen's ashes. He shoved Bud, both hands on his chest, and barked, "Touch me or my things again, and I'll get your ass fired, you clown."

"Oh, really?" Bud laughed.

Nathan turned. "You bet your ass, mister." He could hear Bud laughing as he jogged to the hotel, stumbling over the little hills of powdery sand. His knees were so weak, he was about to collapse in the lounge chair in front of his cabana, but the door to the room next to his was open and the same woman he'd seen at the Tropical, dining alone, reading a map, was standing there, haloed by the light from her bedside lamp, staring at him. He needed to man up just to save face, so he fumbled in his pocket for his key, his hand still shaking, unable to speak. When he looked up, she was still in the door, still staring. "You okay?" she asked, her voice deeper than he might have thought.

"Yes," he said, in as manly a way as he could, after having been humiliated in front of her. "Thank you." He closed the door behind him, sank down on his bed in the dark, and listened until he heard her door close as well, until there was nothing else but the sound of crashing waves dragging shells along the beach.

4

CALLIE

The guy next door? He seemed nice enough—a bit refined for around here, but nice. I had to wonder, though, what he was doing with Bud Delano, one of Fletcher's contacts, and what that little dustup was about. It would be worth chatting up my neighbor, unless, of course, it wasn't. I reminded myself I had five days. All I could afford to take off work. *Cinco días.* However you said it, not that much time.

You have to stop him, Callie. Rosie's voice was on a loop in my head, over and over, and all I could think about was how years and years of injustice had now landed in my lap. I was the most powerful person Rosie knew. I had a responsibility, certainly. I just didn't have as much leverage as she thought. Not yet. I was working on it. That was the goal, right?

I'd ended up here at Cabanas del Mar because the Ventana Azul place was full. Of course it was. Whoever answered the phone didn't know me from Adam and would have been told to say it was. It was that exclusive. But I thought if I could just see the place, get the lay of the land, get into this resort or whatever, know the players, I'd have a start at figuring out what Fletcher was up to down here. Motivation, opportunity, means—had to have those, or I had nothing. Rosie said she knew someone who could help me in Vallarta. So here I was. Waiting.

Back in Del Rio, I'd left things in Padhma's capable hands, told her I had a family emergency, would talk about it when I got back, long story, some such baloney. The upcoming week was pretty low-level in terms of trials—nothing Padhma couldn't handle.

My mind wandered back to the guy in cabana number 9, next to me. How had he ever ended up in funky San Benito? I couldn't help having overheard—who couldn't have?—Bud Delano call him a professor type. And that seemed to fit. His lips did seem rather pursed around an invisible silver spoon of PhD-ness, whereas I, in my new incarnation as Del Rio DA, looked like I was country before and after country was cool, as the George Jones song went. At least—and this was my major accomplishment so far—I had gotten a glimpse of William "Bud" Delano in action at dinner. Wow. I wouldn't have given that guy a license to float a rubber ducky in a tub, much less pilot a deep-sea vessel. Still, the professor might be able to get me to Delano. Or something. Anything. I should be nice, flirt a little. Did professors flirt? Sam McCall was never a flirt. Too uptight. He was born in a fucking Brooks Brothers suit.

All this was just something to think about while I waited for Guillermo Sanchez, the Mexican cop Rosie had set me up with. "Don't tell Berto I'm getting involved with this," she'd said when she stopped by the office and handed me the name and phone number of someone she claimed was a cousin in Vallarta, a policeman. "Berto sends him money. He doesn't know I know. Typical macho guy. He wants to protect me, which means trying to keep me in the dark. You call this cousin. Tell him Berto sent you. Tell him we think your brother is in trouble." Rosie was not letting me off the hook. Fletcher was *muy mala gente*, and Mike was my family. And that, to a Mexican, required no further explanation.

Above me, the ceiling fan circled, one of its blades bent so that it dinged every few seconds, the metallic clank driving me nuts. The room seemed hotter from the fan's noise, if that was even possible. I pulled my phone out of my pocket, checked the time yet again. Quarter to nine. Fifteen more minutes, and I'd figure he was blowing me off. Then what?

The humidity was sapping all my energy, and it took effort to push myself up from the bed and walk over to the table under the window where I'd laid out my evidence, such as it was. Brochures? Check. Copy of email from Alain Chiu to State Senator Jim Fletcher that had been in the record cover? Ditto. Copy of financial reports from American Transport Solutions, one of the companies included in Francois's equity firm's portfolio? Yup. And so on. Picture of Fletcher from a newspaper, plus my most recent photo of Mike. The real docs were in a safe deposit box in a Bank of the Sierra in Sanger, along with the kiddie-porn shot of Fletcher. I'd save that for later. My little secret. Mine and Mike's. Wherever he was. Once I found him, we'd go after Fletcher, the sick bastard.

I ran my hands over the missing-persons report and read it again. I'd moved into action after the night in Berto's attic, called San Francisco and leaned on a public-defender friend from law school to look into any filings about Mike. He'd come up with this, filed the day Fletcher met me for lunch.

Mike had last been seen on August 9 in a dim sum restaurant–massage parlor called the Flower Lounge out on Geary Street in San Francisco—the new Chinatown. The masseur claimed Mike had been there, said he came often, slipping through the restaurant kitchen into the massage parlor upstairs, which was—guess what?—not a massage parlor. That night, he had been snorting a lot of coke and, well, doing the other thing you do with masseurs who are really rent boys, when, apparently, a woman had shown up to confront him.

I unpacked this bogus story for the thousandth time. *Número uno*, not Mike. Mike didn't do drugs. He didn't even take aspirin.

And rent boys? Please. Mike? Not a damn chance. He was truly in love with Francois. And the woman? Guess who that was supposed to be? His sister. Me.

Not me. Obviously. But in spite of that fact, I had been named as one of the people who had been there with Mike. They had witnesses and fingerprints and so on. I was what a civilian would call a person of interest, and I was what I personally would call a sucker.

Of course, the evidence was all faked. I'd been at home. Alone—I really needed to get a social life—and so no alibi. So, yeah, it was pretty much all faked, and it pretty much didn't matter—the finger-prints were mine, no doubt about it. I kept thinking of that damn Diet Coke glass from the Starlight. My fingerprints all over the place. The surveillance photos? Photoshopped. They'd get thrown out, the photo and the glass both. Enough people had seen me at the Starlight. Reasonable doubt and all, even with a generic bar glass. It was a threat, though. Fletcher had friends in high places, obviously. This police report meant he intended to use them to get his way. He could be worried that Mike was onto him, which he was, and maybe that I was, too. That's what the lunch date at the Starlight had been all about: trying to figure out what I knew.

The screen door squeaked, and I turned around. "Yes?'

"*Buenas noches.* Good even-ning." Guillermo Sanchez stood at the door, waiting for permission to enter.

Oh, Jesus, I thought, taking one look at him. He wasn't much more than a kid—skinny, burdened with thick glasses, a battered briefcase, and a badge on a lanyard around his neck that read SEMARNAT, whatever that was. When I nodded and invited him in, he approached, hand outstretched. "*Mucho gusto.* I am, I hope, not too late?"

All I could think at the moment was that regardless of what Rosie had told me, this guy was most definitely not a cop. I needed a little time to get my bearings, because my brain was shrieking, *Hell no, hell no.* I walked to the bathroom and returned with my duty-free bottle of Jack Daniel's and two glasses. "Want some?" I asked, hoping he really did speak English as well as it seemed. In my recent line of work, I could easily spend the whole day listening to cops speaking prison Spanish—things like "Okay, *pendejos, manos en la cabeza*"— but right then, my command of that language was failing me.

Turned out he did pretty damn well with English. In short order, I learned that he did not drink, that he worked for a government environmental agency, that he was only two years out of college, and— last but not least—that he had no idea why Alberto Rodriguez would have suggested I call him. And, of course, it had been not Alberto but Rosie who had dragged him into it by telling me he was a cop.

"Mr. Sanchez, listen. To be honest, I don't need, you know, an environmental agency. I need a judge—*un juez, policía. Comprende?*" I wiped my sweaty hands on my slacks and tried to rein in my rising panic. "Someone with law enforcement experience, access to data-bases, stuff like that. B-Rod—I mean Berto—thinks my brother, Mike, is in trouble. I'm sorry I pulled you into this."

"B-Rod?"

"Yeah, you know, like A-Rod?" I belted back some bourbon, felt it burn my throat. Why was I talking American sports to a Mexican, considering the deep pit of problems I was trying to climb out of?

"Yes, *el béisbol*. A-Rod, I understand. But B-Rod?"

"Your cousin is Alberto, right? Well, we call him Berto, and then sometimes just B-Rod."

"I see." Guillermo nodded. "He is not my cousin."

Great. Another screw-up.

Guillermo repeated, "He is not my cousin." He paused. "He is my father."

"Whoa." I set my glass on the nightstand. "Your what?"

Guillermo shook his head. "Is not important. My mother and father were very young. He was visiting his family's village. He has sent money. His actions have been correct. My mother says I must repay, so I am here." He turned to the table under the window and studied my papers.

"Ah," he said after a few minutes. "This becomes more clear to me now. I know of this company of Mr. Alan Chiu." He pointed to the name on the email.

The name swirled around in my head for a while before it landed on Francois. This was one of the companies connected with his private-equity firm in some convoluted, tax-avoiding way.

"American Transport Solutions. I know," Guillermo continued. "Is very funny because is neither American nor solution. This company is Chinese. They lease very old, leaking oil tankers, which have been polluting our beaches and destroying our marine life. I would like to have evidence to issue a *demanda*. How you say? Law sue? We can work together and be win–win, no? We help each other must be my father's idea."

At least Guillermo *had* an idea, because I sure didn't. I wondered if Rosie knew any of this. Maybe this was just the universe unfolding the way it should, but it was sure looking like a fluke, and in my line of work, I didn't do flukes. But that was all I had, so, in the event that this would work out, I ran Guillermo through the whole rodeo, as we said in Del Rio: the meeting with Fletcher; the phone calls from Mexico; the brochures and the rest of the stuff in the attic; Ventana Azul; Pescado de Oro; William "Bud" Delano; Mike's disappearance; ditto Francois, of the equity firm with a large interest in American Transport Solutions. "And so Rodriguez hooked me up with you. Said you knew the area, could help." Not exactly true, but I decided to leave Rosie out of it. I walked over to the table and unfolded a map I'd bought in one of San Benny's tourist shops. "I think Ventana Azul is right here." I pointed to one of the areas I'd circled.

Guillermo turned the map sideways and squinted at the Mexican coastline, the larger towns in black boldface: Manzanillo, Puerto

Vallarta. San Benito was somewhere in between, and Ventana Azul, a little to the north.

"I know of this resort, this Ventana Azul. Very exclusive."

"Can you get me into it?"

"I do not think this is wise."

"Oh, really?" I reached for my glass on the nightstand. "Is that a fact?"

"Yes, that is fact number one."

"Fact number one? You want to tell me what fact number two is?"

"Fact number two is that Ventana Azul is owned by very big drug lord, Don Cacho. Very dangerous man. Some Italians run it for him, so the gringos can think they are on the coast of Italy at Mexican prices. What do you think to find there?"

Good question. Smart guy. What *did* I think I would find? I threw the question back into Guillermo's court just to buy some time. "Why don't you tell me how you think I can help you? What the win–win part of this whole deal is."

"That is very easy. I need you to get papers from American Transport Solutions. I need to know the schedule and the names of tankers. When they will arrive and leave Manzanillo."

SEMARNAT, Guillermo's environmental agency, occupied an office on the third floor of a government building behind a bunch of other ugly municipal buildings, the kind of bureaucratic dump that made the Orange Cove police substation look like a million bucks. No air-con, no elevator. Okay, there were those things, but they didn't work. The elevator, Guillermo told me, was *fuera de servicio*, and the air-conditioning system, same, was being worked on. I gathered it had been in the process of being worked on for a very long time.

It was 9:00 a.m., the sky gray with humidity, the temperature having reached sweltering level a couple of hours earlier. Guillermo flipped on a couple of table fans, one on each desk. "This is for you." He pointed to the desk by a small side window and pulled over a folding chair that had been leaning against the wall with a bunch of others, as if this room got used for an AA meeting during off-hours.

I sat down on the creaking metal, closed my eyes, and let the fan's breeze blow back and forth over the film of sweat covering my face and neck. Guillermo handed me something, and I opened my eyes to see a SEMARNAT badge on a lanyard with the word *huesped* under the letters. It meant I was a guest. "Want to tell me what SEMARNAT is?" I figured it was something I needed to know, since we had a plan of sorts.

Well, Guillermo had the plan, and, aided by his pals in the enviro business, I was given a file from Save the Oceans, some group out of San Diego that had been down here checking out mangrove die-off. Apparently, they'd given up on the mangroves and Mexico, not that Sanchez seemed too surprised, but the file proved how the oil leakage had damaged marine life. His plan also included my pretending to be a translator for someone named Emilia Nava, who worked in the port of Manzanillo. A real person, as it turned out, because Sanchez gave me a printout out of the girl's ID and information. I was supposed to use my made-up position as an official translator for the port to get information from the American Transport Solutions US headquarters in San Francisco. That was our deal. How I was supposed to do that remained to be seen, but Sanchez seemed to think I had some super-ninja American law-enforcement power, and I did not want to destroy his illusions. I looked at the sheet of talking points he'd handed me, questions all nicely laid out in a column. I was to ask for the last port of call and the next port of call after Manzanillo, knots per hour, number of crew, registration and dates of cholera certificates, numbers of containers and cargo tonnage. All this was for our records, I was to say, which we had lost in a computer crash and had not been able to retrieve. How Guillermo planned to use the information I procured was a mystery to me, but *whatever* was my attitude. For now, Guillermo's faith in my abilities meant I had a desk with a stellar view of the back of the Reina de Hong Kong restaurant: garbage cans; rags on a line; a couple of chickens I thought of as Kung and Pao, pecking around in the garbage. Charming. WTF had I gotten myself into? I felt like an idiot—a scared idiot, but an idiot nonetheless.

A large map of Mexico occupied the south wall, and above Guillermo's desk hung a formal portrait of Mexico's president, some handsome guy who was a movie star or married to one. The east wall consisted of a large window covered in drooping venetian blinds that obscured the view of another crappy-looking building. There was a file cabinet, a water cooler, exactly one ancient-looking computer, and a landline. All very up to date if it had been 1993.

Guillermo opened a drawer. "Many Americans come to the back of La Reina Restaurant from time to time. Up to nothing good is my suspicion. If this Mr. Fletcher you are interested in was at La Reina Restaurant, he may come back." He pulled out a pair of binoculars and handed them to me. "You can use these to see what goes on there. And SEMARNAT means this." Sanchez rifled through his wallet and handed me a card. "SEMARNAT: Secretaría de Medio Ambiente y Recursos Naturales," I read aloud. Secretary of Environment and Natural Resources.

"We have not much funds, as you see."

"You want to tell me how you get anything done?"

Guillermo snapped open his briefcase and pulled out a MacBook Air. "Is all courtesy of powerful businessman I cannot name. He wants to keep his private beach clean, and this company of your brother's friend, this American Transport Solutions, is causing problems. He will be very happy we can help. Then he will help you get into exclusive Ventana Azul, and he will ask some questions of you. You will give him answers. Is the only way."

To that end, and to keep both Guillermo and Powerful Businessman happy, I made a few phone calls to the American Transport Solutions office in San Francisco. Each time, all I got was an answering machine, no human to ask any questions, so I just hung up. My mission was, and would be tomorrow and the next day, until my time ran out, to get the name and number of the person who answered the list of questions, and Guillermo would take it from there, using the name to drill deeper.

I was getting pretty far off the beaten path here, but until something better came along, I was going to have to go along with Guillermo's scheme. I had to find some way into the resort, start connecting the dots back to Fletcher. The resort had something to do with the porn photo of the kid, or Mike wouldn't have put them together. He was organized that way—an "a place for everything, and everything in its place" kind of guy.

By lunchtime, my stakeout of the Chinese restaurant had rendered nothing.

"Hey, Guillermo," I called out over the sound of his relentless computer tapping. He was doing what? I wondered. "Why don't you go to the Reina and grab us some takeout? Maybe you'll overhear something useful."

He shook his head, not looking up.

"You scared they'll discover our top-secret hideout?"

He snapped his laptop closed. "Yes, is true. That place makes me afraid."

"Really?" From where I sat, all I saw was an old Chinese grandmother whose job seemed to consist of sitting on her chair, leaning on her cane, and shouting at someone inside, and a man who pushed through the beaded curtain between the kitchen and the courtyard every so often to throw a bucket of water toward a drain in the middle of the concrete. That was it.

"Afraid of food poisoning. I will go for tortas. Chicken is good, yes?"

"Sure, chicken."

"Keep the door locked. I have keys."

Pointless. I might as well go back to the States now. "Moron," I said out loud to the empty room once Guillermo had departed. At least he wasn't there to hear the crazy gringa talking to herself. I picked up the binoculars and stared at Grandma, trying to remember what I'd learned in criminology classes about perps' behavior, how they become more brazen, something about how the thrill of getting away with the crime required greater and greater risks. Fletcher would come back to the resort. I knew it. I had to get there.

I looked at the time on my phone again. All of five minutes had passed. This was going to be endless, and besides, it was too damn empty in the room—just the sound of traffic outside, some door slamming in another office, rapid-fire Spanish echoing down the stairs, and then a silence that seemed like a reproach for my stupidity.

A brief movement caught my eye, and I lifted the binoculars just in time to see a new person join Kung and Pao in the Reina's grubby little courtyard. A movie-star blonde—Kim Kardashian sunglasses, white pantsuit, red high heels. She went over to Grandma, who pulled something out of her housecoat. I couldn't see what but knew the gesture. Coke was Sam McCall's drug of choice. He snorted to relax, if you can imagine, to watch the NBA playoffs with his feet on the coffee table. I'd seen it many a time. Blondie held her hand up to her face, thumb and forefinger spread wide apart, stuck her nose in the space between the digits. I didn't even need to hear the sniffle. How do you say "doing a little blow" in Spanish? Just then, someone else pushed through the beaded curtain—a man. He turned and looked up at the window.

Fletcher. Oh, sweet Jesus. I had been right. Not so stupid after all. In fact, I was a damn genius.

I dropped to my knees and crawled to the window. Where the hell was Guillermo? I needed a witness. Grabbing my phone, I kept praying I could get some sort of picture. *Please, God.*

By now, Fletcher and Blondie had been joined by a very dapper Chinese guy, midforties, a central-casting, rich investor type—nice suit, big gold watch. Fletcher seemed nervous, pacing around, gesturing to Grandma. The Chinese guy listened, then said something. Maybe translating. I was guessing here. Blondie put her arms around Fletcher, did a little sexy move. He pushed her away. Definitely nervous. Finally, the beaded curtain parted again and out walked the fishing-boat guy, Delano. There they were. The local chamber of criminal commerce.

I kept punching away on my phone, taking as many photos as I could, thinking, *Yes, yes, yes.* Delano went back into the restaurant, pushed open the curtain, and gestured to another man to pass. It took me a while, or maybe it didn't take any time at all, to register who he was. Time slowed down; my arm holding the camera felt weak.

I'd know this man in my sleep. Lanky, dark haired, stylish. Behind his horn-rimmed glasses resting on his perfect aquiline nose, I could imagine his dark eyes, eyes that tended to see right through people. Francois.

The fourth person was Francois.

I lowered the phone, heart racing, vision blurring, and, peering over the windowsill, my heart having dropped into my gut, I saw that it was indeed Francois, which made no sense. Wrong brother-in-law. Francois was the kind one, the charming one, so in love with my brother. I could still picture the wedding toast he gave to Mike, the poem he read in his lovely accent, about wanting to give his groom the "silver branch, the white flower, the word that would protect him from grief." Not a dry eye in the room with the beautiful view of the bay and the Golden Gate Bridge on that perfect, sparkling day in May only a year earlier. Francois? How was this possible?

I was in trouble, or Mike was, or we both were now, and there was nothing I could do. I couldn't take back what I had seen.

I heard voices on the stairs, Guillermo greeting someone, and then his key in the door. I tried to pull myself together.

"There are some people who have arrived at the Reina," he said, a little out of breath. "Did you see them?" He noticed my phone on the floor.

I lifted it. "Let's hope." I wondered if my hand was shaking.

"If your pictures are not good, I have these." He dropped the tortas on his desk and tapped the top of his computer. "In here. They've been here before."

"So, you knew this was going to happen, right?" I couldn't tell whether I was pissed or stunned. Had I just been played in some way? I'd have to figure that out later, too. Right now, I needed details. "You've seen all of them before? You're sure?"

"I can check after they leave," Guillermo answered. "Maybe you should just stay down." He sat at my desk and gave me a running account of what he had seen.

After everyone had abandoned the courtyard, Guillermo walked to his desk and pulled up the file with the photographs. One was definitely Fletcher, the others Bud Delano and the Chinese guy with the gold watch. "Always they are there at this time of the month. But there is a new man today." He said he hadn't recognized the fourth one. Had no idea.

He meant Francois.

"What do you mean, 'this time of the month'?" I changed the subject from the men's identities. I really knew all I needed to know, and I didn't want to call attention to Francois—not until I knew a lot more.

"No. Right before new moon. And then oil on the coastline. I get complaints. Chinese man is from American Transport Solutions." They call him Pez Dorado—Goldfish. He is a gangster. Big Chinese gang, but also important businessman. He works with the Zetas, buys illegal petrol they siphon off from pipelines. Everybody makes money that way. You know who they are?"

Sure, I knew who the Zetas were. The feds came in and did a two-day workshop for all county law enforcement on the different cartels: Sinaloa, the lunatic Zetas, the Knights Templar, Los Caballeros—a bunch of violent maniacs. And now they were up-close-and-personal crazy. The Zetas were the craziest of all.

"Is even worse," Guillermo continued. "The woman is girlfriend of *el brazo de* Cacho. The right-hand man, yes?""

"The big drug lord, right? She's taking a risk, then, flirting with Fletcher." A life-threatening risk. Drug lords and their henchmen were known to be possessive of their girlfriends and not exactly forgiving types.

"Yes," Guillermo said. He picked up the bag of tortas and handed me one, walked to the light switch by the door, and passed his hand over it, plunging the office into a murky gloom. "Better they not see us if they come back." He unwrapped his torta, took a bite, swallowed, and added, "Perhaps Cacho will deal with her at some time." He took another bite, stared past the Venetian blinds. "Life is full of risks, no?"

I had a feeling he was talking to himself as much as to me.

Around eight, Guillermo packed up his computer and cut off the fans on the desks. "I need to get my car out of the garage," he said. Taking his car keys from his pocket, he motioned for me to pass through the door and then locked it behind him. We headed down the stairs, out into the streets, teeming with people, and maneuvered our way through the throng on the way to the *estacionamiento*.

Night had fallen on the town, and Mexico's tropical heat pressed against me, sticky and dense. I followed Guillermo along the narrow sidewalk, stepping aside for sunburned tourists, mothers with strollers, vendors with glass jugs of lurid-colored *aguas*, still shaky from having seen Francois, wondering if Mike was with him. Could I really be that close?

The shops were still open, bright caves filled to the brim with beach paraphernalia, bikinis, sarongs, bug spray, straw hats and bags, their too-bright lights making the dark street itself even darker, their familiar tourist items making the street life more foreign. Mexican junk food spilled out of wire shelves, and the harsh odor of cleansers and laundry detergent filled the air. I felt queasy from the smells, the garish colors, and the crowds, sick to my stomach from seeing Francois. Catching Fletcher in the act of something criminal had seemed like a victory at first, but not so much—maybe not at all—now that Francois was involved. I'd opened the famous can of worms. More like a storage container of pythons, in this case.

I kept my head down, tried to avoid looking into the shops, afraid I would see Fletcher or Francois in one of them, buying suntan lotion or cigarettes. But they'd send their people out on those errands, right? They wouldn't be shoulder to shoulder out here with the hoi polloi, bumping into broom sellers and clusters of plastic buckets hanging against the shop walls.

We reached the street leading to the parking garage half a block off the main drag, Guillermo turned to see that I was still following, then walked briskly up the hill and headed into the looming structure on the right. All I wanted was to be back in San Benito and to hear my motel room door close behind me. I needed to be alone to figure out whatever I could, although none of it seemed good at the moment. Was there really any reason to stay here, to try to get into the fancy resort? If I saw Fletcher, what would I say now that Francois was involved? I reached into the hobo bag I carried everywhere and pulled out my phone to check my texts. Nada. Nothing from Mike.

I felt ill, really ill. When I looked down, the sidewalk beneath me appeared far away and blurry, as if I'd come down with a fever.

"Callie," Guillermo called out. I looked up to see that he was not alone but standing beside a stocky, muscular man dressed in cowboy garb, a Western shirt and jeans. "There is someone I would like you to meet."

I dropped my phone back into my bag, walked toward Guillermo and the stranger, and reached out my hand to shake his. After the usual pleasantries—*mucho gusto* and so on—he turned and began leading us into the far reaches of the parking garage. "What's going on?" I asked, the smell of exhaust fumes adding to my nausea.

"Is powerful businessman. He wants to meet you." Guillermo told me.

"Wait a minute. How does he know I'm here?" I stopped in my tracks, the buzz of fluorescent lights too loud, the greenish glow ominous, the smell of leaked motor oil overwhelming. A car swished by, heading down the ramp. "Hell no, Guillermo." I turned to go, but he grabbed my arm.

"It is no problem. You will go."

I looked at the cowboy and understood that neither Guillermo nor I had a choice.

The SUV's door opened automatically, and in front of me, the man known only by the name Powerful Businessman was seated on what looked like a leather lounge chair. The van had been customized. I could see why, once Powerful Businessman swiveled in my direction. I found myself staring at his large head, beautiful coif, and elegant, custom-fitted suit, just his size. He was a dwarf—a handsome, elegant dwarf with the face of Benito Juárez and the white hair of Santa Claus.

"Please, come in. Sit." The door slid closed behind me; I heard the click of the lock. The cowboy got in the driver's seat, and Guillermo climbed into the front passenger seat.

"I am Señor Carlos Garza *a sus ordenes*. Please tell me how I can help you."

"How you can help me?" I echoed his words. I was expecting a request, an interrogation, something, not an offer of help, which anyone with half a brain would know was probably not genuine at all. "I'm not sure you can" was the only answer I could come up with. It was pretty much the truth, and I was stalling while I formulated some story.

Señor Garza reached for his drink from a mahogany cup holder in the armrest between us, and I could smell the peaty scent of scotch—probably, from the looks of all this, very expensive scotch.

"My friend Memo here tells me you are trying to solve a mystery, something to do with American Transport Solutions, and so am I. You see, the beach is my happy place." He raised his oddly large hands and made air quotes. "And those boats are ruining my happy place."

Pivot, I told myself. *If this were a trial, you would go in a different direction.* I took a deep breath, deciding to leave Mike and Francois out of this. "Actually, I have a more pressing problem. There was a murder in my town. I'd like to solve it." I reached into my bag for my phone, tapped on it for my photo album, and pulled up the picture of the arm and bracelet. "A child, or a young teen, perhaps. Maybe even an orphan." I let that word linger in the air and watched as a slight smile lifted Carlos Garza's lips.

He sipped the scotch, eyeing me, and said, lowering his glass, "I am no bird, and no net ensnares me." He waited for a response, and when he didn't receive one from me, he continued, "From *Jane Eyre*, one of my favorite books in English. I, too, was an orphan. I have a special sympathy for them."

I could feel the sweat under my armpits, on my forehead. "What do you know about these bracelets?" I pointed to the photograph. "Do they mean anything? I'm told they come from the west coast here."

Garza reached for my phone, lifted some reading glasses from his pocket, looked for a minute, and handed it back, shaking his head. "The bracelets are Huichol Indian, traditionally from here on the west coast, but cheap imitations can be found everywhere—the streets, the airports. Many of our traditional crafts are mass produced in China." He shrugged. "I have a strong feeling, señora, you are not telling me things."

He waited, and I began to panic that he would put a gun to my head and demand to know everything I knew. And what would I say? Because what *did* I know, really? Fletcher was a pedophile. Mike knew, and Francois was here with Fletcher, for some reason. Seriously, who was I kidding? There was a 99.9 percent chance Garza already knew all this and more. But I couldn't make myself say anything. I froze.

"No problem," he continued. "I understand loyalty. It is an honorable trait, one I value highly. But you also care about this crime, and so you have a conflict. Conflicts, I understand as well." He sipped his drink and stared at me. "All right. I know some people in the States. I will see if they have resources perhaps not available to you. What do you say to that?"

"I say thank you. *Gracias.*"

Garza laughed. "No, señora, you must answer with the following: You must ask what you can do for me. I need a favor from you as well." He patted me on the arm. "Don't be afraid. Just a small favor. I will let you know soon what I want."

"An offer I can't refuse, right?" I immediately regretted the snarky comeback. Who did I think I was messing with here?

But Garza laughed. "*El Padrino. The Godfather.* Like the movies. Yes, an offer you can't refuse." He laughed again.

And then the driver laughed, and Sanchez did, too. It seemed almost required, so I forced myself to smile, to chuckle. "Just like the movies," I repeated.

A scary movie. And I was in it.

5

NATHAN

A couple of other passengers had already boarded the Ventana Azul van when Nathan climbed in: a blond movie-star type in a white suit, and some French guy. Well, he'd seemed French to Nathan, because he'd greeted him with a disinterested Gallic nod and a mumbled *bonjour* before pushing his chic glasses up on his straight, thin nose, tossing his perfectly cut hair, and returning to his newspaper. Neither of them looked like the bird-watching type, so where they came from, Nathan had no idea. Anyway, the birders weren't due until the day after tomorrow. He planned to use the time to read up on hummingbirds. Perhaps, he'd like to do more of this in his free time, which he seemed to have an abundance of.

"*Bienvenidos*, Señor Bernstein. I am Consuela, owner of Ventana Azul," the blonde said, reaching her hand across the front seat and placing her red-tipped fingers on his arm. "So pleased to finally meet you. So many charming emails from you and your company. Lovely name, Birds of Paradise."

"Ready to roll?" Bud hoisted himself into the driver's seat, all smiles, and turned the key in the ignition. Now on the resort's payroll and pilot in command of their expensive ride, Bud no longer drove like a maniac. He avoided ruts and potholes, taking the curves slowly enough that the French guy could read and Nathan could take in the tropical scenery—the lush greenery, the flowering tabachines trees. Every now and then, a roadside marker indicated a village—San this or that—some Gauguin-like settlement of wooden shacks next to questionably sanitary streams where half-naked children played while bright yellow butterflies flew around them. Or, at least, that was how travel magazines would describe them, omitting the words "questionably sanitary."

Bud and the señora had a little sotto voce chat in the front seat. Very friendly—the usual stuff about the terrible traffic in Mexico City, the fantastic changes in the zocalo, the new shops and restaurants and fabulous boutique hotels, and how wonderful Carlos Slim was to provide all the funds.

Nathan caught Bud eyeing him in the rearview mirror and thought it best not to reveal he'd been interested in the conversation. To hear the two of them talk, it sounded like an advertisement for visiting Mexico City. Maybe they wanted him to inquire so they could recommend a friend's hotel there, which he had no intention of doing. Anything that had anything to do with Mr. Bud Delano was off the list of possibilities. He closed his eyes, leaned his head back on the seat, and pretended to sleep.

About forty-five minutes up the road, the van parked in front of an elaborate wrought-iron gate in the middle of the jungle. Surreal, the whole setting, the gate more appropriate for Buckingham Palace than for the jungle. The señora punched some numbers on her smartphone, the gate opened, and, within minutes, Nathan found himself in the breezy corridor of Ventana Azul, staring past purple bougainvillea toward the Pacific Ocean, a shimmering, teal-colored expanse.

"Nathan, Nathan." A very bronzed man, sporting a white guayabera shirt and a bright red woven scarf, came striding toward him, arms outstretched, calling his name. "*Benvenuto, benvenuto, amico americano.* I am Marco." He grasped Nathan's shoulders and stared into his eyes as if he were Odysseus finally returning home to Ithaca. Next, he aimed his blue headlights at the French guy. "Francois Richter. So glad to meet you." He beamed and shook the Frenchman's hand. "*Ça va?*" Turning back to Nathan, he laughed. "You have met Francois, I see. He has come to try to persuade us to sell the hotel. His equity fund wants to buy our little establishment. I will not sell. *Non, non, non, je ne le vendrai pas!* Rodrigo?" he called out. "Rodrigo! Now, where is he? Excuse me a moment, please." He left his two guests standing by the desk. Nathan nodded and shrugged at Francois. Francois sat on a bench, lifted his paper, and continued reading. Soon Rodrigo was found, the guests' bags handed off to the help, and Marco draped his arm over Nathan's shoulder. "Let me show you around."

They wandered from the corridor to the patio, with its view of the azure sea, where, in the hotel's little private cove, a yacht was anchored—the dolce vita set, Nathan imagined, sunbathing topless on its decks. Marco directed him to a covered pavilion, its roof dripping with more bougainvillea, and down some steps to the stone paths leading along the cliff into the jungle. "We believe Ventana Azul is a sacred space, and we want our guests to experience the spiritual element of descent, as in the Eleusinian mysteries. If it seems a bit intimidating"—he paused, closing his eyes, and breathed deeply, before opening them again—"then our guest is projecting his own demons and needs to confront them. What better place than here?" Marco stopped and waved his arm around the circular pavilion, the patio, the sea, and the jungle. "Here, where we are watched over by the monkey god, the coyote god, and the jaguar god."

They continued down the stone path, through tunnels of foliage, hibiscus, and palms, past the rose-colored villas that made up the resort. Marco pointed out the art gallery, the meditation *palapa*, the gym, the aromatherapy center, and the *palapa* for lectures on alternative healing conducted by a variety of spiritual healers. "We camped here, you know, to feel the earth before any of this was here, before we began the building *nostro paraiso*. The Aztecs built no enormous monuments on the coast. They were seduced by the environment into a state of ecstatic complacency. As was I, my friend. As was I."

Ecstatic complacency. The monkey god. Oh, good grief. Marco was handing Nathan the same guru spiels his other guests got— probably well-heeled ladies of a certain age. He wouldn't be expected to mimic this malarkey on the bird-watching tour, would he? Nathan could hear Karen scolding him. *Stop being such a tight-ass, Nathan. Relax.* So he nodded and murmured approving statements at what he hoped were appropriate moments as Marco babbled on about indigenous architectural styles, explaining why he and his *compagna*, Consuela—whom Nathan had already met in the van, no?—had been careful to adhere to the *palapa* structure: It had developed here on the coast in magnificent isolation and was a timeless, structural vernacular.

By the time he got around to explaining how distinctions between interior and exterior should be blurred, how angles must be replaced by sensuous curves, they'd entered Nathan's villa. Marco pushed open the rough wooden shutters, and the sea appeared in the window, the sunlight dancing off its surface, blue water turning to silver sparkles in the early-afternoon light.

"We have no window glass here, as you can tell, no separation from the sea, the sky, and the earth. That is how we try to live. In harmony. Well, I must attend to our French guest. Luncheon is at two, in an hour. You will hear the chimes. We have no clocks. We are on sacred time here."

Nathan had heard versions of this one-with-nature song and dance at every winter watering hole of the one-percenters he'd ever been to. Truth be told, Nathan's family was one of them, and he had been dragged around as a child to, let's see, Ibiza, Mykonos, Sardinia, where the same lines involving sea, air, indoors, outdoors, nature

were recited. Amazing how close to nature and the cosmic spirit
money could get you. Ventana Azul was just a different version. The
Riviera on peyote. Of course, this whole inner monologue was for
Karen's benefit, for her ghost, which was always with him.

He leaned against the window ledge and stared at the sea, listening for the call of the trogon: *ka-COW, ka-COW*—a sound he had
heard only in Audubon recordings. But all he could identify were
the songs of a yellow grosbeak and a western scrub jay. They were
ubiquitous, but the trogons, they were the prize, and their habitat was
higher up in the foothill scrub. Still, he kept listening, looking. The
thrill of bird-watching relied on seeing the unexpected, the unusual,
or so his mother used to say.

Nathan pulled his binoculars out of his backpack, grabbed his
mother's old birding book—Howell's, the best—and lifted the glasses
to his eyes. Turning to the sea and focusing on the sugar-white yacht,
he watched as a few men pulled up the anchor. No topless women in
sight. Soon he heard a motor start up, and the boat began to move.
The sound of the motor faded, and the sails fluttered and filled.

Nathan turned back to his Howell's, pulled out his notebook, and
began a list of birds his little tour group should look for. Something
kept nagging at him, though. Why here? Bird-watchers just didn't
seem the luxury-resort type—they of the sensible shoes and safari
hats, early to bed and to rise, loaded up with sunscreen, like his
mother and her pals on their birding days.

He'd filled up a page and was beginning to jot down notes, when
he heard the lunch bell chime, the temple gong of sacred time echoing through the hibiscus. He set the notebook on the bedside table,
relieved to have gotten a start on what he considered his class. If he
could do this, he might be able to get back to work. It would be a
trial run, he told himself as he walked up the flower-lined path to the
upper patio. The nice thing about bird-watching was, you didn't talk.
Talking sort of defeated the point, scared the birds. And whatever

lectures he gave would be short and to the point, because everyone would be eager to get started. The hard knot he'd felt in his chest or thereabouts began to loosen, to melt, almost, like something warming in the sun, which he supposed was the whole point of these places: sun, warmth.

Not just the sun and warmth, Nathan. It's the monkey god, watching over you, Karen said. He was certain he heard it, Karen's voice whispering in his ear as she slipped her ghost arm around his waist and led the way.

Francois Richter, the only one seated at the table under the pavilion, raised his glass as Nathan pulled up a chair. "*Santé,*" he said, taking a sip.

"Are you really trying to buy the hotel?" Nathan lifted the wine out of the ice bucket and poured a splash, swirled, smelled the bouquet. *Nice nose, no cork. Okay, we're good here.* He noticed Francois watching. Was the French guy amused? "My folks own a winery," Nathan admitted. "Full disclosure."

"I see you are well trained, and yes, of course I am trying to buy this piece of paradise. Why not?" Francois turned to face the sea, saying nothing more.

"Will he sell?"

Francois cut into the red snapper on his plate, took a bite, and dabbed his lips. "Eventually, yes. They all get tired. They have all gotten tired, the little hoteliers along the Costa Alegre. My company is much more efficient. The others sold. He will sell."

"I don't know if you are interested in my opinion," Nathan said, looking around for Marco and Consuela—where were they, anyway?—"but I think tourists like individually owned places. They have more character, and besides, Marco's passion for the resort is obvious."

Richter set his glass on the table. "And do you know a great deal about passion, *mon ami*?" He raised his glass again in a little salute.

Ah, yes, Nathan was reminded of one of the more annoying traits of the upper class: how they acted like they had a handle on the whole passion-for-living thing. As if the good life were all wine, women, and song. And it was, for them, at the expense of the rest of the world's poorer inhabitants, many of them suffering from diseases that a simple antibiotic could cure and who needed to be cared for by people like his wife.

"Yes, well, passions can change," Richter continued. "Grow suddenly cold, can they not? And now, with everything that is going on in Mexico, especially here on the west coast, we have more resources for security. Our friends Marco and Consuela would hate to be sued, would they not? Are you not the least bit afraid a drug kingpin will come down from the hills and murder you in your bed?"

"That drug thing is overblown. You don't get involved, and nothing will happen to you." Nathan repeated what Birds of Paradise had told him.

Richter stared at him for a minute, started to say something, seemed to think better of it. He just shrugged and returned to his meal.

"Here it is. Here it is." Marco arrived at the table, carrying a large coffee-table book. *Design and Alchemy*, one of Nathan's mother's productions from her very chic design service in both San Francisco and St. Helena. "In California's wine country," he explained to Francois, an explanation that Nathan thought was probably unnecessary, since Francois seemed underwhelmed, to say the least, by the information.

"So remarkable that I should meet the designer's son."

Nathan's heart sank. To say he and his family were estranged would have been too extreme, but there was a distance he wanted to maintain, especially in places like this, where the source of his family's wealth—industrial cleansers, seriously—would be the stuff of lore. An American success story. His Jewish immigrant relatives had done all the heavy lifting, and it had then been up to his parents and Nathan to polish the rougher surfaces of that history. This task required that he be fluent in the language of the club, able to toss off tidbits like "What did you think of the new exhibit at the Tate Modern? Worth crossing the pond for?" Or this one: "Just got back from the Rio Douro area. Portugal is the new Tuscany, you know." And, last but not least: "We're thinking about wading into a bit of derivative trading. How about you?"

The first time Karen had ever heard him trot out this stuff at one of his parents' soirees, she had looked at him like he was speaking in tongues, like he might have just had a stroke. Which brought up another sore point between him and his parents. They had never approved of Karen. Why? 1) She was not Jewish. 2) She was not Jewish. And 3) She discussed things like curing giardia and the lingering side effects of malaria, and who, asked his mother, wanted to hear about diseases? Nathan once overheard his mother wondering aloud to his father if Karen was on the spectrum, but his father, Nathan had to hand it to him, shut her down. "What are you, a psychiatrist? You know about spectrums from what, Miriam?" And frankly, if anyone were on the spectrum, it would be he, Nathan, Mr. Introvert, himself.

"You can Google anything." Marco interrupted Nathan's dive into his family's more troubled side. "We can't have just anyone here. Everyone has to be vetted. I believe that is the word. You and all of your bird-watchers, too. A very exclusive group of people from California. Birds of Paradise organization is top of the line." He returned to the subject of Nathan's mother, Miriam Bernstein. "Very spiritual, very spiritual woman, your mother. We used many of her ideas. Really extraordinary. Such taste, but please." He handed Nathan a pen and pointed for him to autograph under his mother's epigraph: "To all who seek the beautiful life, may your dreams transform you."

Nathan signed and passed the book back to Marco. When he

looked up, Francois was staring at him like some secret had been revealed, and at least one secret was beginning to dawn on Nathan, too: His mother was the one who'd set up this whole bird-watching thing. She was on the San Francisco Audubon board, had heard some fascinating—her word—presentation by Birds of Paradise at some fancy luncheon and gotten all excited about tropical migration zones for hummingbirds. All it had taken was one quick call to Birds of Paradise to get Nathan hired as a tour guide. She meant well, of course, but he knew she also wanted him out of university work and back into the fold, managing the family foundation and so on, now that Karen was dead. And for that he'd need to hobnob with the wealthy and powerful—the having-connections theory of getting ahead in life. He reached for more wine and bit into his *huachinango veracruzano.* "Nice complement with the wine, Marco," he said. He might as well play the expected role, now that Google had outed him as a member of the 0.01 percent club of wealthy and rarefied jet-setters.

The rest of the lunch chatter went on, as Nathan expected. Have you seen *Sideways?* Can Napa wines really compete with French wines? Terroir and vintages and the whole boring repertoire. *It's just booze!* Nathan wanted to scream. *Booze, people!* So when Francois and Marco decided to take coffee in Marco's air-conditioned office and left him alone, he closed his eyes and savored the quiet for a while, sipping coffee and listening to the gentle splash of waves from the cove down the hill.

He pushed aside his coffee cup and wandered to the pool, deciding to stretch out on a chaise lounge. His irritation at having seen his mother's book and the feelings it had stirred up about his role in his family—his *obligations,* as he'd been told many times—were still churning inside him. He was reminded once again of his resentment—okay, let's use his therapist's word, *rage*—at his mother's lack of appreciation of Karen. And didn't everything return him to thoughts of her? Even this place. Especially this place. Ventana Azul was pretty much the perfect setting for romance—lush jungle teeming with night-blooming jasmine, the sound of the sea, the smell of the salt spray, the negative ions he'd once read about that floated around in the marine air like molecular particles of joy. Why had he and Karen never come to a place like this? Because he'd been too busy working, he realized, getting tenure, an international reputation, making it on his own, away from his family. He'd thought he and Karen had all the time in the world, and now guilt and sorrow pressed on his chest with a heavy, burning hand. He'd been selfish and stupid, fighting some Oedipal battle with his mother, and now his conscience was forcing him to face it, along with everything else.

"You, my friend, are carrying a lot of psychic baggage."

Marco's voice floated down from above, shocking Nathan with its abrupt pull into the here and now. He opened his eyes and squinted into the form of his host, backlit from the sun. Swinging his legs around the side of the chaise lounge, he dropped his sunglasses on the table and said, "Don't we all, Marco, after a certain age, have some sort of past? I mean, I would hope so. You know, the well-lived life and all that."

At that point, Marco, in all his white-linen finery, squatted in front of Nathan and stared into his eyes. "Breathe in." Marco demonstrated, closing his eyes, inhaling audibly. "And breathe out. Let the past go. Let go of the grief. Breathe in the possibilities in the universe. I am sorry about your wife, Nathan. But life, as the Buddha said, is suffering."

Ah, so word had gotten around via his mother to Birds of Paradise, to Marco, and, Nathan supposed now, to the universe that he was a grieving widower in need of some sort of spiritual guidance. For all his mother's attachment to her Jewish heritage, she had no problem going off in this cockamamie direction on occasion, as long as it wasn't the High Holy Days or something.

Nathan was now even more desperate to return to his thoughts of Karen and leave behind old battles with his family. "Hey," he said, hoping he sounded exuberant and psychologically healthy enough to be left alone, "I was just thinking of a swim."

Marco apparently approved of Nathan's throwing himself, *avec tout le* psychic baggage, into the pool. He bowed, hands together, like the Dalai Lama, and let him pass.

The pool was one of those infinity constructs where the edge of the basin and the ocean seem to merge. He swam across in a few strong strokes and rested his arms and head on the side of the deck. Someone had scattered hibiscus flowers on the surface of the water, and the blossoms floated around in his wake. The place was a veritable women's-magazine photograph, which made him wonder something else: Where were all the rich girls? Maybe it was off-season, but did bikini wearing and tequila shooters have a season? There were usually a few models or would-be models lounging around these places, game for whatever.

He turned over and floated on his back, pushing the tropical flowers out of the way, drifting back and forth in the water. Every now and then, he dove under the surface, and each time he came back up, the softness of the tropical air surprised him. California was either too bright or too foggy or too windy. It was rugged. This was definitely not rugged. He swam back to the pool's edge, rested his chin on his forearms again, and stared out to sea. The yacht was back. Someone was lowering the sails. Nathan flipped over on his back and tried to become one with the universe, tried to connect with his dreams, the alchemy, and all the folderol, but really with Karen.

How long, he wondered, had he been floating there? At some point in his dreamlike state, someone had lit the citronella torches by the side of the pool and he hadn't heard a thing. A little disconcerting, he thought, entertaining a moment of paranoia. Paranoia. One of his demons, Marco would have told him. He heard a voice, sharp, commanding, but definitely female.

"Kate, William," the voice called again. *"Ven acá."* Yelps and barks followed, and then the scratching sound of claws hurrying against the tile floor of the main *palapa*. Two white Afghan hounds, elegant as the royals they were named for, loped down the stairs from the reception area. *Rich people's dogs*, he thought. They were followed by Señora Consuela from the van. Nathan sank back down into the water, but the Afghans had spotted him and were bounding in his direction.

"Oh, there you are, Señor Bernstein. What a good idea. A swim would be so pleasant." She cast off her suit jacket and trousers. All she was wearing underneath were two white strips of bare skin where her bikini had been at some point, and a diamond tennis bracelet. Nathan turned away. Jesus, was he such a prude? Soon, a current of water swirled around him and up came Consuela, who put her hands on his shoulders and brushed the side of his face with her cheek, kissing the air somewhere in the vicinity of his ears, first the right one, then the left. Consuela, he noticed, wasn't as young as she'd looked from a distance, which made all the rest of her that much more impressive.

"So glad to finally have a chance to talk with you," she murmured. "You can call me Concha. Everyone does." She leaned her head back on the rim of the pool as if it were a pillow and extended her body, just under the water's surface, in front of Nathan. *"El agua. Delicioso,"* she said, closing her eyes, daring Nathan to look, which he forced himself not to do.

How long had it been since he'd been with a woman? He didn't like to think, couldn't imagine being with anyone but Karen. But he didn't trust his body not to just act reflexively, out of desperation, starvation. He turned around and faced the ocean, pressing himself against the pool's plaster, while Kate and William, in spite of their House of Windsor names, did decidedly doglike things: snarling and leaping about in mock turf wars, drinking out of the pool, peeing on the side of the bougainvillea pots. To all of this, Consuela or Concha seemed oblivious. Of course, she had a squadron of maids just to clean up after the dogs, maybe even a nanny for each of them, like movie stars have for their kids. He wondered how long she would stay floating in front of him like this, waiting for him to make a move. Maybe he was kidding himself—a scrawny, Berkeley professor was certainly not her thing. And bird-watcher? That, too. Too wimpy. Ah, but the wine millions. How that changed things. Maybe he could make a quick getaway. But halfway out of the pool, he heard Consuela call out, "Don't get out of the water. I need to get someone to take care of Marco's *pinche perros*. They'll devour you."

The translation, Nathan knew, was basically "Marco's fucking dogs." Very ladylike. He slipped back into the water. "Sure, no problem," he said, wondering why he was being so polite. Some kind of survival instinct told him it was a good thing to do.

Concha lifted her arm, and the diamond bracelet fell a few inches, from wrist to forearm, flickering as she reached for a bell by the side of the pool. A tiny chime in her hand. "I need the water to balance my *dosha* type. Do you know your *dosha* type, Mr. Bernstein? *Dosha*. Hindu. From an ancient healing method. Ayurvedic. One of our practitioners will explain tomorrow when she tests your radial pulses."

A vision appeared to Nathan: microscopic Michelin tires rotating along the blue veins of his wrists. Probably not what Concha meant.

"The treatments are part of the bird-watching package. We feel all the birders are *vata* types. I'm feeling strong *vata* energy coming from you. Air energy. I'm fire, myself."

Just then, three young Mexican women in some kind of traditional garb appeared at the edge of the pool, like dancers in a Cinco de Mayo parade. Concha gave instructions in a language Nathan could not understand, and they trotted off, taking the white dogs with them.

"The girls are lovely, are they not? We saved them from their dreadful little Huichol village. Disgusting place, really." Concha closed her eyes again and leaned her head against the tile lip of the pool. "I've ordered a lime-honey infusion for you and some cedarwood incense. *Vata* energy is difficult energy to handle."

Settled back in his villa with the Huichol maids fussing over him, Nathan sipped the herbal drink Concha had ordered while they waved smoke around the room, lifted the mosquito netting from his bed, passed their burning sticks across the cover. They waved incense over the candles in the corner, and they even waved the little bundles around Nathan himself. It was sort of like being psychically frisked by cosmic TSA workers. He tried to feel his *doshas* balancing, but it wasn't working for him. Wasn't the monkey god a trickster god in a number of religions, or was that the roadrunner he was thinking of? He told himself to stop with the sarcasm already. Realigning *doshas* was not such a bad way to spend the day. Hadn't he spent whole days in his pajamas in bed, doing crossword puzzles and sudoku—anything to fill the time? He closed his eyes and listened to the evening sounds, the frog racket. The room almost vibrated from the noise. Some of the frogs had even leaped through the open windows and had stuck themselves to the walls like brown, croaking suction cups.

Open windows. That was what was wrong with this picture. Nathan put his cup down on the floor and called to one of the maids. "*Señorita?* Uh, *momento.*" The cosmic fumigators stared back at him, mute. He didn't care how fabulous this place was supposed to be—anybody who traveled had learned from near misses and close calls to be careful. The last time he'd had no window screens, in Playa del Carmen with Karen, their problem had been rats the size of Volkswagens. The rodents had managed to climb up a two-story-high palm tree outside their eco-chic hotel room and spent the evening commuting across the bedspread. Never again.

"Excuse me," Nathan asked one of the dumbfounded maids, "*seguridad?* Is there any security here? How can I lock?" Rats were one problem, theft another. He was starting to count the days until this job was over—it was all too strange—and he definitely did not want to have to deal with a stolen passport, no cash, you name it.

The maids chattered all at once, the gist of which was that there were people out there.

"What people?" he demanded.

"*Gente de seguridad,*" the older one answered. Security people. The maids seemed a bit anxious about this, too, which was no comfort. Nathan had heard too many horror stories of what happened to college kids camped on beaches in Mexico. *Gente de seguridad* was not good enough. He wanted to speak to the owner.

As if on cue, he heard footsteps on the pebble path. Torchlight reflected on the leaves of a large banana tree in front of the villa. Sometime during the altercation, one of the maids must have slipped out and told Señora Consuela, because there she was, standing in his doorway, hair still dripping from the pool, tiki-torch bearers at her side. His mood soured further at all this East-meets-West hooey.

Concha didn't look too thrilled, either, her stare as lethal as Lady Macbeth's in Kurosawa's *Throne of Blood*. She looked like she might start shrieking in Japanese while the torchbearers pulled out samurai swords.

"I hear you have concerns," she said.

"Yes, I have concerns." Nathan did not care one whit that he looked like a wuss. "It's entirely one thing to be watched over by the jaguar god. It's the murderers and thieves I have a little trouble with. Oh, yes, and the rats that live in palm trees. I want a room with windows and doors I can lock."

Concha waved her hand in the air, as if that would suffice to brush away all anxieties. "We understand the difficulties of tourism in Mexico and have taken all necessary precautions."

"Which are?"

The maids were still swabbing the spiritual decks with their incense. "*Basta*," Concha hissed in their direction. "Enough. Go." Concha's Hindu-healer act evaporated, and she now used the same peremptory tone with him that she had used with the maids. "This is a sensitive matter. Most of our guests know us and know our, how shall I say it, reputation. When a person of a certain stature in Hollywood, let us say, or in a large, multinational corporation, says to an equally important friend in Hollywood or in another corporation that this person will be well taken care of at Ventana Azul, it is understood that security issues have been addressed. Obviously, for people of such importance, people who must often travel with armed bodyguards even in the United States, it is not enough to have locks on the door. You must understand, at our prices and with our waiting lists, we do not count housewives from Iowa among our clientele. Come. Let me show you." She waved her arm in his direction. "What do you see?" Concha didn't wait for an answer. "I'll tell you what you see: nothing but palm, fern, mangrove, and banana trees. You see the creeping *matapalo* vine. You see volunteer coffee bushes growing below, in the tree understory. You see a bird-and-butterfly habitat, because that is what we have planted here. However, it is what you *don't* see that is most impressive. What I am about to tell you is completely off the record. Do I make myself clear?"

"I gather we're not talking about the coyote god here?" Nathan said.

Concha sneered. "We live here, my friend. We do not just visit. We have accepted all the paradoxes and contradictions that are Mexico." Ventana Azul, she explained, as if to a tedious child, had a unique relationship with the Mexican military. There was a thousand-man garrison nearby, and she and Marco took advantage of off-duty soldiers. It was beneficial to all. Ventana Azul paid more per day that the army paid per week. Commanding officers got a finder's fee, Concha called it, to compensate for any inconvenience. A bribe, in other words. As a result, the jungle, which had already been cordoned off with high-tech electrical fencing from a private American prison corporation, was swarming with Mexican soldiers with the necessary tools of the trade and training provided by American security experts. "Should you need anything . . ." Concha didn't finish her sentence. Instead, just to prove the point, she lifted her cell phone and pushed a button. *"Una botella de mezcal, y dos vasos."*

It had been some rent-a-soldier, Nathan realized, with slow horror, who'd informed Concha about his questioning the maids. Jesus. He tried to figure out what else they'd seen. Had he picked his nose? Talked to himself? But before he could inventory his past actions, one of the maids appeared with a tray, a bottle of mezcal, and two brandy glasses, as requested.

"We have technologically efficient ways to communicate, even here in the jungle," Concha said, waving her cell phone before pouring the mezcal into the little saucer her brandy glass was sitting on. "We must pay respects to the animals first." She carried the saucer over to the corner and set it down next to a saucer of what appeared to be milk.

"Is that for the watch cats? Are they heavily armed as well?"

"No." Concha told him. "I learned this from the Rajneesh. It's for the . . . how do you say in English? The *cascabels.*" Rattlesnakes. "It will keep them out of your bed." She poured the mezcal into the two other glasses and offered Nathan one. "And, of course, the *ratones* you are so worried about."

He could hardly imagine Hollywood types staying in a place where they might find rattlesnakes lapping up mezcal like kittens, dipping little forked tongues into the bowl in the corner. These people were delusional.

"*Salud*," Concha said. She downed her shot in one gulp. "Oh—
Marco wants to see you in the office. Business details. So tedious."
And with that, she was gone.

"You create your own reality, Francois." Marco was in the middle of
some argument with Richter, who was lounging on one of the sofas in
his office, flipping through an Italian *Vogue*, when Nathan entered the
room. "If spiritual enlightenment is important to a person, he will find a
way to manifest the wealth necessary to come here as a guest. Let Bernie
Sanders worry about the poor people. Your company will never make
a profit by turning this place into a crowd-pleasing Best Western just to
achieve a high volume of traffic. The jungle and the wild coast are never
going to appeal to budget-conscious families—please. Your guests will
need to be more, how do I say, citizens of the world."

Marco waved an elaborate, Aztec-looking, silver letter opener
with a little hummingbird on the end in Richter's direction. "It is
important to stand in the space of abundance," he said, before he
sliced through another envelope, glanced at it, and threw it in the
wastebasket. He lifted a pill from a silver tray and knocked it back
with some murky-looking water, while motioning for Nathan to
have a seat. "Chromium picolate and lemon water," he announced.
"Clarifies the skin."

It could have been valium and tequila he was drinking, for all
Nathan cared. A few more days in this place, and he'd be standing in
the space of substance abuse. He was starting to yearn for Berkeley,
the grimy fog, the sound of the BART train.

Marco abandoned his argument with Richter and turned his
attention to Nathan. "Ah, my friend, we are so sorry, but I have an
email just now from Birds of Paradise. The tour group will be arriving a day late. Something to do with the charter flight. This will be no
problem for you, I assume."

At this, Richter stopped turning the pages of the magazine. *What's it to me?* Nathan wondered. *But yes, it is in fact a problem.* "Just a day? Sure. Any more, I don't know."

Marco's computer chimed, announcing incoming mail. "Yes, here it is. Mr. Fletcher, a state senator, will be arriving tomorrow. Mr. Chiu from American Transports, too."

"What about the rest of them?" Nathan asked.

"There is no rest of them. That is all. Very, very private, Nathan. Very exclusive. These men need to relax, as you will find out when you meet them. Very important men. After looking at birds, they will then go fishing with Pescado de Oro, a company we recommend because of Señor Bud. They will do a little business."

Nathan felt goose bumps on his arms and legs—a strange sensation out here in the tropics. But the air in Marco's office was frigid from air-conditioning. Now, the announcement that the birding tour was basically a boondoggle for corporate lobbyists made his blood run cold. He needed some air, humid as it was. "Hey, Francois," he said, as he headed for the door, "it's a small group. Want to join us? I'm sure they wouldn't mind."

"No, no." Francois said, returning to his magazine. "I saw Hitchcock's *feelm* with *Teepee Aadrun*. Birds flying everywhere are not for me."

6

CALLIE

I locked the door to my room, walked down the beach about a quarter mile, hung a right past some bungalows, and circled back along the main drag to the front entrance of Cabanas del Mar. I wanted to scope out the scene this morning, after what I'd seen in the Chinese restaurant the evening before, make sure Bud wasn't lurking around. He could easily make a quick call to Fletcher to tell him about some American woman showing up in San Benito, and Fletcher would connect the dots right back to me. It was a chance I didn't want to take. I peeked into the breakfast-room windows, which were open to the street, and the coast seemed clear. The only folks there were a couple of gray-haired retiree types whom I had never seen around the place before—maybe they were staying at the RV park by the lagoon—and a dark-haired girl on her phone, texting with a vengeance. Even my neighbor who'd had the fight with Bud seemed to have disappeared.

All in all, the place was pretty empty, so I relaxed a little, walked in, grabbed a table, and pulled out a chair facing the entrance, lifting a coffee cup in Garcia's direction. "*Café con leche? Por favor? Azúcar?*" I picked up the menu on the table and studied the pictures of different egg combos. Pictures. Simpler for the tourists. A couple of eggs over easy, more coffee, and then I would call Rosie, tell her

Berto's "cousin" Guillermo had been very helpful and that I would explain more when I returned. Really, I had Fletcher dead to rights, with photos to prove it. He and I, along with our good friends in the FBI, would have to have a little heart-to-heart when I got home. The real worry now was about Mike, about his being in imminent danger, even from Francois. With what I knew now, I would confront Francois and, God willing, Mike, who, I fervently hoped, would be safely home. I wouldn't even have to ask for Fletcher's endorsement. I would demand it, would run against his corruption, clean the place up. No need to take Powerful Businessman up on his offer of help. It was definitely time to get home and find Mike.

"You're an attorney, right?"

I jerked my head up from the pictures of *huevos rancheros*. The dark-haired girl with the iPhone pulled up a chair and sat down. No "May I?" No nothing.

"Hold on there, honey." I said. "I'm not really in the mood for company."

"I am not company. I am Eva. Guillermo's friend. We need to talk."

Oh, no. A friend. A jealous hissy fit. I was absolutely not in the mood, and where, by the way, was my coffee? "I think you've made a mistake," I said, looking around for Garcia, who seemed to have disappeared.

Eva's phone dinged as a text came in. She tapped rapidly, pushed SEND, and turned her attention back to me. "No. Not a mistake. These people you saw yesterday when you were at Guillermo's office are very, very bad. I need to show you something. We need to go."

"Wait a minute. First of all, I don't know you. Secondly, I need coffee and breakfast. And finally, I'm not going anywhere with you until I talk to your"—I made air quotes—"*friend* Guillermo. Actually, upon reflection, I'm not going anywhere with you even if I do."

"*Joven.*" Eva snapped her fingers at Garcia, and he came running, nodding his head as she spoke rapid-fire Spanish in a tone that would have gotten service at the Ritz. "I got you a large coffee in a paper cup and a breakfast burrito. We must go now to my car. We'll discuss it there. You have a gun?"

"As a matter of fact, I don't carry a weapon. Last I checked, it's hard to get them through airport security and illegal to carry them here. So, no gun. Are you a cop? You seem to be pretty good at getting takeout food. It's one of the job requirements."

"I have Glock 40 in my bag. 'Illegal' is subject to debate here. I will give you my gun. That way, you'll feel safe. You can shoot me if I turn out to be a dangerous woman."

"Eva. Tell you what. You go get Guillermo, and the three of us can have a little chat. I need to make sure you're not out of your mind. Cancel the to-go order or take it with you. We're done. *Adios. Comprende?*" I stood up. If the girl didn't walk away, I would. Turned out Eva left in a huff.

Three cups of coffee, two eggs, a couple slices of not-bad bacon, and some okay toast later, I was in the mood to regroup. I would go back to my room, pack up, check the flights and the transportation out of here. I'd gotten what I came for.

But since it was pretty much mission accomplished, a major miracle, I might even go for a swim, a plan that involved buying a suit. They all looked pretty hideous, from what I could tell by walking past the beachside shops, but desperate times called for desperate measures. I'd earned a swim, at the very least. It might even help dampen my fears about Mike. I paid the check and walked back to my room, keeping an eye out for the neighbor or Bud.

At first I thought I'd opened the wrong door. A muscular man, dressed sort of like a cowboy, or a Central Valley farmer, for that matter, was sitting on the bed, and I slowly registered that I'd seen him the night before. He was Garza's driver, and it was my room, all right, my T-shirt thrown over the chair, my suitcase opened.

"Señora," the man said, as he stood and shut the door. "I am sorry for the inconvenience, but you will please come with me."

"Oh, hell no," I said, before I saw the gun. A Glock 40. Popular little item down here. Not something you argue with. "Let me guess: You're with Eva, right? Garza sent you both."

The man nodded.

"Can I at least use the ladies' room first?"

"Of course," the man said, walking into the bathroom and checking that there was no escape route available. "It's going to be a long drive."

About an hour and a half later, after driving through a tropical version of hell and gone, Eva, plus the driver with the gun who'd escorted me to Garza's tricked-out, armored Range Rover with mirrored windows, leather bucket seats, and surround-sound speakers, and I were parked under a half-defoliated mimosa tree off the side of a red dirt road, the engine running, air-conditioning blasting. Beyond the darkened window stretched a hundred feet of dirt runway that ended near a twig shack, its roof covered with palm leaves. A black narco-van was idling near it—same mirrored windows, the whole bit. So far, I'd said only two words to my kidnappers. Actually, three. "Fuck you, Eva."

"You'll feel differently when you see what I have to show you," Eva had said. "Trust me."

"Right. Trust you."

"Here, take this." Eva handed me a card with the words *Casa de Maria* written on it, along with an address in Puerto Vallarta and a couple of phone numbers. "Casa de Maria is an orphanage. Call the Mother Superior." Eva reached for her phone. "She'll tell you I'm on the level."

I shrugged, took the card. Some nun's word out here in the jungle wasn't going to do me a lot of good.

"*Como quieres.*" Eva reached into a large bag on the floor, pulled out binoculars, and handed them to me. "Here."

"What am I looking for?"

"The shipment."

"The shipment of what?"

"You'll see. Then we hope Jim Fletcher gets out of that other van. He's waiting, too."

I sank back against the leather seat and stared at Eva. "You're serious?"

"You help me. I help you. You help Señor Garza. He helps you. That is the way it works here. As you said, *comprende*?"

I focused the binoculars on a group of men waiting under the shack: a couple of soldiers and Bud Delano, the fishing guy who was hooked up with Fletcher.

"You speak good English. Lived in the States?"

"I'm not from here. I'm from California. Mandarina. You know Mandarina?"

"Mandarina? Really," I said. Yeah, I knew it, and Eva knew I knew it, and Garza knew I knew it. "How'd you get here?"

"I think the question is more, how did I get to Mandarina?" She paused, stared out the window, and then turned back to face me. "From the orphanage." She pointed to the card. "Anyway, this is better than Mandarina." She waved her arm at the red-flowering tabachines trees and the palms. "It's a tropical paradise, no?"

I scanned my surroundings, imagining that outside the van's closed windows and above the air conditioner's drone I'd hear the sound of cicadas shrieking, the harsh call of crows. I'd smell the rotting foliage of the jungle, damp and muddy like compost, filling the steamy air. So much for what you call paradise. Eva was staring out the same window, biting a thumbnail, her leg jiggling restlessly. *She's scared*, I thought. *Not a good sign.*

"Look." She finally turned back to me and said, "Guillermo says I can trust you, and I trust him, so here's the deal: My father is Mayor Parra. My foster father, actually. He takes money from Fletcher."

I had been hearing rumors for years. The new skateboard park in Mandarina? Bought with cartel money. The new motor home Parra bought? Ditto. Cops would get close to nailing a meth distribution ring over there, and then—poof—all the witnesses would evaporate. It hadn't been the cartel after all. It had been Fletcher's dirty money all along.

"You're from Mandarina, but you're here. How come?"

"We are part of the protection service that Consuela Mendoza has retained. At least, that's what they think." She pointed to Bud and the men circling around the black van that Fletcher was supposed to be in.

"What about the real security, over there?" I nodded toward Fletcher's van and two army convoy trucks.

"Don't worry. Everything is arranged." She said something in Spanish to the driver, and the truck filled with the sound of those shrieking cicadas I'd just imagined, followed by a man's voice, coming from the speakers, scratchy and amplified by the high-tech system. Someone or someplace around Bud Delano had clearly been wired for sound.

"*Que mas hace?*" One of the soldiers lifted the barrel of his rifle and shoved it against Bud's forearm, right above his diving watch.

"What else does it do?" Eva translated.

I didn't need it, but I was glad not to miss any of the nuances, so to speak.

Bud didn't move his arm away, just stared at the soldier until he lowered the gun. Then he looked at the large gold dial glinting on his wrist. It probably told him what the dashboard in the SUV told me: It was 2:07 p.m. and 93 degrees in the shade.

Bud laughed. "It's telling me, '*Este pinche calor es de la chingada.*'" This heat is a son of a bitch. He waved his other hand in front of his face, a futile attempt to keep the mosquitoes from swarming around his mouth and eyes.

"*Los insectos siempre molestan a los gringos.*" Another soldier laughed, lighting up a cigarette.

"The bugs are bad for the gringos," Eva continued.

Every now and then, one of the men walked out onto the runway and scanned the sky over the southeast horizon for the plane they were waiting for. Nothing. No sound, either, just the screaming cicadas coming over the mic as well. The heat had gotten them going.

"*Siempre lo mismo,*" Bud complained.

Eva translated again. "He is saying each time he waits with Señor Fletcher is the same." She continued over the sound of Bud's nasal twang. "Five hours wasted time, two clowns for company at the *aeropuerto*. Is a joke. But hey, that's what he loves about this place. If a pathetic dirt runway is an airport, then a redneck from Oklahoma like him is king of the world."

Bud stood on the fender of the army transport truck and, holding his arms out like wings, shouted, "I'm king of the world." He jumped down, and the two soldiers, squatting on their haunches in the shade of the palm leaves, playing cards, looked up briefly and then went on with the game. "*El gringo loco,* right?" Bud asked.

He pulled a gun from a shoulder holster under his loose-fitting shirt, twirled it around his fingers, and then aimed it at the skinnier of the two. "*Si, soy loco. Soy un gringo loco.*" The skinny soldier aimed his rifle at Bud before Callie could blink.

"Shit, man!" he yelled. "You're as mean as a damn snake! *Olvídalo.* It was a joke."

"*Cálmate, guey,*" the pimply soldier told his companion. "Sr. Bud is joking. Él *no bromeará más. Cálmate, flaco.*" It took the skinny soldier a while to put the gun down. His reflexes had ratcheted into place and wouldn't budge. I wondered where they trained these guys, wondered if they could even read. They were probably just good for blowing people's brains out. Not necessarily a bad skill to have around these folks.

That's when the pimply soldier started in with the watch again. *"Cuánto costó?"* How much did it cost? he wanted to know.

"Amigos." Bud stuck out his left arm so the two rifle-carrying kids could get a good look. He twisted the dials and punched little buttons.

Eva continued translating. "Señor Bud is showing them how the watch can read the ascent velocity underwater, where its depth display is, how it can measure surface time for after-dive safety."

"This here is a Citizen Hyper Aqualand 260-meter dive watch with computer interface. It'll do everything except give you a blow job." The pimply-faced soldier leered. "What are you grinning about?" Bud taunted him. "You never had a blow job in your life."

The skinny one laughed at his companion.

The soldier changed the subject. *"Cuánto pagaste?"* How much did you pay?

"You want to know how much you have to pay to get a watch like this? Well, my amigo, *you* would have to pay about thirty-five thousand pesos to get a watch like this." Bud, of course, must have known that was more money all at once than they had ever seen in their lives. "I, on the other hand, didn't have to pay a cent. A woman gave it to me."

"Una gringa, verdad?" A *gringa* gave it to you, right? The soldier wanted to know.

"Now," Eva said, "they are talking about girls. *Gringas. Gabachas.* These boys are having a hard time understanding that *gringas* go to bed with men *and* buy them expensive gifts. They think women from the North are freaks of nature. Typical male bullshit talk."

Bud closed his eyes and seemed to tune out while the two soldiers talked about friends of friends of a guy in Acapulco, or Cancun, or Cabo, who'd basically been supported in lavish style by some *gringa* who didn't even know the guy was married. "Hey, Sr. Bud." Skinny grinned at him. "When the *gringas* try me, they'll be giving me los Rolexes. *Si, señor.*"

Bud appeared to be tiring of all the macho hooey. He stretched out on the ground in the shade next to the army truck and pulled his hat over his face.

It was already past 3:00 p.m. I knew they would have to land before sunset. This place wasn't exactly JFK. A pilot would have to deal with an unpaved runway, no lights, and a stand of coconut palms at the southwest end.

Bud lifted his cap, started reminiscing. "Out here, guys, this is easy. You should have been in Quintana Roo. Those flights from Belize, you had to time just right, light enough to land, too dark for anyone to find them once they did. I can still feel my balls freeze, thinking about it. That was before Raul Salinas's green days, *los días verdes.* That was when you had to have real *juevos* to run drugs. Hell, a man's gotta do what a man's gotta do, as my old man used to say every time he broke the seal off a brand-new bottle of Wild Turkey."

"Señor Bud." Skinny called his name, and Bud opened his eyes. The other soldier pointed to the southeast horizon over the mountains, and Bud looked up.

"It took them long enough," Bud groaned, hauling himself up from the ground.

The plane was descending over the sierra. I could hear the dull roar of the engine. The two soldiers put away the cards, put on their shirts and berets, wiped the dust off their boots. "Jesus, you'd think General Patton was on that plane," Bud yelled over the sound of the engine. He said it in English. Eva did not need to translate.

The driver cut off the sound, and Eva motioned for us to cover our ears as the plane's wheels touched the ground and taxied to the end of the strip, sending dust flying everywhere. I pulled out my cell phone and prayed I could get these shots. Neither Eva nor the driver tried to stop me, but I tapped Eva on the arm and mouthed, "Okay?" anyway.

"*Claro,*" she said, and then pointed to the driver, who lifted a Nikon, then started clicking away, one picture after the next, as the plane's door slid open. "But I'll see you get better pictures. Or Guillermo will. One of us." It sounded like a done deal.

"This is what Señor Garza wanted you to see. This is the pilot. Now wait." Eva said.

Another man came out, dressed in army fatigues, carrying two plastic cradles with handles. Baby car seats. "Are those what I think they are?"

"Baby carriers," Eva confirmed. "Chinese babies. From ships in Manzanillo port. They bring in bigger profits. The couples up in San Francisco who buy them think Chinese babies are smarter than Mexican babies. Sometimes they can pass off a Maya baby as Asian. They make even more money that way."

The soldier climbed the plane's steps again and brought out two more carriers, and then two more, and two more and two more.

"Each baby brings in about seventy-five thousand dollars, the girls a little less. You're looking at about a mil right there. Every month, it adds up."

And that's when a man got out of the plane with a Chinese girl, maybe about fourteen, maybe a little more. "The bastard." My chest tightened.

"This is where the real money is. You sell a baby once; you sell a girl infinite times at truck stops, at conventions, online, on the dark web. That's what they'll do when Fletcher's through with her."

The girl threw herself to the ground, refused to walk. A soldier came over, yanked her up, and slapped her, once, twice. Our driver turned up the speakers, and we could hear the girl's wails.

The pilot walked over to the other van. There was some conversation I couldn't really hear and Eva didn't translate. The car filled with the sound of crying babies from the speakers. I turned back to the girl, could see the end-of-the-world look in her eyes. "Oh, Jesus," I said, trying not to scream. "Oh, God."

Another soldier stepped off the plane, holding a rope and leading a chain of children down the steps, like a train of pack mules, toward a makeshift shed along the runway. The girl who couldn't walk found her strength, scrambled away, and ran over to one of the girls in the chain, pulling on her, holding on for dear life. Another soldier dragged her back by the hair, put his hand over her mouth. He pulled her to the van where Fletcher was supposed to be waiting, opened the door, and threw her in. The mic picked up Fletcher's laugh. "We got a wild one," he said.

I reached for Eva's hand.

The van's door shut. "Shit," Eva swore. She leaned over the front seat and spoke rapid-fire Spanish. *"No puedo acostumbrarme. Nunca."* The driver nodded. Eva repeated, in English, "I will never get used to this. I feel sick for days. Sick." She reached back into her bag and pulled out a folded-up red silk scarf. She unwrapped it to reveal a velvet cross studded with silver medallions. She closed her eyes and mumbled something in a strange language. She kept mumbling until another man stepped off the plane. The same Chinese guy I had seen at the restaurant trotted down the stairs and walked quickly to the van. That's when Fletcher stepped out of the car in his perfectly pressed blue shirt and khaki pants like some preppy frat bro ready for a day at the country club. Eva kissed the cross, wrapped it back up in its red silk cover. "We need to see him with that man. We need to hear what they say."

Who's the man?"

"Alain Chiu, vice president of American Transport Solutions. Big trafficker—humans, meth precursors, whatever. Wait. They are having some discussion." Eva put her finger to her lips.

Fletcher said, "I haven't gotten paid. What's the deal here? You will not double-cross me, Chiu." His voice screeched over the speakers.

"You'll get the rest when the cargo has been distributed as you promised. Nothing missing this time, not even one kid," Chiu answered. "That was our arrangement, and now you are getting greedy. I am not responsible for your debts."

Fletcher again. "I could have you arrested in the States. I could have your assets seized. *Hasta la vista, amigo.*"

Chiu turned and walked to the other side of the van, stopped, and turned around again. "Very funny, my friend. I will remind you, your hands are not clean. I know your dirty little habits with these girls."

"Who's going to believe some Chink, Chiu? You people lie all the time." Fletcher laughed.

Chiu stood very still for a minute and then walked toward Fletcher. "I can have you killed, Fletcher, just like ordering room service. Deliver all the products. Then you'll get your money." He spat near Fletcher's shoe, turned, and went back to the van, where a man stood, opening the door. "*Saca la chica del coche! Ahora,*" he yelled. The bodyguard pulled the girl out of the van and dragged her to the line of waiting children next to an army bus.

I was totally over my pay grade, but the threat came loud and clear: *I can have you killed like ordering room service.* Fletcher was in trouble. Francois had to know. He was here, and Mike? What did Mike know, and where was he? My throat was dry, and the cicadas kept screaming like the hot flames of hell, which was what this must have been. The palm trees, the dirt runway, and the van's complicated dashboard went in and out of focus, blurry one moment, sharp and bright the next, like something glimpsed from a spinning carousel. I was frightened, true, but something else—fury, I guessed it was— pounded in my heart like a hammer. I would get Fletcher if it was the last thing I ever did.

I watched Fletcher's van back up, turn, and drive away, along with the other van and the army bus with the soldiers, the crying babies, the terrified children. The plane revved its engines, taxied, sped up, and was soon gone over the Sierra Madre, leaving only the sounds of cicadas.

"What happens to them now?" I asked.

Eva threw her head back, closed her eyes, and sighed, exhaling from somewhere deep inside her where grief resided. "They starve, they get worked to death in some poultry farm in some shithole in Arkansas. They get raped, die of infection, or drop dead of dehydration on a tobacco farm in North Carolina. Their bodies get hacked up and thrown into some Walmart Dumpster, and the traffickers hightail it out of town." She turned and faced me, staring hard, her eyes full of anger or despair—both, probably. "Here's my question: How have you not known all these years that this was going on? The blindness of white people blows me away. This is something every one of us brown people knows. The ghosts of these children, all our dead, whisper to us at night on the orange-scented breezes from the groves, from the stench of the hog farms, from the rotting trailers by the sides of casinos in the Mississippi delta where they trick these girls out. How have you been so blind?"

My throat tightened, felt raw and scratchy with tears I held back. What right did I have to cry?

Eva smoothed the silk covering the cross and gave it to me, saying, "Take this for protection. I will see that you get those pictures once you are back in the States. You may not believe me, but you have the power to stop this. *Vamos*," she said to the driver, and we were off.

There was nothing more to be said. What *could* be said that could make the horror go away? We rode back to San Benito in silence.

7

NATHAN

Nathan looked up from the glassy face of his iPad, where he'd been trying to lose himself in the *New York Times* book review, and surveyed the pool, the vacant chaise lounges. From the hotel's kitchen drifted the sound of a wailing accordion, and with it laughter and the clattering of dishes. But that was about it. Still no bird-watchers. As he'd indicated to Marco last night, he would stay only one more day. If the bird tour didn't start, he wasn't willing to stick around, drinking hibiscus water and floating in the pool, forever.

He had to admit, though, that 99 percent of people in the world would want to be where he was right now, stretched out under an umbrella on a cliff above the Pacific, iPad in hand, and a glass of the aforementioned beverage on a table just within reach. Paradise, in his experience, he wanted to tell them, wasn't all it was cracked up to be. Maybe that was why God put a serpent in the garden—as a reminder that when things seemed too good to be true, they usually were. This place was not totally on the level, but he just couldn't figure out what the serpent was this time. Concha? Marco? Francois. And, lo and behold, there he was.

"*Bonjour*." Francois waved and swung one leg over the rope that stretched across a rock stairway leading down to the cove. The yacht was still anchored there in the blue-green water.

"Hey, Francois, it says *paso prohibido*. I don't think you can go down."

Francois shrugged, stepped back over the rope, and walked toward him. "*Mon ami*, do you always obey all the rules?"

"Yes, I suppose that's my general inclination. Especially when my lawyer resides in another country."

Francois sat down on the chaise next to Nathan, grabbed Nathan's iPad, and shoved it into his satchel. "Hey. Forget rules. France has rules—many, many rules. I don't need rules here in the new world. Which is why we must go to the beach and swim in the water where the fish swim. Get up. *Viens*." Francois grabbed his arm and pulled.

What the hell, Nathan thought. *I could use some exercise.*

He followed Francois, stepping over the rope, and began the steep descent down the rough stones. Bright blooms poked up from the scrub, and the bougainvillea tumbled over the wall bordering the stairs. With each step, the sound of the waves lapping at the curve of the beach got louder. He could even hear the rigging knocking about on the yacht still anchored in the cove. A flock of pelicans flew over, calling, and Nathan wondered when he and Francois would hit some barricade that would halt their progress down the side of the cliff— the armed security Concha had talked about. There seemed to be nothing wrong with the path, something he pointed out to Francois.

"*Oui, je sais*. It makes me pissed that they don't allow us the beach. We are the guests."

"Actually, Francois, I'm the help. You, I can't say. You came here all the way from France to buy this hotel?"

"*Non*, I came from Hong Kong."

"Lot of rules in China, too, I've been told. A lot of people."

"A lot of money, my friend. Money the Chinese want to get out of Hong Kong. They think luxury hotels are a good investment."

Francois sat on a rock and looked out over the ocean. "Sometimes Bill Gates's yacht passes by. Like an ocean liner. He has a place in Vallarta. That"—he pointed to the yacht in the cove—"looks like a canoe in comparison, even though it's a Pacific Eagle, a state-of-the-art sailing ketch. They tell me it's been around the globe twice." Francois reached into his bag and pulled out small binoculars. "Amazing." He sighed. "Do you sail?" He lowered the glasses and looked at Nathan. "Rich people usually do."

Nathan thought of the family's boat anchored at the yacht club in San Francisco: *The Premier Crew*. He nodded.

"Don't be modest. Our friend Marco told me it's a three-masted, 112-foot boat built by Sangermani."

"Wow, Marco seems to know all about me." Nathan was not pleased.

"You won the San Francisco regatta."

"I didn't. The crew did." Nathan reached for the binoculars. "These are really more like opera glasses, Francois." Before he could look at the boat, Francois took them back.

"Yes, I need them to view the opera that is life." He lifted the binoculars and looked toward the yacht, humming "Nessun Dorma." *None shall sleep. My secret is hidden within me.* "Turandot, you know?" he asked, without taking his eyes off the boat anchored in the cove.

Nathan watched as a skiff was lowered from the boat and someone climbed down the rope ladder into it. No life vest, Nathan noticed. Living dangerously, he supposed.

"*Bien.*" Francois, hopped up, brushing off his khakis. "I think this is not the time to swim."

"Why not?" Nathan asked, not that he cared one way or the other.

"Too much activity. And with the motorboat? Pah. The smell of gasoline. Not aesthetic, really."

The climb up the cliff was steeper than he'd gauged on the descent. Always the way, Nathan guessed, huffing and puffing and realizing he was pretty out of shape, which should have been no surprise. Karen's treadmill had become more of a clothes hanger, a landing zone for household detritus. Nathan would have liked to stop and rest, but Francois was ahead of him, zipping up the hill. Of course, he was younger, and even though he sported those ridiculous sandals Frenchmen always wore during the summer, he walked swiftly, almost as if he were in a rush, for some reason. Nathan wondered if he'd missed something that had happened on the boat, if something other than aesthetics had made Francois no longer want to swim with the fish, as it were. He wondered if Francois knew the Mob meaning of that expression, if he was indulging in a bit of French irony or even fatalism, which seemed appropriately creepy for this place.

Trudging up the hill, Nathan thought about what he'd seen. Everything had looked pretty normal. A skiff had been lowered from the yacht and had motored over to a small dock, where a van or some kind of truck was idling. Supplies, probably. Or drugs. That was what one always expected in Mexico, wasn't it? It was probably canned milk and peanut butter. Anyway, Nathan was just as happy to get back to the *Times*. As surreal as the news was, at least it was in English. At least it made him feel as though he were home.

Francois lifted an arm and waved to someone, who responded with a loud whistle, and when Nathan reached the guard rope, he saw why. Two men were sitting on chaise lounges, a dark-haired guy on the very one he'd vacated to accompany Francois. The other one was none other than Bud Delano.

"Looky here, Fletcher," Bud called out. "It's the birdman."

Francois walked over to the men, shook hands with the guy called Fletcher, handed Nathan his iPad back, and then took off, leaving Nathan to introduce himself.

"Howdy," Fletcher said. He didn't get up.

"So, you're on my tour." Nathan tried to reconcile the hunched figure on the lounge chair with images he had of state senators or other bird-watchers, for that matter. It didn't work.

"So it seems."

Fletcher's hair was graying, greasy, and unwashed, and the guy was sweating. Big, wet stains marred the underarms of his blue shirt. Not that Nathan was the epitome of sartorial splendor, but these political types always seemed impeccable, not a drop of perspiration anywhere. Maybe this guy had health problems, and the last thing Nathan needed was some senator or whatever to have a heart attack on his watch. Then he noticed the glass in the guy's hand, heard the familiar rattle of ice cubes, and smelled the scotch.

"You two have met?" Fletcher pointed to Bud and then Nathan. "He'll be coming with us. We'll need protection, and he's armed." He swirled his drink and sipped. "Isn't that right, Delano?"

"I'm not sure that was part of the arrangement," Nathan stated, he hoped forcefully.

"Don't worry, Bernstein. I won't shoot the bluebird of happiness. Hey, Jimbo, isn't that what we're looking for? The damn bluebird of happiness."

Fletcher glared at Bud, rattled the ice cubes in his glass, and downed his drink in one gulp. "I am not in the mood for your humor, Bud, so put a lid on it, okay? I'm just not in the mood." He turned to Nathan. "He will be joining us whether you or I like it or not, Mr. Bernstein."

Nathan slammed the door to his villa. No way was he going into the jungle understory with an armed-and-dangerous Bud Delano. He may have lived a sheltered life, but he'd watched enough TV crime shows in the past year since Karen's death to know this reeked of a drug drop or something. He had no intention of sticking around to find out what that something was. He pulled out his phone and started searching for car services. He'd probably have to go as far north as Puerto Vallarta. Who cared? He was leaving. That much couldn't be clearer.

"Car service," he tapped into his phone, "Vallarta," and, sure enough, there it was: Limo Ejecutivo. He punched in the numbers and heard the buzz of the Mexican dial tone. "*Bueno*, Limo Ejecutivo," a woman singsonged into his ear. He explained that he needed a car to pick him up at the resort Ventana Azul, at which point she interrupted and said they did not have a contract with the resort.

"*Contrato?*" he questioned "This is necessary? *Necesario?*"

"I am very sorry," the woman answered in English. "Goodbye."

Nathan tried another service, with the same results. There seemed to be no point in continuing.

He sat on the bed, holding the phone and listening to wind rattle the palm fronds outside his window, trying to remember the drive up to Ventana Azul. Wasn't there some little village somewhere? He'd seen children playing in a stream, hadn't he? How far was that on foot? An hour, two? He could make it, no problem. Certainly, someone could call a taxi service from some restaurant. Even *pueblitos* had a cantina or two. Or maybe they served as third-class bus stops for those school-bus contraptions that were all over the place.

He grabbed his birding book, his binoculars, the silk pouch of Karen's ashes. Everything else, he would leave behind. He snapped a photo of his suitcase and the few clothes he'd brought. He'd see that Birds of Paradise reimbursed him for his expensive carry-on. For pain and suffering, too, just for good measure.

Walking down the long, palm-lined drive, Nathan wondered why he hadn't done this sooner, instead of sitting around, feeling uneasy. He nodded at an old gardener who was raking leaves with an antiquated implement, stopped, asked how long to the nearest village, and was told it was ten kilometers, *mas o menos*. Seven miles. He'd get there before dark easily.

Just then, the large wrought-iron gates opened and a black van entered the compound, pulled up, and stopped. Marco rolled down the window, and Nathan saw that he was not alone. A burly guy in a cowboy shirt was riding shotgun. Marco did not look pleased.

"Hello there, my friend," Marco called out. "*A dónde vas?*"

"I thought I'd take a walk outside the resort, kind of get the lay of the land, Marco."

"I can't let you do that, I'm afraid. It is not safe." His good-natured grin was starting to dissolve into taut lines. "Not safe at all."

"Seems safe enough to me. I'd like to see a real village, you know, see the real Mexico."

Marco turned to the burly guy and repeated what Nathan had told him. "*Quiere ver el México verdadero.*"

They laughed rather mirthlessly and repeated the words *México verdadero.* The laughter stopped. "Get in the car, Señor Bernstein," Marco ordered.

Nathan shrugged. "I'll be back in time for dinner, Marco, don't worry." He waved, turned, and headed back down the road. The van did not move.

A few yards down the drive, Nathan heard the van back up. He heard the door open, and someone called out the name Eva. As footsteps approached him, he turned to face a dark-haired young woman. "You need to do what they say. And anyway, the gate will be locked. I am afraid you are like a prisoner here. But it's a nice jail, no?" She took his arm and led him to the van.

Nathan had been stretched out on the bed for about half an hour, staring dry-eyed at the woven leaves of the *palapa* ceiling, his heart racing from the panic attack that always hit him when he felt trapped. Claustrophobia began suffocating him the minute elevator doors closed; when cars slowed to a halt in traffic jams; or when planes, sealed up, ready to take off, idled instead for hours, or what seemed like hours, on the tarmac. And now this. Trapped here in the jungle. There really was no way out of here, was there? It was a jail, like that woman had said. *Think again*, he told himself, wiping the sweat off his face with the bottom of his T-shirt. *Think harder.* The boat in the harbor, maybe. Was he strong enough to swim out to it? Doubtful. What about Francois? Maybe he could spring Nathan from this tropical San Quentin, sneak him out. Maybe the kitchen staff could be bribed.

The harder he thought, the more panicked and desperate he became. His legs jerked with the old restless-leg syndrome that flared up at the worst times. Could his mother be called upon? God, how humiliating. But it was the best idea he could come up with. He could tell her he had contracted some awful disease, like hepatitis, and needed to be medevaced out of here. Or he could claim erratic cell phone coverage. The last thing he wanted to do was to blow the whistle on this ridiculous bird-watching tour until he got out of here, at least. If he told his mother the truth, she'd probably call the governor. Then all bets would be off—who knew what these folks down here were capable of if someone made *real* trouble for them? Besides, knowing his mother as he did, he was certain that the mere mention of the word "hepatitis" would send her into a frenzy of activity on his behalf. And, now that he thought about it, what if the cell phone coverage in his room actually *was* erratic? He hadn't tried to contact anyone since he'd called the limo service that morning. Lifting his hips, he reached into his pocket and pulled out his phone to check, when he heard a knock on the door and looked up to see Marco breezing into his room with the entitled air of a welcome guest.

"Calling an Uber?" Marco laughed, lifting a joint to his lips and taking a long drag. He held the joint out to Nathan, shrugged when Nathan shook his head, and exhaled, coughing. "Pure Acapulco gold buds. The finest. Life is good, Nathan. You should relax." He sat down on the other side of the bed and then stretched out, thoroughly enjoying himself and his stoned buzz.

Nathan stood up and walked to the far side of the room. "Do me a favor Marco, okay? Just get the fuck out."

"Now, now, my friend. No need to be difficult." He sat up, folded his legs yogi-style under him, and took another toke. "The rich are different from you and me, as your great writer Fitzgerald once said. And Mr. Chiu from American Transport Solutions, one of your bird-watchers who should be here soon, is very, very"—Marco waved his arms in the air like a conductor—"very rich. He wants privacy most of all, which is why he and Mr. Fletcher are going on your little bird-watching tour. No spies watching them, no spies recording them in the room. All very private out there in the *campo*. The whole bird-watching—what do you call it?—ruse is bullshit."

"Good." Nathan opened his suitcase, walked to the closet, and began throwing what few items he'd brought with him into it. "Then you don't need me. You can have Bud take them on a nature walk. We're done here, Marco. False imprisonment is a big crime. You let me go, and I say nothing to BOP. Otherwise, I will absolutely sue. I'll see to it they shut down this whole phony resort."

"Nathan, Nathan, Nathan." Marco wet his thumb and forefinger and squeezed the burning end of the joint. Once it was cool, he dropped it into his shirt pocket, stood, and walked to the door. "Ah, yes, one more thing." He turned slowly. He sighed, his shoulders drooped.

Jesus, what a performance, Nathan almost laughed as he threw another shirt on top of the pile of clothes. He turned back just in time to see Marco streak across the room, and before he could really process that Marco had slammed him against the wall, Marco's hands were around his neck, pressing hard. Nathan couldn't breathe, couldn't speak. The blood vessels in his head felt like they would explode.

"Listen, you little prick. You will do everything I tell you to do. Don't threaten me. If I even thought you would do something so stupid, I'd never let you out of this country alive."

His thumbs pushed harder against Nathan's throat, and Nathan's vision tunneled, narrowed to a point where he strained to see. Just before he blacked out, Marco miraculously let go and Nathan collapsed on the floor, shaking, feeling like he would puke.

"Dinner is at eight, *pendejo*. Mr. Chiu likes cultured conversation. Think of something intelligent to say. I expect you to be charming."

Nathan felt a burning pain in his ribs. Marco was kicking him over and over. He curled into a ball, his hands wrapped around his head to avoid the blows, but there were no more. He heard footsteps, then nothing. Marco was gone.

8

NATHAN

He lay on the floor for a long time, curled in a fetal position, the pain still burning in his throat and ribs. After a while, after the pain subsided a bit and Nathan felt the cold tiles underneath him, he began to weep, big, gulping sobs, snot running down over his lip. Had his life passed before his eyes? No. Nothing had passed, just his hold on life narrowing into black emptiness, and that was all there was. Marco had almost killed him. He had almost died. And what did he have to show for his time on Earth? A degree, a house, a dead wife. He didn't even have a dog. The tears and sobs kept coming. He had no idea how long he'd stayed on the floor like that, but eventually the tears stopped, the gulps subsided, and, in their place, a strange peace settled over him.

At first, he didn't understand, and then it all made sense, where the calm had come from. A simple fact: He was not dead. He was still alive, still here. Relief ran through him like a shot of morphine, like honey flooding his veins. He let himself lie there in a pool of sweat and tears, feeling all of it. For the first time since Karen's death, he wanted desperately to be alive. And he was. He was.

By the time he finally pushed himself up off the floor, showered, and changed, the bruise on his throat had bloomed into a lurid, deep-red splotch. He tried speaking, saying his name, and his voice came out rough and scratchy, but it hardly mattered. He would be out of here in a day or two, just like the stalled elevator he'd been trapped in once had lifted, just like the delayed flight had eventually taken off from O'Hare. He would call his department chair as soon as he returned to Berkeley and tell him he was ready to be put back on the class schedule. Of course, Tom, the chair, would ask if he was certain, and he would be, he thought, looking out of the window at the sky, now turning rose gold in the sunset, a few perfect streaks of clouds shimmering like prayer flags. It was time to move forward.

He tied his sneakers and stepped out of his villa and onto the path, still feeling drugged from the aftermath of the surge of adrenaline. Floating past the palms in the sunset's pink-colored light, he headed toward the patio where dinner was being served. He didn't even dread seeing Marco. Nathan was the victor, the way he felt now, no longer the sniveling crybaby Marco had kicked as he lay curled on the floor.

He reached the top of the path and looked past the hibiscus to the patio. Marco was not there. Nathan saw an overturned chair; a well-dressed Asian man, forty-five or so, pacing in front of the patio wall while talking on his phone; the same dark-haired woman he'd seen in the van; and a rather misshapen, silver-haired man in a kind of elevated wheelchair that looked like something Stephen Hawking would have ridden around in. He was pouring himself a shot from a bottle when he noticed Nathan and waved him over.

"Please, join us. Have a drink. It's a very fine *añejo*."

No Marco, no Concha, no Bud, none of them. Still, it was quite the crowd assembled in this strange, slightly upended tableau, but in his dopamine-fueled state, the usual anxiety he experienced when anything was out of the ordinary got shoved into some unreachable part of his brain. All he knew was that the muscles in his body seemed fluid, his body weight not very weighty at all. Even the corners of his mouth seemed to be lifted into what must have been a smile.

"You missed the excitement," the dark-haired woman said. "There was a snake." She downed her tequila. "I'm Eva, by the way. I suppose that sounds very biblical. Eve and the snake, doesn't it? Well, it scared the shit out of Marco. I can tell you that."

The Asian man returned to the table. "I sent a picture to one of our ships' pilots—he's from Australia—and they know all about snakes. He says it was a python, a small, burrowing python, only six feet, typical of the area. How terrifying. Six feet does not seem small. Does it?"

"Don't worry," the silver-haired man said, looking at Nathan. "He was dispatched with, shall we say." He pointed to a smear of blood on the concrete. "Machetes are a wonderful tool to have. My driver took care of it. I'm Carlos Garza, but my friends call me Cacho. Well, Don Cacho—out of respect, you understand." He indicated again that Nathan should sit. "Dinner will be a bit delayed. You know Eva and Mr. Chiu? I believe Mr. Chiu was to have been one of your bird-watchers."

"*Was* to have been?" Nathan shrugged. "Interesting choice of verb tense. Does that mean . . ."

"Canceled," Mr. Chiu told him. "Will no longer be necessary, it seems." His phone rang, and he walked from the table to answer.

Canceled? Ruse? What was it? Nathan knew something was a scam, but which one: scheduling the tour or canceling the tour? And there was no one with whom to pursue this line of thought. Don Cacho was still focused on the dead python.

"Snakes have such different connotations in Western culture," he said, pouring Nathan a small snifter of tequila, then topping off his own. "The Mayans believed that snakes carried the sun and the stars across the heavens; the Aztecs worshipped the fire serpent and the feathered serpent. It was all about renewal, rebirth."

"Snakes give me the creeps," Eva interjected, pulling them all down from the serpent stratosphere. She refilled her snifter, raised her glass. "*Pa arriba*," she said.

Then, out of nowhere, an explosion. The noise, the brain-scrambling moment of making sense of it. Fireworks? A bomb?

Nathan heard the sound, felt its percussion, really, and looked around as each head jerked back. Don Cacho and Eva shared a glance, and the man shrugged. *"Mis muchachos,"* he said, shaking his head. "They are like children with toy guns—*pow, pow, pow."* He aimed a make- believe pistol, pulled an imaginary trigger.

Another shot, but this time a scream and then another *pow, pow, pow.* Immediately, Chiu was standing at the table. "You should send someone," he said.

Don Cacho nodded and pulled out his phone, and when someone answered, he asked. *"Todo bien?"*

All Nathan heard was *si, bueno, okay, si.*

Don Cacho snapped the phone shut. "Jungle pigs. *Jabilis.* One of the maids got scared. They can be vicious. Let us return to our tequila, shall we?"

Mr. Chiu sat down. "Wild boar is big delicacy in Italy. Too ugly to eat." He wrinkled his nose. "Let's drink" He lifted his snifter. "To seeing birds at another time, not pigs and snakes. My friend Don Cacho was explaining *añejo* tequila to me. A sip of good *añejo* should be felt first in the chest." He sipped and held his hand over his heart. "Yes, that's where the warmth begins. It should strike like a good marksman, wouldn't you say, Don Cacho, my good friend?"

The conversation was too bright, Nathan thought, a bit flinty and sharp, like water running over granite rocks. An undercurrent of tension. But not his tension, and not his problem, so nothing he had to figure out.

Eva had turned and was facing the sea, swirling her tequila and biting a nail.

"Now, Eva," Cacho chided. "Don't drink this like an American. Sometimes, I must say, your compatriots show no appreciation for subtleties."

Mr. Chiu nodded. "None whatsoever."

Nathan had a sense they weren't really talking about appreciating the finer points of alcoholic beverages, but he saw no reason not to play along. He had actually read the in-flight magazine on the way down to Mexico, which included an article on the finer points of the country's national drink. He began to hold forth on the particulars of extra *añejo*, how it was smoky, with floral overtones. He even convinced himself that he knew what he was talking about, and, of course, since these two gentlemen never flew commercial, they would have no way of knowing he was regurgitating the most superficial content imaginable. Only Eva seemed not to be listening.

"What happened to your neck?" she interrupted, absent-mindedly placing her fingers on her own.

"I fell."

"On your neck?"

Nathan scrambled a minute. "Against the sink. It looks much worse than it is. I know it's ugly. Too bad I don't have a cravat or something."

Eva just stared at him, unblinking, and then turned back to gazing at the horizon, biting a hangnail or whatever it was on her thumb. Nathan began to wonder if she was a little off. Well, who wouldn't be around here? All this weirdness could get to you after a while. He desperately wanted to hold on to the blissed-out feeling he'd had lying on the floor, but it was starting to fade like the rose color in the sky, which was now being swallowed up by twilight.

He almost regretted that Marco wasn't here. He'd been prepared to regale Mr. Chiu with his knowledge of Chinese opera just to show Marco he'd survived his bullying threat, was capable of cultured conversation.

Chinese opera: something he actually knew a little about. His mother had for the past year been excited about the San Francisco Opera's decision to perform the Chinese classic *Legend of the White Snake,* speaking of snakes. "With real members of the Peking opera," she'd gushed, "which no one appreciates over there anymore." Much of her preparation involved designer gowns, and, yes, she had considered flying to Paris but then thought it would be much better to utilize the talents of a Chinese American designer like the one who dressed Michelle Obama. The big problem, apparently, was that other society ladies were having the same idea. She needed to get in line—a rather new experience for Nathan's mother. In between her own couture concerns, she found time to nag him about his tuxedo options. "Do not even tell me you are thinking of renting."

Prodded by this memory of his mother, Nathan now found himself lecturing, as if to one of his classes, about the *White Snake* opera. "It's an unbelievably complicated story involving one of the eight immortals and a white snake who turns into a beautiful woman." Nathan sipped his tequila and continued, "When her husband uncovers her true nature, he dies of shock, only to be brought back to life to swear undying devotion to Lady White Snake, as she is known. The tale is full of magic potions and immortal gods. Nothing as simple as our fairy tales."

Chiu waved his hand. "Those old superstitions just keep Chinese people backward. They believe these things in the countryside. Ghosts and spirits and so forth. We need modern ideas. We need capital investment. We have to make deals with the devil sometimes, without worrying about being haunted." He crushed out his cigarette on a saucer.

Nathan got the distinct impression Chiu knew what he was talking about, that he had firsthand knowledge of deals with the devil. All those tech sweatshops would be a place to start, all the censorship. But it was the dullness of his eyes that gave him away, Nathan realized, like even his pupils and irises had seen enough evil and were exhausted.

"Suffering is the price of modernity," Chiu continued, as if he were reading Nathan's mind.

"Life is suffering," Nathan offered up. His sum-total knowledge of Eastern religion.

"Exactly," Chiu said.

Don Cacho slapped the table. "No one is suffering here in this Mexican paradise."

Nathan saw Eva shoot him a glance.

"At least not us," Cacho added, lifting his glass.

Dinner came and went. A prawn first course with mango and melon, paired with a Baja chardonnay, followed by quail in *mole rojo* and a Baja tempranillo. All very civilized, Nathan thought, which was the whole point, wasn't it? Maintaining the achievements of the realm against a backdrop of pythons, wild pigs, and the menace lurking in the jungle. Otherwise, one could go all Kurtz and Conrad. One more day, he told himself. He promised never to complain about summer fog in Berkeley again once he made it out of here.

Don Cacho interrupted his musings about *Heart of Darkness*. He wanted to know if Nathan had been to Guadalupe Valley. And so the conversation drifted into the safe harbor of wine-and-food pairings—polite, twenty-first-century conversation that had replaced the safe zone of Victorians discussing the weather.

"One day," the wizened old man said, "all your Napa vineyard workers will come back to Mexico, and then where will California be?"

"Where will Mexico be, Don Cacho?" Eva blurted out. "The States need Mexican workers, but Mexico needs their MoneyGrams. You want complicated, Nathan? Somebody should write an opera about that." She got up and began refilling glasses.

"We'll have Chinese investment. Isn't that right, Señor Chiu?" Don Cacho laughed.

"Exactly." Mr. Chiu lifted his glass. "Here's to our excellent partnership."

Nathan waited for Eva to join in the joke. She caught his eye briefly but just as quickly turned away and raised her glass. "To partnerships," she said.

By then the twilight had slipped into night, and they were now leaning, elbows on the table, candles flickering, their faces in half shadow, warm, tropical darkness all around them. It seemed to Nathan like a Rembrandt painting rendered in black velvet. Chiu and Cacho, a globalized version of Dutch merchants; Eva the barmaid, pouring wine from a green bottle, instead of a pewter pitcher. Nathan realized he was a little drunk. No, a lot drunk, but he didn't stop Eva from pouring more wine into his glass. *One more night*, he thought, *so why not?*

Eva announced, "It's not a Mexican party until someone cries and someone fights. We need to keep drinking. And we need to sing."

On cue, Don Cacho began to sing a romantic ballad. "*Bésame mucho*," he crooned, "*como si fuera ésta noche la última vez.*"

"Mexican opera." Eva nodded toward Chiu, who was more interested in his wine and whatever was on his phone.

Eva pulled Nathan up and began to dance with him. He really was drunk, but she didn't seem to mind, nor did he. It was strangely enchanting to be dancing in the dark jungle with a beautiful woman, to the tune of a single voice. Cacho crooned in a deep, melodic baritone that suited the romantic words. Over Eva's shoulder, Nathan could see that Cacho's eyes were closed, his hand over his heart. Soon the table and chairs began to swirl, and Nathan held up his hands, as if to say, *Enough.* "I've had a lot to drink," he mumbled, sitting down. Eva turned to Cacho and wheeled him around the patio as he sang.

Nathan held on to the arms of his chair, steadying himself, when the singing stopped abruptly. Across the pool, as far as Nathan could make out, Francois was carrying a bundle. But the bundle began to make a sound, which took Nathan a while to process. Crying. That's what it was. A baby, crying. Francois was gesturing, motioning that Cacho should come over to him, and he waved back. "My guests, it seems, have arrived. The boat can set sail at last." He pointed to the yacht.

Cacho pushed a knob on his chair, and the chair hummed and turned, carrying him toward Francois and the baby. Eva followed. "See, Don Cacho," she said, "a real Mexican party, no? Someone is crying."

Chiu stood. "Good night," he said to Nathan, and walked toward Francois.

Within minutes, they were gone.

Nathan poured himself the rest of the wine. He was already smashed, but Baja wine was impossible to get. Even in Mexico, this bottle retailed for close to $100. He listened to the frogs, he felt the black warmth of the night, he put his head down on the table.

He woke as rough hands shook him, and an equally rough voice called to him from somewhere far above his chair, the table. "*Señor, señor,*" the voice kept saying.

When he opened his eyes, he was staring at a soldier. Two soldiers, actually, unless he was seeing double, which was entirely possible, and the other soldier wasn't there at all. Ah, but he was. They lifted him from his seat and more or less carried him by the armpits back to his room. They sat him on the bed and then pushed him down onto it. "Stay here. Is better," the rough voice said. And then the blackness covered him again.

He didn't know what woke him. Maybe it was the crashing head-ache, the sandpaper-dry mouth. But he was awake, in pain, and still in the jungle. Nathan swore. How much had he had to drink? He was dying of thirst and rolled over with much effort, reaching for the pitcher of purified water the maids kept filled. Only it was empty.

No one had replaced his water bottles. So much for the great service he was used to.

Lifting his head and then the rest of him required a heroic effort. Fortunately, he was still dressed, still had his shoes on. Going to the kitchen would not require another epic battle with his clothes, at least. Then he remembered the soldiers. Had all that been real? In spite of his pounding head, he was aware of an eerie quiet. Until now, he had always been able to hear the sounds of some sort of domestic industriousness outside his villa: sweeping, scrubbing, the sloshing of water, the lilting voices of maids.

Nathan pushed open his door.

The path was strewn with thick leaves, blown palm fronds, and when he reached the patio, he saw that the table had not been cleared. He didn't even want to get close. Just the thought of congealed food, wine residue crusting in the glasses, flies everywhere, made what was churning in his stomach turn to full-fledged revolt. He glanced at the cove far below the cliff. Indeed, the boat was gone. Nothing but a rippled half-moon of blue water. When he turned to head to the reception area, he noticed a soldier. So, they *had* been there. He had not been dreaming. The soldier, dressed in camouflage, was sitting on a lounge chair, weapon at the ready. Nathan froze, and then the soldier got up and walked to the reception desk. Nathan wanted to run, but to where? He was in one of those awful dreams where you need to move but you can't. A minute later, the decision was made for him. The soldier stepped out from the flower-covered arch and walked over to him. "Please. You will come now." It was the same voice from last night. And yes, Nathan supposed he would.

The soldier pushed open the door to Marco's office. "Please. You wait."

Nathan sank into the white sofa and gripped the edges, his legs shaking. Where the hell was Marco, and what the hell was going on? He pushed his sweaty palms down onto his thighs, trying to keep his legs still while his mind raced with possibilities, all of them frightening. His upper lip felt damp, and he swiped it with an equally clammy forearm. Just as he was considering standing up and walking around, as if pacing would somehow calm him down, the door opened and the soldier reappeared, this time walking behind Don Cacho, who motored in on his chair, smiling.

"I thought you'd left," Nathan said, before he thought better of it. Maybe he shouldn't have said anything. Maybe it was too dangerous to speak. But hadn't Don Cacho said he was leaving last night? And the boat was gone.

"I didn't go. I lent my boat and my crew to my guests. Beautiful morning for a sail up the coast, don't you think?"

"I'm wondering where Marco is. Did he go with them? I have to settle up with him, since I'm checking out. I *am* leaving today, right?"

"Yes, yes, leaving today, of course." He lifted a manila envelope, waved it at Nathan, then added, "Marco is, I'm afraid, no longer with us. He was fired, so to speak. I did not approve of the way he was managing my affairs here. I am, you see, the owner."

From what Nathan could tell, the current management was not doing such a remarkable job. Of course, he had no intention of commenting on the rather poor service.

"You need something for the *crudo*, the hangover. *Joven*," he yelled, and, much to Nathan's relief, one of the waiters he'd seen around rushed in. *"Menudo por el crudo."* Don Cacho laughed at his little rhyme.

The last thing Nathan wanted was tripe soup with chiles. "Water, please. Let's just start with that. Then maybe coffee, black, if it's okay."

Don Cacho nodded and translated. The waiter rushed off.

"Well, let's settle our affairs, shall we?" He wheeled himself to the desk, motioned for Nathan to take the seat in front of it, and pulled a piece of paper out of the manila envelope he'd waved at Nathan earlier. Next, he took out a stack of $100 bills, counted out fifty, and set them on the table. "This is your invoice for services rendered. Please read it over and see if you have any questions. You may need this at customs, though I doubt there will be a problem. I have made some calls."

Nathan read the letterhead: MEXICO MAGICO RESORTS INC. LIC. CARLOS GARZA, PROPRIETOR.

Cacho pulled out another paper, pushed a pen Nathan's way. "You will sign that you have received payment."

"I thought Birds of Paradise was paying me."

"What does it matter? Me, them—you are being paid." He seemed tired, like the gracious-host act was wearing thin. Nathan was not about to push it further. He reached for the pen.

The waiter came in with coffee and water. While Nathan gulped the water, Cacho got down to business.

"After your fortifications"—he waved at the beverages—"I will also need you to sign this: a letter explaining to Birds of Paradise that all went according to plan and you had a lovely time guiding the tour. The paper underneath is a nondisclosure contract, which you will also sign."

Nathan set his water glass on the table and started to object.

Cacho lifted his hand. "This is not up for negotiation. You will not want problems with my lawyers, I assure you."

It was then that Nathan noticed the armed soldier at the door. Yes, non-negotiable. Nathan signed his name and reached for his coffee.

"*Hecho*," Cacho said. It is done. "The *muchacho*"—he waved at the soldier—"will escort you to your room to pack. You will be ready to leave in a half an hour, yes?"

"Sure," Nathan said, hoping he sounded like everything was totally acceptable, instead of downright terrifying. Probably not a necessary action on his part, since this Cacho guy most likely didn't care one way or another whether he was scared or not.

"We have arranged transportation for you back to San Benito."

"Señor Bud?" Nathan asked, dreading the answer. But he was wrong.

"Señor Bud? No, no, he is otherwise occupied. But *mis muchachos* are very good drivers. You will be safe. It has been a pleasure, Mr. Bernstein."

And with that, he nodded once more to the soldier, who stepped up to Nathan and motioned that he should leave.

9

CALLIE

I watched from my beach towel, where I'd been swatting sand flies and in general lying low, literally, and looked on as my former neighbor opened his door and hauled his duffel into his old room next to mine. So he'd come back from wherever, and looked a little ragged, at least from this distance. Really, I was surprised he'd returned to San Benito, a town whose charms were limited, to say the least. Maybe he'd gone on some tour. By now, I was the world's expert on local tours, like the "famous" deep-sea-fishing excursions run by that criminal Bud Delano. I would never look at these golden-ager activities the same way again.

I rolled over on my back, throwing an arm across my eyes to block out the sun and to keep those frigging gnats or flies off my face. I had bigger things to worry about than my neighbor's whereabouts. Those other concerns festered around me in the soupy air.

For argument's sake, I asked myself, if I had never seen the kids yesterday, had never actually seen Fletcher with them, would I have walked away from this? Would I have just kept a wary eye on Francois and at the first appropriate moment told Mike about what I knew, let him deal with it? And where was Mike? That last question played on a loop in my head all day. *He could be dead* was the answer that came up with increasing frequency, like a sped-up record, the sound rendered no longer in funny chipmunk voices but as something sinister and shrieking. I couldn't continue to push down the big question of my brother's whereabouts. What if Francois and Fletcher had done something to him? And by "done something," I knew what I meant. What if my brother was dead? *Dead, dead, dead!* screamed the hysterical, ratlike voices in my brain.

Back in Del Rio, I'd been feeling my oats, hadn't I? Feeling pretty powerful. I'd had a goal, and I'd been sticking to it. Of course, I'd felt overwhelmed by the fact that Rosie had pressured me into finding out about the kid, and I was pissed that Mike had put me in this situation. But secretly, hadn't I relished the sense of being, you know, the law? Hadn't I been practically pumping the air with my fists, swaggering around my has-been farm town, thinking, *I got this*, a mere five days ago? Less than a week. What an idiot. I waved the flies away with my hat.

What was I, really? A small-town DA. And before that? A litigator in a big law firm, capital "B," capital "L." Sure, not for the faint of heart. But really, 90 percent of the time we settled out of court in cushy offices with agreements written up on creamy bond paper. No guns, and the evil was mostly abstract: sums of money someone was cheated out of, a questionable prenup signed under duress. Even the date-rape case that I had walked out on seemed, in retrospect, genteel and refined by comparison. My client was a scumbag, no doubt, but I never saw him do it. I held at arm's length every crime I worked on.

I sat up, pulled my knees into my chest, and watched as a family down the beach wrestled with an umbrella, the two sons running around, kicking sand at each other. Looking at them, I couldn't help but think of that mule train of children destined for what kind of torture.

A week earlier, my feelings about Fletcher had run from mere distaste all the way to contempt, pretty tame stuff compared to what I felt now: loathing, rage, and, okay, fear. Real fear. What if he had done something to Mike and the whole lunch meeting at the Starlight had been just a decoy? People did that. What would I do? What could I do? Try to find his killer, of course, and who would that be? Fletcher, most likely. He had the motivation—those photos—and if it hadn't been Fletcher personally, he'd have paid off someone to do it, one of those soldier thugs I'd seen the day before, or even Bud Delano himself. Bringing to justice a murderer that well connected would be a life's work, wouldn't it? It would be my life's work—of that I was sure.

Part of me wanted to be the kind of person who could just run away, sell the farm, and move to the South of France. Wasn't that what everyone in San Francisco always threatened to do? But then, how would I live with myself, having let everyone down, having failed those desperate kids? It was a Gordian knot. The harder I pulled on it in one direction, the tighter it became in another—it could never be cut. I'd be choking on it in Provence, no doubt. I'd turn into one of those expat alcoholics with a secret from the past that they were trying to drown with Châteauneuf-du-Pape.

From the east, toward the mountains, I heard the sound of helicopters, their rotors rat-tatting from above. They flew toward the town, probably patrolling San Benito's lagoon and bay. I lay back down in the lumpy sand and listened to the sound, its thrumming almost comforting, holding out the promise of rescue.

But then they kept getting closer, louder—too loud, really.

I sat back up. The three helicopters were flying low, toward the beach. Too low, and in a kind of menacing formation. The two parents had stopped trying to put up their beach umbrella, and it listed to one side, its canvas panels flattened against the pole. The father shielded his eyes as he looked up, straining his neck. He lowered his arm and said something to his wife, who began frantically pulling at her children's arms, dragging them up the beach toward the row of palms, while her husband loaded up the soda bottles and plastic bags, pulled the umbrella behind him, and began to run.

I figured I should follow the Mexican family and seek shelter, though I couldn't see where they'd gone after they passed the palm trees. Jumping up, I jogged through the sand to the cabanas. It was slow going, and meanwhile, the sound of the choppers was deafening. The first one in the formation got close enough to bend the nearby palm trees in its path like feathers. I got to my room, locked the door behind me, sat on the bed, and waited, though for what, I had no idea. I thought about crawling under the small desk, as if that would protect me if they started firing machine guns. But I was too late. The room shook, the bed shook, my neck jerked back from some impact. I slid down to the floor and managed to get my head under the bed.

I started counting to try to keep track of time: one Mississippi, two Mississippi, just to know how long this assault lasted—if *I* lasted long enough for it to matter. At 310 Mississippi, the noise seemed to abate, as if the choppers had moved farther down the beach or out to sea. At 815 Mississippi, they were gone, leaving a creepy silence behind them. I slid out from the bed, crawled to the window, and peered through the venetian blinds. Papers littered the beach, blowing and settling and blowing again. A few fell from the palm trees outside my window. For a long time, or so it seemed, no one came to gather up the papers; no one walked the beach. Even the gulls had retreated to safety, even the rolling waves arrived at the shore small and subdued in the now still air. I picked up where I had left off: 816 Mississippi, 817.

I heard my neighbor's door creak open and, peering through the blinds, saw him reach down and grab one of the pieces of paper. Flyers of some sort, I guessed. He disappeared from my view, his door closed, but not for long. Within minutes he emerged, the paper still in his hand. He waved it in my face when I opened my door. "Warnings," he said. "This is some kind of warning."

Then he looked up at the roof and began to scream. I followed his eyes, staring up at the tin overhang. A man's body dangled half off the porch roof, its horrifying, open-eyed stare leering, its mouth a gaping cavern, frozen by rigor mortis, his white shirt covered in blood, half his white hair blown off, the right side of his head with it. My neighbor ran back into his room. I could hear him retching.

In the distance, the high-low wail of sirens approached, and as I scanned the beach I noticed another body, this one near a blown-over plastic chair, the pant leg of its white suit ripped, one shapely thigh rigid against the chair leg. I bent and picked up one of the flyers that had blown onto the porch and read the words *Aviso!* Warning! *Asi trata el Caballero a los quienes no son caballeros.* This is how the Gentleman treats those who are not gentlemen. And then I remembered where I'd seen the white suit: on the woman in the Chinese restaurant when I'd been spying from Guillermo's office. She been with Francois, as well as Fletcher. Oh, Jesus. I started to move toward her, when I saw a third body and changed course, running through the soggy sand, so fast my lungs ached. Francois had been there at that bizarre meeting. Doing what, for God's sake? He wasn't stupid enough to betray a Mexican mafia kingpin, was he? Did I really know how stupid he could have been? Or Mike, for that matter. I wanted desperately to stop and breathe, but there was no time. The sirens were right there, screaming against the roar of the surf.

Camo-wearing soldiers emerged from the side road and sprinted toward the beach, two by two, assault rifles ready, black boots kicking up sand. The soldiers were getting close, were yelling something, and the last body seemed miles away. I had to get there before the soldiers stopped me. I had to know if Fran was lying there in a grotesque heap. And I made it. I found out. There he was. In the same blue oxford shirt, the same khakis I'd seen him in yesterday.

Fletcher. His was the third body.

The soldiers were running toward me, screaming. I sank to the sand, my face in my hands. Of course it was Fletcher. What had the Chinese man at the plane said about how quickly he could have my brother-in-law done away with? Relief flooded me. It was not Mike. It was not Francois. It was Fletcher. Thank God.

Someone was pulling my arm. I looked up and saw my neighbor, his hair and shirt matted with sweat. "Get up!" he shouted. "Get away from here. Get up!"

The soldiers were still screaming, still running toward us. *"Quienes son ustedes? Quienes son ustedes?"* Who are you? Who are you? Their faces were contorted with menace.

My neighbor dragged me with both arms, until I obliged and stood. He put his arm around me. *"Mi esposa,"* he called out to the soldiers. *"No comprende que hace."* My wife doesn't know what she's doing.

"Fuera," they kept yelling. Get out. And, we ran, my neighbor and I, as fast as we could.

Back in my room, my neighbor wrapped the hideous bedspread around me, its musty pom-poms in my face, and handed me a glass of water. "You okay?" he asked. "Can you take some deep breaths?"

I didn't say anything. I couldn't really talk. My teeth were chattering, my hand shaking too much to hold the glass. I gave it back to him. Jim Fletcher was dead. Not that I intended to spill any material facts to this man. Actually, I wanted him to leave, just leave. Jim Fletcher was dead. I needed to think about what that meant. I needed to be alone.

"I'm Nathan, by the way."

I nodded and pulled the bedspread more tightly around me, thinking, *Go, go.*

He stood up, but he didn't walk to the door, just stood by the window below, where the body was still hanging off the roof. I realized Nathan and I were stuck here. Neither of us was going to be able to leave until the soldiers removed it.

"Here's the weird thing." Nathan sat on the bed next to me, his words almost a whisper. "I knew those people."

As soft as his voice was, it was as if he'd slapped me, like in the old movies where the cop smacks a blubbering dame and says, "Snap out of it, Myrtle."

Snap out of it, Callie, I told myself. *Focus. Don't give anything away.* "What do you mean, you knew them?" I hoped I sounded normal, at least for the situation at hand, not overly anxious to know the answer.

Suddenly, he was telling me more than I could have imagined. Ventana Azul, Birds of Paradise, Marco and Don Cacho, a dwarf, Bud and Fletcher. All of them. "And then there was this French guy named Francois. I think he took off on this Cacho guy's yacht. It was all very weird, like some horrible dream." He started to laugh. "Sorry," he said. "Inappropriate, I know. I was just thinking the stupidest thing. I should have bought trip insurance. I had a friend who went to India, and someone died on this expensive trip. He'd purchased trip insurance, and they paid him back because someone else died, paid him every last dime he spent. Wonder what I could get for this experience. Sorry, not funny, I know. I'm just babbling."

I held up my hand and motioned that I wanted to get past him. Dragging my bedspread with me, I walked to my bag, pulled out my bottle of Jack Daniel's, and waved it in Nathan's direction. He shook his head. I got a glass from the desk and poured a slug. "So, Nathan, you have a last name?" It was probably too pushy, but he surprised me. He handed me a card. NATHAN BERNSTEIN, it read. PROFESSOR OF ART HISTORY, UC BERKELEY.

"How'd you get here?" I mean, who knew who this guy really was? So far, no one here was what or who they said they were. Even me. Seriously, I was not about to believe some card from a fancy university. I pointed to the huge bruise on his neck. "What happened?"

"Long story. Marco. It was stupid. I'm kind of an amateur bird-watcher. That's why I was here. My wife died." His shoulders sank, and he looked at his hands, folded them in his lap, unfolded them again.

He did seem to be babbling, and I tried to figure out how to handle this. "I'm sorry about your wife," I said. He appeared to be searching for something in his hands and wasn't really listening, which was fine by me.

I sat down on the bed next to him, and neither of us said anything for a while. Eventually, this Nathan guy sort of snapped out of it and turned to me. "You?" he asked. "What about you?"

What about me? No one but Rosie was supposed to know I was here. "I'm a citrus farmer. Central Valley." I told him. It wasn't a total lie, but I was hardly giving up vital info. Anyway, Nathan seemed miles away, and he never asked my name, or where in the Central Valley I was from. Good.

I let it go at that.

PART
TWO

10

CALLIE

Chuy's Creekside Package and Sundries Store was still open when I drove by around 5:00 p.m. after the long flight home from Mexico. I pulled into the dirt lot next to a couple of pickups, hopped out to shop for a few things—milk, eggs, and dog treats, to make amends for having been gone—threw them in the trunk, and headed over to the taco truck one of Chuy's relatives had set up in an old nectarine orchard next to the store. I was really too tired after everything I'd gone through even to boil eggs at home. I ordered a couple of carnitas tacos, extra green salsa, and an agua fresca, and sat down at an oilcloth-covered picnic table under a string of lights that drooped between the gnarled fruit-tree branches. Banda music, the whining accordions, blared from speakers on top of the truck. Had it not been for the dry heat of the Central Valley, the smell of dust and fertilizer, I could have been back in Mexico. In my head, maybe I still was, leaning over Fletcher's body on the beach, the sound of the choppers pounding in my ears.

I pulled out my phone and texted Rosie. "Back home," I tapped onto the screen. "At Chuy's now. Will come by for Vato." In my bag next to the phone, on a cocktail napkin from the plane, were notes I'd made. I pulled them out, too, my scrawl blurry from having bled through the paper. "F at S," I'd doodled, meaning "Fletcher at the Starlight." Was that the start of this whole mess? Or was it "M," for "Mike," and Fletcher's telling me my brother wasn't answering his phone and didn't seem to be home? No, it was the arm of the kid with the strange bracelet that had been found in Fletcher's grove. I'd scrawled "K," for "Kid," as a reminder. Wasn't that where it all began? No, it was really what had been hidden at Alberto's and Rosie's—those photos—and Rosie's demand that I do something. I'd written "R and pics." I wanted a road map back to where I'd begun, back to when I'd planned to get Fletcher's endorsement for his senate seat.

Fletcher's death had changed everything. If he was responsible for any harm to Mike or the death of the kid, well, it was too late to do anything about it, at least, as far as he was concerned. Mafia justice had been swift and ugly. I would let myself rest tonight and start calling Francois first thing tomorrow. Who knew if he'd even answer or where he was? He could still be in Mexico, but I doubted it. It would be interesting to find out, to say the very least, and I'd have to think about how much I was going to tell him about what I knew. Probably nothing at the moment. I needed to get my bearings.

I was going to have to make my move to run for the state senate much earlier than I'd planned, now that the governor would certainly call for a special election. Other than leaning on Fletcher, I hadn't really made a plan. Now, I would have to rely on Mia, and good luck with that. Well, women were running for office right and left these days. I would get in touch with their support networks. I could figure it out.

My phone pinged. I tossed the napkin back in my purse and checked the text. It was Rosie. "Stay there," she wrote. "Be there in 10." A woman stuck her head out of the taco truck window and hollered, "*Veintidós.*" My carnitas *plato* was ready. I was starving.

I was finishing up my second taco when I saw Rosie's minivan wheel into the parking lot. She got out, waved at me, and hurried to my table, where she slid onto the bench opposite me. She pushed her dark glasses back on her head and reached for my hand. "*Como estas?*" she asked.

"*Mas o menos,*" I answered. So-so.

Rosie reached into her pocket, pulled out a vape pen, and took a long drag. "Is the stress," she said, exhaling into the twilight. "All this with Mike and Fletcher is too much. Did Guillermo help?" She used her purse to swat away the meat bees swarming over my taco basket. "They've been worse this year. I think it's the drought." She took another drag off the stick and shrugged. "It's always something. One year it's bugs; the next it's snakes." She fixed me with a stare. "Well, did he help?"

I said yes, he'd helped, and gave her a general rundown. Fletcher was there, had some meeting at a Chinese restaurant, was clearly up to no good. I left it at that.

Rosie reached over the table and took my hands in hers. "I have some good news. Mike came home, *gracias a Dios.* He called us from the Fresno airport, said he'd flown in from San Francisco, and I took him to your house. Good news, right? After all that." She vaped up again.

"What?" I screamed, slamming my hands on the table. "You are kidding me!" Even the meat bees scattered, abandoning the taco remains. I jumped up, knocking over the picnic bench, as an electric charge, volts of relief and rage over all those unanswered texts and emails, surged through me.

"*Cálmate,* Callie." Rosie got up, righted my bench, and pushed me back down. Looking around, waiting to make sure no one was listening, she pulled me close. "There's more," she whispered. "Don't scream again. More news, not so good, maybe, or maybe good. I don't know. Fletcher is dead. That's what Mike told me and Berto. Fletcher is dead. Why Mike is at your house."

I turned away. Mike was at my house. Mike knew Fletcher was

dead. What did Rosie know? What should I say? In the background, Los Tigres del Norte's voices blasted; four Cal Fire guys at the next table burst into laughter over some joke, one of them spitting out his drink. Rosie tapped my arm. I spun around and faced her. "Tell me what you know." I'd just start there.

Mike had called the house, and Lupe had answered. "She told him you were away and that he should call us. We were watching the dog."

"And he told you Fletcher was dead. How did he know?"

Rosie shrugged. "Mia, I guess. A massive heart attack. The funeral is tomorrow. He was cremated."

That was fast. There was absolutely no legal way they had gotten Fletcher's body to the States and cremated in one damn day. For all I knew, they could have scraped the ashes from a bunch of cantinas' ash trays, or they could have dumped the contents of someone's Weber grill into an urn. But I would bet good money those cremains did not belong to Fletcher.

"That's all we know, Callie. Maybe Mike can tell you more. Anyway, we're keeping Vato. You know how allergic Mike is to dog fur." She got up, walked around the picnic table, and kissed my cheek. "I gotta go, *chica*. I wish I could say I was sorry, but I'm not. I'm glad he's gone. Maybe we can get back to normal around here now."

Normal, I thought, driving toward home, over the river, past the field where we'd found the kid's arm, up my long drive to the tree-shaded farmhouse, where I caught my first glimpse of Mike, alive and well, as he got up from the porch swing and all six foot one of him jogged out to meet my car. I almost knocked him over opening the door. There was nothing normal about what was going on.

"Hey, hey." He held up his hands, then ran them over his cropped head of silvery hair. "I know, the prodigal brother. My bad."

"Your bad? That's what you have to say?" I charged to the trunk, pushing him aside, and grabbed my groceries and suitcase. I could hear him following me, his shoes crunching in the gravel. "You have a phone!" I yelled, not turning around. "Use it, why don't you?"

"Callie, stop." Mike grabbed my suitcase, set it down. "I went to Tassajara for a weeklong meditation class with a disciple of Thich Nhat Hanh. I know I mentioned it at some point."

Had he? I wondered. Could I have possibly spaced that out? I had a little gaslight moment. Was Mike lying? Was I getting senile?

"So don't blame me, "Mike continued. "We couldn't have phones. One week of peace and bliss. I get out, and all hell has broken loose." He grabbed my arm, and I shook him off. "Listen, Callie, we can sort this out later." He straightened up and took a deep breath. "Something serious has happened. Fletcher is dead. He had a heart attack."

"I know," I said, lifting my suitcase and walking up the porch steps. "Rosie told me."

Sitting down in my grandfather's rocker, I waited for more. I needed to know what else he knew, what Francois might have told Mike, if anything.

"Mia called me. You, Mia, Fletcher. Jesus. I had no idea how essential I was to everyone's life," he said, looking in my grocery bag at the milk and eggs. "These need to go in the refrigerator."

The screen door slammed, and I waited, listening to the frogs and the creak of the old rocker. Maybe I could just let all this go. Fletcher was dead. He could do no more harm. And Mike was here. I was home, and all this was over. I could pretend it never happened. Rosie wouldn't tell anyone. She'd gone behind Berto's back by giving me Guillermo's information. She wouldn't tell anyone any more than I would. As far as the dead kid went, I'd ask Chief Karkanian to keep the case open, keep the undercover guys' ears to the ground. The arm of the law might be long, but it reached out with glacial speed.

Mike pushed open the door and handed me a cold beer. "Cheers," he said, sitting on the porch swing, lifting his bottle in my direction. "Where were you, anyway?"

"The coast," I told him, which was sort of true. "How's Mia?"

"About like you'd expect. She sounded, I don't know, distant, but maybe that was just the valium talking. She said he died on some fishing trip in Mexico, that they didn't tell her right away, so she never got to identify the body. Does that seem okay to you?"

"Not really. But it's Mexico, Mike." And, of course, Fletcher could have dropped dead or been killed right after I'd seen him at the airstrip. What did I know? Just what everyone else did: Fletcher was dead. As a doornail.

"Someone in the consular office signed the papers, she said," Mike continued, "so I guess it's legal. And then they cremated him."

We rocked in silence for a while, my thoughts going back and forth with the movement of the chair. Should I tell Mike everything I knew? How Fletcher really died, how Berto had the child-porn photographs Mike had hidden? What was I waiting for? I was thinking more like a prosecutor than a sister. I wanted to know the answers to my questions before I let go of any information. Wow, was I ever becoming a control freak, which was ludicrous, considering how out of control the whole situation was. To tell the truth, I just didn't have the energy for any of this. Talk about needing a meditation trip to Tassajara. I'd put that on my to-do list in the near future, but for now, I was going to bed.

I stopped rocking, stood up, said I was tired and that the next time he scared the shit out of me like that, I was going to be the one to have a heart attack. I told him I'd see him in the morning. "I'm sure the sheets on your old bed are clean. You know Lupe." I wondered if Mike would look for the pictures hidden under the mattress and ask about them. They were pretty much useless at this point—nothing we could hold over the head of the deceased.

"Thanks, but I already made up the daybed on the sleeping porch. Too much dog fur, Callie."

I stood up, stretched, walked over to him, and kissed the top of his head. "I love you, little bro." I was all of ten minutes older, but I reminded him, "I'm still older than you, and my ticker can't take it. When you go away, text your contacts. Please."

The next day, Mike and I stood on the corner of Fresno Street, in front of the large cathedral, sweltering in our formal black clothes, while we waited for Mia's limo to arrive from the funeral home where they'd retrieved Fletcher's supposed ashes, now encased in a gold-leaf urn. The event was turning out to be the spectacle I'd imagined, with police cordoning off the street, detouring city traffic, and the Central Valley and Sacramento political elite pulling up in shiny cars in their Sunday best. I found myself making a mental note of everyone I would have to contact, people who might be allies. *Thank you so much for attending my brother-in-law's funeral. It meant so much . . .* That kept my mind off the last image I had of Fletcher: his body crumpled, on a beach in Mexico, his clothes and face covered in dried, crusted blood. I could almost hear the helicopter rotors pounding in my ears even now.

"Are you ready for this?" Mike asked, pulling me back from that moment. "They're not having communion, just so you know. Not that I could partake, of course."

"None of them could, Mike. Look at this crowd." I elbowed him. "They're politicians—rhymes with 'sins,' venial and mortal. Mia just saved everybody the embarrassment." I would have bet my last nickel half the men here couldn't wait to get to the reception at the country club, have that first drink, and start pawing whatever cute intern they'd dragged along with them. Weddings and funerals were always good excuses for that sort of thing.

"Uh-oh, Callie, something wicked this way comes. It's your ex."

"Oh, hell no." I spun around in time to see Sam McCall break away from a group huddled by the church doors and head our way.

"Callie, Mike," he called, waving, as if he were a host, as if we were the guests. The last time I'd heard his voice was when? Ah, yes. On Fletcher's phone—something he wanted to discuss over an excellent single-malt scotch. I stiffened my spine, flashed a future politician's smile. "Sam." I offered my cheek for a perfunctory kiss, all the while thinking of the hand-sanitizing wipes I was going to use on it the minute he turned his back. "So good of you to come. It means a lot. You were one of Fletcher's close friends." Okay, so I was fishing.

"I was, Callie. When Mia called, I was stunned. He was a quarter-back, for God's sake. He was in the best shape of any of us. I just don't understand how this could happen."

Mike and I murmured all the appropriate words: "terrible," "shock," "our poor sister."

"Poor Mia." Sam shook his head. "I told her if there was anything, anything . . ." His voice trailed off. He turned and scanned the crowd, saw someone and nodded.

I followed his gaze, and not that I should have been surprised, but I was. He had nodded at a portly gentleman in a navy suit. That man was none other than Mayor Parra, of Mandarina. Eva's foster dad. How did Sam know Parra? Well, I would make sure I found out exactly how. You could take that to the bank. And when I got the answer, I would be discussing that matter with Sam over some of his excellent single-malt scotch.

I was about to say something about what a wonderful job Parra was doing in Mandarina with youth activities, but no sooner had I formu-lated that seemingly innocent comment than a swarm of attendees who'd been milling about the church lawn began to move in a group toward the driveway. "Mia," I said, pulling Mike by the arm. "She's here."

"I'm joining you," Sam said, leading the way. "Mia's asked me to sit with the family." With that, he broke into a trot to open the door for my sister. I stood, frozen in place, as I watched Sam take my sis-ter's hands in his and bend to kiss them.

"Let's go, Callie." Mike shrugged. "Sorry, but the guy always was a creep. Some things never change. We need to rescue Mia from his slimy grip."

From inside the cavernous church, the organ began to play a processional. I watched my sister as Sam helped her out of the limo and steadied her when she wobbled on her high heels. Always a fashion plate, she'd dressed to the hilt for this somber occasion in a black, form-fitting suit, a Jackie Kennedy veil covering her face. No expression was visible. No red-rimmed eyes, either. I thought, ungenerously, how she always loved being the center of attention, and now she was, her small frame no longer overshadowed by Jim Fletcher. I wondered what she would do now. Sober up? Marry again? Do charitable work? Her life's trajectory seemed like a ricocheting bullet. There was no telling where it would go. I could guarantee, however, it would not be back to Del Rio, and that after today, she and I would have less and less to do with each other as the years passed.

Walking toward the limo, I decided to make the most of this encounter, and when I reached the corner of the lawn where she was standing now, holding on to Sam for dear life, I embraced her, kissed her cheek, and said how terribly sorry I was. I wedged myself between Sam and Mia, denying him his moment of chivalry, and nodded to Mike, and together we walked toward the arched church doors as a family, letting Sam McCall trail behind.

"Ah," Mike said, as we stood in the lobby of the Sierra View Country Club after the funeral. "This is going to be like prom night. Zombie prom night from hell. Let's get this over with, okay?" He pointed to a sign that said FLETCHER FAMILY EVENT. Before we pushed through the double doors, Mike pulled me aside. "You always said you were going to run for Fletcher's seat when he termed out, Cal. I guess we could say he has definitely termed out. All the money people are in there—I say we work the room. What about you?"

He was right. I was running for the state senate right now, today, in this room. I nodded. "Let's do this thing."

After about an hour of moving through the ballroom, shaking hands, murmuring, "So good of you to come," "Such a terrible loss," "We have to keep Jim's legacy alive," I noticed Mike and another man—thinning hair, beige suit matching the general color of his skin—deep in conversation by the plate-glass windows overlooking the golf course. I headed to the bar and ordered a Pellegrino, and when Mike shook the man's hand and walked away, I took my glass and wandered over to him.

"Who's the guy?"

"Definitely the one in charge of corporate donations, or what the layperson might call bribes. Nigel Wilson, a Brit. He's with Francois's company, ATS. Hong Kong office. They send him around to all these shindigs if it's in their business interest, kind of like a human Harry and David food basket."

"And ATS has an interest in the valley?" Then I went in for the kill. "Speaking of ATS, where is Francois?"

Mike shrugged. "Business trip, as usual." He dropped that subject and returned to ATS. "Study up on this, Cal. Food shipping is big business. Carbon footprint. Don't even get me started. You know who the biggest market for walnuts, almonds, and raisins is, right? China. Well, the fruits and nuts don't get there by themselves. Rumor has it ATS wants to buy up all the nut-processing facilities. You didn't hear that from me." Mike handed me a card. NIGEL WILSON, it read. "Go over there and make an impression. He's on his third drink, and you look like a million bucks."

—

A few hours later, Mike and I sat in my car at the Fresno airport, the AC on full blast. Mike flipped the lever on the side of the passenger seat, and it fell back, taking him with it. He crossed his arms over his chest and stared up at the ceiling. We were waiting for Mia and others to arrive from the reception. A family get-together was being held in Nigel Wilson's private plane, where, as Sam assured us, we would have complete privacy.

"Jesus, who knew Fletcher was such a saint?" Mike groaned, remembering the funeral service.

"And a dedicated public servant," I added. "Always trying to get those job-killing regulations off the back of the little guy." It had been a bit hard, to say the least, listening to the priest commend Jim as "Your servant," and to hear how "God in his mercy and love should blot out the sins Jim has committed through human weakness." Human weakness—right.

Mike and I were quiet for a while, just the thrum of the engine and air-conditioning filling in the silence where all the things I needed to say and couldn't say hung between us. Maybe now wasn't the time, but soon, soon, I would have to tell Mike what I knew about Fletcher in Mexico, about Francois. And then all hell would break loose. I glanced at Wilson's plane waiting on the tarmac, Mia's swanky ride, courtesy of Fletcher's bundlers. I'd arranged to show Nigel, as in "call me Nigel, sweetheart," around Del Rio's various almond and walnut processing plants, have him schmooze with the owners, see if he could make them an offer. If he was the money guy for Fletcher, he would most likely have to be mine at least for this election cycle. I was going to have to show him I could be useful, get my hands dirty, just not as dirty as Fletcher's. Never as dirty as Fletcher's.

Speaking of local crops, I babbled on, covering up what was really on my mind. "I've got a pesticide case right now you wouldn't believe," I told Mike, killing time, waiting for Mia and my ex, that POS, to get here and board the aircraft. "Big-ag lawyers threatening

Old Testament–type retribution, locusts and frogs, practically killing my firstborn, except I don't have one." I wondered what they'd do now that they couldn't bring the wrath of Jim Fletcher down on my head. "What do you think this hush-hush meeting is about, Mike? Is Sam just being a drama queen or what, private planes and all that? And can you believe my ex? Swanning around, all over Mia like a bad case of hives, handing her tissues. What was going on there?"

Mike sat up, reaching for the dial to increase the fan. "You might as well tell Mia now about your plans to run for state senator. Tell her we want to keep Fletcher's seat in the family. Tell her you'll need her to keep doing all the society work she did before Fletcher died when you run for his seat, only you'll pay her. It will be a real job. She needs the status. That's her thing. I'll back you up."

"What do you think is taking them so long? And did you see that big guy in the corner?"

"Yeah. Mia's bodyguard."

"Paranoid much? What she needs is an AA sponsor."

"What she didn't need was that last Botox job."

"Now, now, let's not be catty."

"Well, are you? Going to tell her? Say you'll need her help. She can make TV ads, flaunt the Botox and the fake boobs. She always did like to be the center of attention."

"You don't think she and Sam are an item, do you?"

"Maybe. Who cares? Get over him. He was an asshole. Correction: *is* an asshole. You still haven't answered."

"Short answer: I don't know. I don't want Sam McCall being all up in everything." What had Fletcher said about Sam the last time I'd seen him? He was glad I'd found my "niche." I wondered what he'd think when he found out I considered my niche to be in the state senate. But, to quote Mike, who cared, really? "Okay. You're right. No time like the present." I said, feeling a surge of energy. I was going to make this move. Finally.

"Don't let Sam get under your skin. He's looking a little worse for wear, don't you think?" Mike turned, looked out the back window. "Look who's here," he said, just as Mia's black limo pulled into the adjacent spot, the bodyguard driving and Nigel Wilson in the front. And—wouldn't you know it—Sam and Mia in the backseat, her head buried in his shoulder. Mike opened the passenger door, got out, walked over to Mia's car and then back to me, motioning me to get out. "Sam's waving us on," he said. "We just climb the gangway stairs, and the crew will open the door. Mia and Sam will follow in a bit."

"Ah," Mike said, as he settled into the cream-colored leather seat of the Gulfstream and stroked the polished, curved wood paneling. "Flying private. So, this is how Nigel and the rest of the one percent live."

The icy air smelled like a very expensive luggage store, one in Florence, Italy, maybe. "Nothing like that new-plane smell," I said, sniffing theatrically. I lifted the window shade. Mia and Sam were still in the car.

"Let it go, Callie," Mike said, leaning over me and looking out the window.

"Let what go?"

"The float-queen thing from high school. Surely, you have higher aspirations than being citrus queen of Del Rio County."

"They voted for me, and then she got Dad to change it. Bitch."

Mike pulled the shade down and said, "Sweetheart, let's face it: I was the one in the family who should have been the citrus queen."

I laughed. That was the thing about Mike: He could always make me laugh. "Check out the full bar." I waved to a girl, guessing she was the high-end version of a flight attendant: young, sleek, dressed in a tight blue skirt, a starched white blouse with a gold name tag affixed to it, and an Hermès scarf around her neck.

She glided across the cabin, smiling with seeming delight at the prospect of serving us. "What can I get you?"

All I could think of was a martini, eye-achingly cold, with two olives, but, knowing the announcement I was about to make, I said, "Do you have San Pellegrino with a slice of lime?" And, by golly, they did, along with a number of different bourbons for Mike.

"Thank you, Clarice." Mike squinted at the name tag when the flight attendant returned with our drinks in two heavy crystal glasses, ice cubes clinking. She set real coasters and linen cocktail napkins on the polished wood table in front of us. Mike sipped his cocktail and murmured, "Yes, maybe I will move in."

"Party's over," I told him. "Here they come, the four horsemen of the apocalypse. Let's see—what have we? Plague, war, famine. What's the fourth?"

"Mike ticked off the numbers on his fingers. "Sam, Mia, Nigel. I guess the fourth was death, but Fletcher pretty much had that covered."

The plane's door opened, a wave of heat rushed in, and behind it, Mia ducked into the cabin.

"Sorry, everyone," she said. "Hard day. I needed a moment." She smiled weakly at Sam, who walked over to the flight attendant and mumbled something, and within a minute, Clarice returned with a glass of white wine. "I'm so sorry for your loss, Mrs. Fletcher." That elicited another weak smile from Mia, but nothing more. She lifted the glass and drank like she'd been crawling through a desert. "Honestly, I don't know how I survived this heat growing up. Do you even think that church was air-conditioned?" Mia set her glass on the table in front of her, smoothed her tasteful black skirt, and said, "Well, I'm glad we're all here together. Family is so important, at these times especially." She hadn't even removed her Prada sunglasses, though the veil had been discarded.

Sam sat down next to Mia, Nigel headed for the cockpit, and Mike reached for my hand and held it tightly, less out of affection and more like a race car driver gripping a gear shift, trying to maintain control of a revved engine. I sipped my water, breathed deeply, and did not say, *Can we just stop with the bullshit, please.* Instead, I murmured, "You're right, Mia. It is." I felt Mike give my hand a little tug of approval.

Mia sipped her wine, cleared her throat, and said. "I've brought you here because I needed to tell you something in private before you hear it on the news. I think we all need to be prepared."

I felt a current of anxiety surge through me. Had reporters gotten hold of the real reason for Fletcher's death? If so, my connection to him might not help me. I began to think of ways Mia could shut down the story. I would offer to help, and I was so busy thinking of the legal ramifications that I almost missed the last part of what she was babbling about.

"So, for that reason, and many more, and, of course, with dear Sam's encouragement, I've decided to run for Jim's seat." Mia sipped her wine, set it back on the table. "I doubt . . ." She hesitated. "Well, *we* doubt"—she patted Sam's arm—"anyone will run against me."

I fell back in my seat, pushed by the force of the shock, and then I started to laugh. Mike's hand tightened on mine, and I shook it off. "Mia, frankly, you'd have to get sober and stay sober. Politics, to paraphrase the saying, ain't basket weaving at the Betty Ford clinic."

Mia raised her hand slowly to her glasses, pulled them off, and set them on the table. She lifted her wine in a toast to me. "Good one, Callie. We can always count on you to say such interesting things."

"Medical records: private. You should know that, Callie." Sam spoke up, ready to take over. "Your word against ours, and, well, your word won't be worth much."

"Oh, really, Sam? Why is that?"

"Two reasons." He held up his second and third fingers. "Del and Rio. Do you really think anyone will take a small-town DA's word for it? We have some pretty big people behind us." He waved his arm around the Gulfstream. "They're all in for Mia."

I looked around for Clarice, needing a drink, but she had disappeared, was somewhere behind the louvered doors of the forward hatch, listening.

"Are we done here?" Mike asked.

"Not so fast, Mike. We have a few requests."

"I'm not canvassing for a right-winger in my neighborhood, so forget it."

"Your neighborhood, Mike—that's the point. What's the name of the blog you write? *There Goes the Gayborhood*? Well, we'd like you to shutter that for a while. And, Callie, that case against the growers' spraying. Drop it."

I did what any self-respecting district attorney would do. I lost it, threw my water right in his face—ice cubes, lime, everything. "Screw you, Sam. A slight miscalculation. I'm running for that seat. And those growers who poisoned those workers? They're right in the middle of my target. And my gay brother? Civil liberties for all."

Sam didn't look up, just continued brushing ice cubes off his suit jacket. "You're proving my point. I told Mia nobody would challenge her. And you know what?" He raised his head, stared at me. "You, Callie—you are the nobody."

11

NATHAN

"**A**mazing, isn't it?" the woman asked.

Nathan turned away from the fifth-story window where he'd been eyeing the traffic below, watching as cars inched their way up Sansome Street, feeling—traffic or no traffic—an overwhelming delight in the beauty of San Francisco. Today, just two weeks after he'd returned from Mexico to the gray summer gloom, the fog had lifted. September was here, and the sky was now a rapturous blue, the color of heaven as rendered by Renaissance masters. He'd been planning, after the event he was attending here, to walk the few short blocks to North Beach for lunch at that old stalwart the Original US Restaurant and perhaps include a postprandial stroll through the tumble of pastel buildings near Coit Tower, where the sparkling bay would spread before him, sailboats floating like so many angels' wings. Jesus, he was getting sentimental, wasn't he?

He shook himself out of his reverie. "Excuse me?" he said to the Asian woman with spiky salt-and-pepper hair. She wore bright red lipstick that matched her red silk jacket. Like a flare, she had interrupted his musings.

Not really surprising that she would be Asian, since the event being held on the whole fifth floor of a San Francisco high-rise was the kickoff for the statewide California-China Celebration of Culture and Commerce, to which his family foundation had contributed a great deal of money. He squinted at the name card dangling from the woman's lanyard. DR. MARY YEE, it read. He had absolutely no idea who she was or why she'd singled him out. Maybe he was giving off happy energy. At least, that was what his neighbor's wife had told him when he'd run into her on Shattuck, up by the Thai place, a few days earlier. "Wow, Nathan. Mexico was so good for you. It's like you're giving off happy energy these days. That's so great."

He didn't know about the energy part of it, but he did feel happier, or less sad, maybe, after having gotten out of Ventana Azul alive, after having not ended up dropped from some aircraft, like Marco, and it was a huge gift, as if a rusted, twisting knife had been pulled from his heart. He desperately wanted to hold on to this newfound peace, joy, whatever it was, and at times he found himself afraid to move too quickly, lest this feeling shattered like some fragile glass container inside him.

Amazing. The woman had asked him if it was amazing, and he pulled himself back from the brink of his memories. "Yes, yes, it really is." Nathan waved his arm toward the various exhibitions that had been set up in the cavernous space: a mock stage of the Peking Opera, with elaborately robed marionettes; a twenty-foot-long Year of the Pig parade float in tangerine and fuchsia; a not-so-miniature version of the Donglin Temple. And somewhere behind these incredible creations must have been California's contributions, the whole ugly history of the actual treatment of the real Chinese in so-called Gold Mountain overlooked, he supposed, or at least apologized for, one hoped. The buzz of the attendees' voices, the clanking sounds of dim sum carts filled with savory wares being pushed to-and-fro, were all interwoven with the dissonant twanging of a handful of traditional musicians performing on lute-like instruments. "It's rather incredible."

"I hate to burst your bubble, but I was talking about the traffic."

Dr. Mary Yee nodded toward the street below. "They say it's all the Uber drivers on the road. But really, can't you just imagine the day when one more car added to the mix stops the whole thing altogether and nothing ever moves again? But you're right—the artisanship on display here *is* incredible. That is, if you leave out Ai Weiwei, censorship, human rights violations, and so on. My name's Mary Yee." She lifted her name card and then laughed. "Oh, I guess you can see that. We've met before, you know."

Nathan had no memory of a prior encounter. It was as if he'd plunged into a cloud and could no longer tell up from down, and no distinguishing landmarks presented themselves to help him get his bearings.

Ever since Mexico, and along with the "happy energy," he had been finding himself disoriented like this. Other times, he would be overwhelmed by a flood of raw emotion, accompanied by tears, no less, completely not in control of himself. He'd feel a sudden tenderness for strangers in a café or a supermarket, for dogs trotting happily down the street. Anything could set him off: the rattling of gingko tree leaves on campus outside his office, the beautiful strawberry pastries at La Farine. Even the querulous voices of his neighbors' kids, which used to sound like nails on a chalkboard to him, could make him smile. His therapist had told him this was perfectly normal for people who'd had near-death experiences, or at least felt as if they'd been near death, which he certainly had.

There were moments, though, when his old paranoia would seep into the bliss of his happy bubble. He would start to wonder if, instead of what was considered "perfectly normal," he'd experienced some serious medical event back in Mexico that had caused this radical personality change. Maybe when Marco choked him, he'd lost too much oxygen and had destroyed some part of his cerebral cortex. Perhaps he'd had a kind of stroke. Now, this woman was saying she knew him, and he had absolutely no idea who she was.

"We met at a party two years ago. Doctors Without Borders. I knew your wife, Karen."

At the sound of Karen's name, he felt his throat tighten and tears well up. He turned back to the window, willing himself not to sob, desperately trying to think of the sailboats, the blue water, the past moments of happiness, holding on to them for dear life.

"I'm sorry," Mary Yee said. "I'm . . . I don't know what to say. I lost my husband, too, and it was almost worse for me that no one ever said his name."

"How did you know Karen?" Nathan sniffled, shook himself, his back still to the room.

"We were in Honduras together." Mary opened her purse and handed Nathan a tissue. "I'm a pediatrician. I don't go anywhere without Kleenex. Anyway, I'm sorry. She was wonderful, as a person and as a doctor."

Nathan dabbed his eyes. "I think the traffic has moved a little. The MINI Cooper seems to have advanced a few feet." They stared at the cars below in silence. He didn't know whether he wanted Mary to stay or go, and then, deciding on the former, he turned around and faced her. "What brings you to this event, besides, well . . ."

"Besides the fact that I'm Chinese? My family runs a famous restaurant in the Central Valley, the Imperial Kingdom. We've been there for a hundred years. They drafted me to represent us." Mary looked back at the cars. "I used to live in all this." She waved a hand at the traffic. "But after I was in Honduras and then India, I decided I didn't need to go all the way across the world to treat diseases of poverty; I could go back to the Central Valley. Let's see . . . I've recently treated a nine-year-old kid with TB and a teen with rickets. Unbelievable. Worse, the TB case hasn't come in for a follow-up."

Mary handed him another tissue, but he shook his head. "I'm okay now."

"Well," she continued, "somewhere in the midst of all this elegance from the Ming Dynasty, all the Orientalism, you might call it, is California's contribution to the commerce part. Would you like to see?"

Nathan let her lead him through the maze of exhibitions and stalls until they reached an almost life-size photographic display of Chinese life in California during the gold rush. "Did you know," she said, "that it was the Chinese who introduced the whole concept of canals, or irrigation ditches, to the Central Valley, the ones that enabled so much farmland to be created from swamps? Many Chinese were from a very rich farming area, the Pearl Valley. Anyway, most Chinese stayed up near Sacramento, in basically Chinese ghettos, like Lok. Have you ever been?"

Nathan floated along on her chatter. He could see how she would be able to charm some kid into rolling up his sleeve, and before he even knew the needle had punctured his skin, she would be swabbing off the vaccine site with alcohol. Nathan enjoyed her lilting voice, enjoyed her tales of Gold Mountain, stories of her great-grandfather, the famous chef for presidents, and before long they were standing in front of an installation of a traditional Chinese storefront, a balcony above the front door covered in latticework. Mary pushed aside a beaded curtain and revealed a huge photo of the great-grandfather, a young girl clinging to his knees. "Is that you?" he asked.

"No, no, my mother."

"Oh, is she a chef, too?"

The dim sum cart passed, and Mary grabbed a few dumplings, handing a couple to Nathan. "My family's *baozi* are better, but these are pretty good. No, my mother doesn't make dinner; she makes reservations. She was an orthopedic surgeon, like my dad, so she never cooked. When she retired, she didn't take up cooking or knitting or anything reasonable; she heard the call of religion and went back to school to study."

"She's a Buddhist priest?" Nathan dabbed his lips, using the napkin beneath his dumpling.

Mary laughed. "See? Stereotypes all over the place. No, she's a Unitarian minister in Marin. Totally rational. That's her thing. She celebrates UN Day like it's a religious holiday."

Nathan laughed. "Seriously?" he asked, wondering when he'd last laughed so easily.

"Seriously. I'm going to get us some more dumplings. Wait for me."

He turned back to the photographs of the Imperial Kingdom restaurant and of the few members of the small Chinese community who lived nearby in something called Chinese Alley, built after the Chinese Exclusion Act of 1882. The captions led one to believe that they had all prospered in spite of everything, so it was really no big deal. Hardly the case, Nathan knew.

Mary Yee returned with two plates piled with dim sum. "The waiters love me because I can speak Cantonese and Mandarin. Look—*har gow*." She pointed to some glassy-looking dumplings. "The *har gow* has shrimp, and barbecued pork is in the *cha siu bao*. Yum. I'll show you all the famous people my family has served." She passed the photo of the glamorous diners from the '60s and pointed. "They were extras in Charlie Chan movies. And see that guy in the corner? He was"—she raised her fingers and made air quotes—"Number Two Son in the same. He also played Hop Sing at the Ponderosa." She stopped and took another mouthful. "Really, you don't know whether to laugh or cry, do you? Ming vases on one side of the Pacific. The Ponderosa on ours."

"Well, here's Governor Brown, Pat Brown," Nathan pointed out. "So maybe things were getting better then? Yes? No?"

"Yes, for us. For the farmworkers, not so much. Oh, here's one." She pointed to a recent photo, one of Dianne Feinstein standing in front of the Imperial Kingdom's elaborately carved, gold-painted doorway. Her companion, Nathan thought, looked familiar, and no sooner had he remembered who the man was than Mary Yee confirmed it.

"That is our state senator, Jim Fletcher. I should say *was* our state senator. He died. A heart attack or something."

Jim Fletcher. Mexico. The memory landed on him as hard as Marco's body had fallen on the roof of his cabana. Ventana Azul. The bird-watching tour that had ended in dead bodies on the beach. No, Fletcher had not died of a heart attack. Was that how they'd covered it up? *Is that what everyone is saying?* he wondered.

Mary tossed her paper plate into a nearby bin. "He was actually kind of a jerk, but I did hear him refer to Dianne Feinstein once as a great little gal. Probably the only time in her life someone called her a gal. Are you okay? Nathan?"

He needed to say something, but what? Mexico was over, and he didn't want to be dragged back into it. "I've just been standing too long."

"Bend your knees. People tend to lock their knees. It's why they get faint when they stand too long."

Nathan bounced a bit up and down, bending his knees. "This guy Fletcher doesn't look so old that he should have had a heart attack," he said, not really knowing what he was fishing for.

"Like we should talk, Nathan. Neither of our spouses was really old. It happens. But listen, I wanted to talk to you about coming to a DWB conference. That's why I intruded on your private moment over there by the window."

"DWB?"

"Doctors Without Borders. We're going to talk about Karen's work. Dr. Bernstein's work. Would you come? Would you consider saying a few words?"

So that was it. She hadn't connected him with Mexico or with Fletcher, whose name had the effect Nathan had so feared, pulling the plug out of the wall socket of his happy energy. "I don't know. I . . ."

"Here take this." She pulled a business card out of her jacket pocket. "Just think about it. I have to go for a photo shoot with the local dignitaries, including our deceased senator's widow." Mary pointed in the direction of a podium, where a few well-dressed men were hovering around a petite blond woman like bees around a queen's hive. "She's running for her husband's office. Keep the power in the family seems to be the goal. Anyway, that's why I dressed in the whole *Flower Drum Song* outfit, instead of jeans and a lab coat. It was my grandmother's—real-deal silk."

"It's a beautiful jacket," Nathan said, because it seemed the thing to say and because he desperately wanted to get off the subject of Jim Fletcher.

"Call me, okay? Think about it." Mary waved and walked off.

He was not thinking about it now, certainly. He was back in Mexico, with all its creepiness swirling around him: Marco; Bud Delano; Jim Fletcher, drunk and sweating on the patio one day and dead the next. His eyes followed Mary to the podium, where she posed in different configurations with the group assembled, including for a couple of shots of just Mary and Mrs. Fletcher.

He wanted this monkey off his back. That was when an idea crystallized in his mind. He would tell Jim Fletcher's widow what he knew, what he had seen in Mexico, the whole rotten picture, and then he would be free. She could be the one to seek some kind of justice, whatever that would look like in Mexico. As a politician's wife, she would have some pull with international agencies, wouldn't she? Certainly more than he would ever have. That was the ticket—tell her, and be done with it. Then he could let it go, take his walk to North Beach with a light heart, sit on the wall surrounding Coit Tower, and watch the boats, the sun setting behind the Golden Gate Bridge. He could get the happiness back, be free, and relegate the whole episode to no more than a strange and exotic memory.

Nathan milled around for a while, until Fletcher's widow headed for the exit, and then followed her to the hallway, watching for an opening as she simultaneously punched the elevator button and answered her phone. Nathan overheard snippets: "It's on more than just the tenth floor." "Sheaves, eaves." "You talk to him." The elevator arrived, and Nathan stepped into it.

"Going down?" Mrs. Fletcher asked.

Nathan nodded, and when they reached the bottom floor and the doors opened, he cleared his throat. "Excuse me, Mrs. Fletcher." She stepped into the entrance hall and turned to face him, phone still in her hand, a society matron's practiced smile aimed his direction.

"Yes?"

"I need to speak with you. I . . ." Nathan noticed her smile tightening.

"My driver is just leaving the parking garage under the building," she said, putting him on notice.

Nathan blurted out the story that Dr. Mary Yee had told him: Everyone believed that Mrs. Fletcher's husband had died of a heart attack. But Nathan could assure her he had not. He babbled the words "bird-watching tour" and "Ventana Azul" and ended by saying that she should look into it. He waited for some response. Gratitude, maybe, or something like it. Instead, he could see that the widow didn't believe him, that she thought he was some crank. She glared at him, her mouth now a tight line.

"What did you say your name was?" she asked, lifting her phone. "How can you be reached?"

Nathan watched her eyes squint into a fierce glare and decided against giving her his information. If he thought he'd made a difference, that she would pursue the truth about her husband's death, she quickly disabused him of the illusion. "Look, I have no idea who you are or where you came up with these absurdities, but I can assure you my attorney, Mr. McCall, will be in touch." She squinted at his name tag. "Mr. Bernstein, since you are not very forthcoming, I can get your information from the festival organizers. I think you have just engaged in slander. Good day." She turned and headed for the door, her high heels echoing in the vast marble foyer.

Nathan leaned against the wall, aware that he was sweating, that he'd been an absolute fool. Looking toward the large revolving glass doors, he watched Mrs. Fletcher push through them and step to the curb, waving her hand as a black Lexus pulled up. The driver hopped out, and Nathan took one look, his knees almost giving out. Minus the flowered Hawaiian shirt, the man, Bud Delano, wearing a leather jacket and aviator Ray-Bans, was unmistakable. Nathan pressed himself against the wall and turned his face away from the door, hoping the glare through the glass would prevent Bud from recognizing him. It dawned on him with lightning speed that if Bud Delano had managed to survive the Mexico carnage, it stood to reason that he'd had a hand in it. He was even crazier and more lethal than Marco had been. Nathan braved a quick glance at the door just in time to see the Lexus merge into traffic and drive off, and he knew with a sick feeling that this was not the end of it. If Bud had had a hand in Marco's and Fletcher's deaths, he would certainly not want Nathan around to accuse him.

Returning to the China California Celebration event, he wandered through the various exhibits, looking for Mary Yee. He needed whatever information she could give him about the Fletchers. Had there had been any prior whiffs of malfeasance or corruption? But by the time he had woven his way through the many booths and searched the now thinning crowd, he hadn't found her. He wandered back to the exhibit of the Chinese in the Central Valley and took out his phone to shoot some more photos of Jim Fletcher, zeroing in on one of him standing in front of a sign that said FLETCHER FAMILY FARMS: AMERICA'S FINEST CITRUS. Nathan punched the farm's name into his phone's search engine and scrolled until he found an article in the *Del Rio Times*. Headline: "Dismembered Body Found in

Fletcher Family Farms Orange Grove." *Wow,* he thought. *Just wow.* Squinting at the date on the paper, he added up the numbers. Only three weeks ago. Right before Fletcher was in Mexico. This was too weird. Nothing was this coincidental. This was terrifying, actually. He felt sick and still sweaty from his encounter with Fletcher's widow. *Let it go, Nathan,* he told himself.

He calmed down enough after a while to realize that Mrs. Fletcher could threaten all she wanted, but the Bernstein family had access to high-powered attorneys as well. Her threat would, in all likelihood, be resolved in an oak-paneled room by a simple cease-and-desist letter and a handshake. All a misunderstanding. And, of course, the more information he had about the Fletchers, the stronger his case would be.

What had Mrs. Fletcher been talking about on her phone before Nathan decided to drop a bomb on her life? Something about the tenth floor. Wouldn't hurt to have a little look around, would it? If everything was on the up-and-up, then he would feel less guilty about letting go. And if it wasn't? It wouldn't hurt to know. He could tell his attorney and proceed from there. He walked back to the row of elevators and punched the brass button with the engraved number 10.

The doors opened into a drafty hall blocked off with a makeshift plywood wall still smelling of raw lumber and sawdust. The rest of the tenth floor was hidden from view, except for an opening behind a cheap, prefab door on which a large, open padlock dangled. Nathan slipped through the door and found himself in an empty office space, bare and industrial, with visible ducting and windows covered with brown paper. In one corner, a kitchen had been sloppily constructed. Folding high chairs leaned against the wall. Stretching the length of the room were several single beds, like a dormitory of sorts, and about five banged-up cribs. As Nathan got closer, he noticed the mattresses smelled of urine and bleach, the crib sheets worn and stained.

There were a couple of playpens set up, and in one, a lone rattle lay abandoned on the plastic cover.

He didn't have a real name for what he was seeing. The words "trafficking" and "illegals" came to mind, but connecting them with the elegant Mrs. Fletcher was hard. Nathan remembered the leaflets from the beach in Mexico: *This is how the Gentleman treats those who are not gentlemen.* Whom had Jim Fletcher run afoul of? Nathan held up his phone and took a picture. He was definitely having his attorney contact the police.

From the far end of the room, Nathan heard the clanking of tools and headed toward the sound, following it around a corner and down a bleak hallway. A repairman on his knees in the freight elevator, earbuds blaring the tinny sound of angry talk radio, was attaching wires to the side of the elevator door. He jumped when he saw Nathan.

"You snuck up on me, man." He took the earbuds out. "You from ATS?" he asked.

Caught off-guard, Nathan lied. "Yes. Mrs. Fletcher asked me to check on things," he embellished, hoping he sounded believable.

"Hoo, boy, the bitch from hell. Am I right? She ripped me a new one about the damn elevator. Well, you people should have brought us in sooner. I'm Jack." He stood, stretched his knees. "Got a problem with your hoisting wiring. So, what I did was take out the old door unit switches and mounted a couple of proximity switches. They'll control your slowdown and activate the door. Let me tell you people something: Maintenance is the name of the game. Like I said, you should have brought us in sooner." He dropped back down to his knees and popped in his earbuds. Conversation over.

Nathan turned away from the elevator, leaving Jack to his activities and radio. Taking out his phone again, he filmed the kitchen area, opening the cabinet doors to reveal a box labeled PEDIALYTE, a few baby bottles. Good. They could get Child Protective Services in on this. He filmed the folding high chairs and a pile of kiddie booster seats. On the bottom shelf, Nathan filmed a box of crayons and opened a pad of paper. In the middle of the pad, Nathan stopped, brought up short by a child's drawing and writing. *Yo soy José Guzmán*, it said. Nathan zoomed in on what must have been the boy's self-portrait. *Yes*, Nathan thought, *we are definitely looking at calling in Child Protective Services. No child should be living like this.*

"You know what I think?"

It was Nathan's turn to jump now. Jack was behind him, leaning against the wall.

"You all are too obvious with the cribs and shit."

"Obvious about what? What are you suggesting?" Nathan tried to play the part of some corporate middle manager.

"Hey, I fix industrial elevators in this city. Every morning, every damn morning, I drive in from Tracy at five a.m, over Altamont Pass and through that hellhole of the 580–680 interchange. Next, I park in the Third Street garage and have to step over people living in the streets, needles, human waste products, if you know what I mean, all over the place. And then you know what I see? Half these damn high-rise buildings I go into are empty from the third floor up. You gotta be a multibillionaire to live in this town. So, no way do I think you folks are running a daycare center in this pricey zip code. Nah. Anyway, I just fix freight elevators, right? They don't pay me to be the damn border patrol. Your secret is safe with me." He looked down at his clipboard. "What you've got here in addition to the doors is damaged sheaves, and they are going to have to be replaced, which apparently is going to throw off Mrs. Bitch's schedule."

"I suppose you've offered a solution to expedite this."

Jack looked back at his clipboard. "Says here ATS is willing to pay triple for a crew to work straight through to have it ready by Sunday night. Cleared it with my supervisor. I don't have any say-so in it. Hey, it's your money."

"It is indeed."

"You know what I figure?" Jack hoisted up his tool belt. "All this stuff is for anchor babies. I been hearing about it for years on my radio talk shows."

Nathan could just imagine what those were: wall-to-wall Alex Jones and Rush Limbaugh ranting about immigrant invaders. Sure enough, Jack continued in this vein.

"Come in here illegally, drop a kid, and you're set for life, right? Presto-bingo—US citizen. So, how much do they pay you for this, my friend? Or should I say *amigo*?"

"I think you've got it wrong, but I'm not at liberty to tell you."

"I figured you wouldn't be. Just letting you know you don't fool me. Anyway, I'm done with the job." Jack ripped off a sheet of paper from his clipboard, an invoice. "You can give that copy to the dame. The other two are for the company."

Nathan waved the invoice in the air. "You ready to close up? If so, I'll be going. Thanks," he said. Yeah, no kidding. Jack had no idea he would soon be called in for a deposition or that Nathan was absolutely inclined to agree with his assessment of the situation. He nodded and walked to the passenger elevator.

"Wait up. Found this in the door." Jack waved a piece of beaded cloth at Nathan, some kind of band or bracelet.

Nathan took it from Jack's hand and looked at it for a minute while it dawned on him. The bracelet or whatever it was reminded him of Karen's medicine bag from that shaman in Mexico. West coast of Mexico. Ventana Azul. It was all coming together: Bud Delano, this bracelet, Fletcher.

"Tell Her Highness she's gotta be careful with that kind of thing. It could fall and damage the pulleys, and then you'd be shit out of luck, mister."

12

CALLIE

The Bay Bridge metering lights were already on, and the traffic had piled up behind the toll booth to the MacArthur Maze. Oh well. Idling in traffic gave me time to think, something I really needed to do. I wanted to pour my heart out to Mike, but today was not the day. Why not? Because Mike was hosting a baby shower and I was due there in an hour, which was probably how long it would take me to cross the bridge. All I had to do was figure which lane I should be in in case the big one hit. Outer lanes, and I'd go quickly, falling into the bay. Inner lanes, and I'd crash through to the lower deck, killing myself and probably the family below in a minivan. I had to stop being so negative, and I didn't want to rain on Mike's special day. The baby shower was for his baby. I was still in shock.

Actually, I'd been not really myself, whoever that was these days, since Mia's announcement on the plane a few days earlier, so I wasn't surprised when I got a text from Mike, saying he just wanted to check in, see how I was doing. I knew he was worried about me in his own way. I'd waited until after work, until I was engaging in my usual exciting activity of throwing the ball to Vato, to call. I'd had a chance to rehearse a few comments—*Oh, I'm fine; I'll figure something out*—until I thought I sounded convincing. Mike's real motives for the text came out soon enough, however. He wasn't just texting to check on me. He had news of his own, which he blurted out. "I'm going to be a father, Callie. Francois and I are going to be a family. You're going to be an aunt."

An eternity went by before I could muster any words. "Wow," I said. "Wow." I imagined a surrogate, a donor, a birth six months or so from now, with time to adjust, paint the nursery, get used to being Aunt Callie, to losing my brother to diapers and playdates. What I hadn't imagined was that he meant this week. He was going to become a father this week. As in three days. The baby was arriving on Thursday on a flight from China, through somewhere else, to LA. It had all happened so fast. And on Saturday, which was today, they were going to have a shower after a traditional Jewish naming ceremony at Temple Emanuel in the morning, which Francois had wanted to join to give his daughter a sense of identity. Clearly, they'd lost their minds.

"Say something, Callie. Say you're happy for me."

I managed that much. "Of course I'm happy for you. It's just a surprise, a huge surprise." What I wanted to say was, *Why didn't you tell me all this? Why am I in the dark?* Then I remembered his claim that he'd told me about meditating in Tassajara and I'd forgotten. Still, nothing I asked now would change the fact that he'd cut me out of this part of his life. But I rallied anyway; it wasn't all about me, was it? I said I was ecstatic for him, told him I'd be at the shower. I was the aunt, after all.

And then there I was, after everything I'd been through the past week or so, leaning over the deck railing of Mike's lovely home all tricked out with pink crepe paper, nursing my sense of failure, trying not to feel like such a loser. I sipped my wine and stared at the houses that spread up and down the hillside toward the Sunset. Postcard Alcatraz Island, the blue-green bay. Squinting toward Noe Valley, I tried to see my house, the one good thing I got out of my divorce from

Sam. I bet he was sorry about that momentary lapse now. The place grossed me six grand a month from a techie couple who was renting it while their house on Dolores was being remodeled. I could retire to an island in Greece on that. So, why didn't I? Because what would I do? That was the question I asked myself every day now that Mia was running for Fletcher's senate seat.

I could move back here, work for some nonprofit, and basically just live the Cali lifestyle. Nah. Too much Armenian farmer in me for that. Too stubborn. Not a quitter. I'd have to figure out some other way.

I heard the sliding doors open behind me, and turned.

"Hi." A woman approached the deck railing. I'd noticed her before, milling about. She sported a stylish haircut, lots of silver bracelets, and the ubiquitous Eileen Fisher black pantsuit.

"I couldn't take all the screaming babies." She leaned her back against the railing, looked through the sliding glass doors, and shook her head. "Used to be the great thing about being gay was, no one asked you when you were having kids. Now"—she shrugged, shook her head again, and sipped her wine—"I'll stick to cats, thank you. I'm Martha, by the way. Martha Bittner. The attorney. The one who tried to talk them out of this overseas adoption."

"Really? Why?" Suddenly, I was all ears.

"Some of these folks here call me the Stork. I hate to think about how much money I've taken from Mike and Fran and the rest of these folks, but foreign adoptions are getting trickier. They said they weren't getting any younger—a bird in hand and that sort of thing."

"True that." I nodded. "As it is, they could be using walkers by the time she's a teenager."

"They'd had their share of heartbreak." Martha pushed her hair out of her face. We were both getting blown around a bit by the wind coming off the bay. "The surrogacy thing that didn't work out. Mom changed her mind. The complicated donor-egg transfer to another surrogate in Colorado that didn't take. These are the stories no one tells you. It's all some movie star suddenly popping out twins—presto."

I felt a wave of sorrow for Mike, and for me, too, that he hadn't confided in me. "No wonder they did what they did," I said, as much to myself as to Martha.

"People get desperate. I've seen it." She raised her glass, sipped more wine. "Well, all's well that ends well. They got lucky." She lifted her glass toward the room behind the sliding door. "Looks like we're being summoned, so here's to Mike and Fran. Mazel tov. You know what we should do? Pray to the Great Goddess that we don't come back as Chinese baby girls. They get treated like crap over there. Anyway, everyone got lucky." She raised her glass once more, then passed me to join the party.

From inside, I could hear someone tapping a glass with a spoon, calling out, "Okay, everybody, settle down. We're about to begin."

"Would you look at that?" Martha said, motioning me to go in front of her. "All the gray hair in there. I feel like I ought to be at a retirement party, instead of a baby shower."

The lights in the room were already turned off, the babies and toddlers downstairs in the first-level bedrooms with the sitters, and the guy with the glass and spoon motioned for me to draw the curtains, which I did. On a screen against the wall, the name Mei-Lin—Beautiful Jewel—was projected from a computer set up for a PowerPoint presentation. Below the name, I saw her birthday—July 10—and began to get a sick, dizzy feeling, a memory of all those baby carriers coming off the plane in the jungle in Mexico. I began to calculate how old she was when I was there: something like six weeks, small enough for one of the carriers. Could Fran have been there picking her up, purchasing her, really? My suspicions were mounting by the minute. A woman sitting at the dining table called out, "Have you done her chart?" which started a lot of chitchat about Chinese horoscopes versus Western and distracted me from my morbid thoughts. The man with the glass wandered around the room, shushing everyone. "We don't want to scare her when Mike and Fran bring her out."

And then there she was, more like a bundle attached to Mike's chest with a kind of bag. She had a small, perfect head covered with silky black hair and large black eyes that blinked often, in disbelief, it seemed to me. Her mother must have been beautiful. Mike walked through the crowd, turning this way and that, showing her off, his finger pressed to his lips to keep everyone quiet. I had to admit I had never seen him happier. Francois followed, beaming, shaking hands with all the well-wishers. Given what I'd seen in Mexico, I felt like the evil witch arrived to curse the fairy-tale princess. I wished I could not know what I knew, and wondered again about the attorney, if she had her doubts about the legality of this. *Remember her name*, I told myself. *Martha Bittner*.

Mike sat down in a rocker as best he could with a small baby attached to him, and Francois gave him the remote for the PowerPoint.

"Thank you all for being here. You know how much this means to Fran and me. We've tried not to be jealous as we watched you guys start families." He began to choke up, and as I looked around at all the guests dabbing their eyes with cocktail napkins, I couldn't have felt shittier. Mike clicked the remote and began. "We named her Mei-Lin, which, as you can see, means Beautiful Jewel, and I just want to show those of you who couldn't be at the airport when we welcomed her home to San Francisco the photographs we had taken."

Mike began to click through the images. "Okay, here I am being allowed onto the plane. The airline's customer service helped arrange all this with TSA. The flight attendants were so excited. Remember, Fran?"

And there was Mike, greeting his baby for the first time. I teared up. God, the look on his face when Fran handed him that pink bundle. Mike clicked again, and we saw the two of them beaming as they entered the airport waiting area, where friends waved shiny Mylar balloons that read WELCOME, BABY and sported headbands with bouncy, glittering stars. But soon enough, we were all brought back to reality when a loud wail pierced the background lullaby music that ran under the photos.

"That's mine." The horoscope woman at the table got up. "Sorry. I knew it was too good to last." She squeezed through the crowd and headed down the stairs.

There were more photos, more tears, but finally Mei-Lin awoke from her trance and bellowed like a banshee.

"Thank God," one of the guests yelled. "I was beginning to think she wasn't real."

None of this was real, or, rather, it was surreal, I thought, gathering the glasses and plates and carrying them into the kitchen. The guests had left, all parting with the usual jokes—"You're crying now—wait till you see what college costs," that sort of thing—their children piled into strollers and car seats. Mike and Fran warmed up a bottle of breast milk purchased from a company called Mother's Is Best and retreated downstairs to put Mei-Lin to bed.

And then it was quiet. All except for the loud remonstrations in my head. *I'm Mei-Lin's aunt*, the voices reminded me while I loaded the dishwasher. I had a responsibility to get this all out in the open. If Fletcher had arranged for this baby to be delivered in some criminal fashion, it could all come back to haunt us, especially Mei-Lin. Couldn't Mike and Fran see that? No, they'd been desperate. And now they were blind with love. And me? I'd be guilty of a felony if anyone found out I'd been in Mexico and knew anything about this. I could get disbarred. Accessory after the fact. Bittner. Martha Bittner. I grabbed some paper from next to the phone and wrote down the name, shoved it in my pocket.

"She's sleeping." Francois stepped into the kitchen. "I need a cigarette, so I'm going outside. Pretty soon, he's going to make me walk down the block to smoke." He grabbed an ashtray from the dish drainer.

"Pretty soon, he's going to make you quit."

"Yes, to be sure. He's already talking about how we need to stay healthy so we can walk her down the aisle."

And then the words came out of my mouth. "You have other problems than planning her wedding, Fran. I know."

Fran turned, looked surprised, and hesitated at the door. "Yes?"

"I was in Mexico. I saw you at the Reina de Hong Kong restaurant."

I don't know how long we squared off, staring silently at each other, waiting for someone to say something, show their hand.

"I have absolutely no idea what you are talking about, Callie," Francois said finally. "And now I'm going to smoke my cigarette while you come to your senses."

"Yes, you do, Francois." Mike stepped into the kitchen from the hall. "You don't have to protect me. You know. I know. How did you find out, Callie?"

I told him I'd seen the pictures he'd hidden in an album cover, pictures that Lupe had found of Fletcher with a kid—sick stuff. "I put two and two together after Fletcher wanted me to find you. Rosie said Fletcher was a danger, told me I needed to figure out what was going on at Ventana Azul, so I followed the trail to Mexico. You used those pictures to blackmail Fletcher and get a baby, didn't you? Oh my God." This was not the image I had of my brother, the do-gooder.

"Look, I'm going to do you a huge favor. I'm going to forget about this, and so are you. Nobody knows anything. Fletcher is dead, so that just leaves Mia, and she is paying me—us—a lot of money never to let this come out. Enough for private school, for college."

"You're telling me you're blackmailing her now?" I gripped the side of the counter, almost faint with horror. This could not be true.

"I'm telling you to forget everything you know, or think you know."

"I can't do that, Mike." I turned back to the sink and began scraping bits of dip and cheese off the plates. "There are laws against this."

Francois left the kitchen. I heard the front door open and, and from the kitchen window, watched as he walked to the sidewalk and flicked his lighter. I wiped my hands on a dish towel. "Mike, you don't understand."

"No, *you* don't understand. We did all this with an attorney. It's as legal as it can get, even the prior financial arrangement we made with Fletcher to ensure our silence, which, according to a codicil in his will, his widow has to honor. So, you see? Very good legal advice. You will not destroy my daughter's life because you are still riding on the famous, vengeful Giritlian high horse. You will not destroy my family."

"What high horse? She's a stolen baby. You got her with the aid of a child molester through blackmail, Mike. I saw it."

"You have no way of interpreting what you saw when you were snooping on Fran, do you? Really? I'm going downstairs to be with my daughter now. When I come back up, I want you gone."

"Mike," I called out. "Mike, listen."

He didn't say anything. I cut off the kitchen light, walked to the guest room, and sat on the bed, waiting. Maybe he would change his mind, come back up. I heard Francois open the front door, heard the lock click. I heard him head downstairs. I waited maybe a half an hour. Nothing, no one.

I threw my few things in my bag and headed to my car. It wasn't until I'd made it over Pacheco Pass, along with a bunch of long-haul truckers tanked up on Red Bull, gunning for the Grapevine, that I pulled onto a spur overlooking the San Luis Reservoir, cold and gleaming in the moonlight, and the nightmare of what had just happened washed over me again, a tidal wave of despair.

The time glowed from the dash: 12:37 a.m. Mike must have kicked me out around 10:30, just two hours earlier. Why was I so dry-eyed, when tears would be such a relief? I felt my ribs, my lungs, my heart being squeezed out like a rag, but not a drop from the tear ducts, just a kind of wide-eyed panic. Now what? Life as I had known it was over.

Resting my head against the steering wheel, I could hear my breath coming in short bursts like rough static from a faraway station, as if a part of me had floated off to some distant place while I'd sped down the peninsula toward Gilroy and was now garbled, lost, and desperate to be heard.

What is it with you two? Fletcher had asked—taunted, really. *The twin thing?* I had thought Mike and I were so alike, both so principled and just. Well, we weren't anymore.

Mike called it adoption. I called it baby trafficking. Who was right in all this? He had a daughter, and all I had was my high-minded desire for justice.

The car shook in some big rig's wake, I lifted my head and stared out across the flat expanse of the reservoir, over the bone-dry hills, toward Los Banos and the broad valley beyond. I had no choice but to keep driving, even though soon there would be nothing in front of me but flat land and huge black skies.

I shifted the car out of park and checked the mirrors, and, when the coast was clear, pulled back onto the highway. I sped up and was soon going at least ten miles over the speed limit with all the truckers toward Del Rio and whatever my life still held for me there.

13

NATHAN

Nathan leaned back on the sofa, arms stretched out behind his head, and stared at the Diebenkorn painting on the wall opposite him, one of the iconic *Ocean Park* series. Through the open double doors that led to the dining room of his parents' San Francisco pied-à-terre, the Sabbath candles flickered on the polished table where at sundown his mother had lit them, saying the prayer. Then his father had passed him the kiddush cup and joked, "Let's see if all the money I spent on your bar mitzvah paid off." But, as with riding a bike, Nathan blessed the fruit of the vine, passed the cup to his father, who drank, and then blessed the bread.

During dinner, with the warm smells of roasted chicken, carrots, and onions, and the yeasty scent of challah, surrounding him, he looked back and forth at the painting, then out through the wide plate-glass windows at the view over Pacific Heights, at the blue evening, at the pastel houses that seemed to tumble down toward the bay. Diebenkorn had gotten so much right, not just about composition and geometry but about the spirit of California in those days, its hope revealed by the painter's shimmering light. Nathan knew that was his parents' California, with its airy freedom of possibility. His own California, the new, twenty-first-century version, was much darker, but why burden his folks with that? They were getting older and seemed more fragile, a little more stooped, each time he saw them. Nothing and no one lasted forever. He should know, and he vowed to do more for them, to be a better son.

He closed his eyes and listened to his mother in the kitchen, praising Marta's cooking in her badly accented Spanish. This time, he didn't allow it to irritate him. Maybe, at age fifty, he'd finally grown up. Maybe, after Mexico and Marco, he'd finally put things in some perspective.

"You like?" Marta asked his mother. "*El tzimmes* is good?"

Nathan heard his father behind him, the clinking of glass. "*El tzimmes*—there's a new one." He handed Nathan a brandy snifter. "Watch and see if she doesn't go back to Mexico and make a mint opening a kosher restaurant. How about *el cognac*, sonny? Keep your pops company."

"Sure." Nathan sat up and held out his glass while his father poured.

"That Diebenkorn was one of the best investments I ever made." Howard Bernstein pointed with his own glass. "Good thing I bought it in the seventies."

"The best investment you ever made? What do you mean, *you*? How hard did *I* have to twist your arm?" His mother set the candlesticks on the coffee table, bringing with her the Sabbath lights. "How did my grandparents, of blessed memory, ever carry those things from Poland? I can't even carry them from the dining room."

"Okay, so, I'm cheap. I should have given your mother all our money to invest in art. We'd be multimillionaires." He sipped his cognac.

"I think you already are," Nathan said.

"I suppose you're right. Sometimes I can't believe it."

"All the time he can't believe it," his mother chimed in. "He still shops at the dollar store for T-shirts."

"You know what one of those Diebenkorns sold for in London recently? Twenty-four million dollars. Good." Howard chuckled. "Now I have something to bribe the Nazis with if it comes to that again."

Nathan's mother lifted her knitting needles from a basket on the other side of the sectional. "They're not Nazis anymore. They're neo-Nazis, and what do they know from art?"

Nathan watched his mother lift her yarn, soft and wispy, like trails of clouds. She was knitting a cap the size of half an orange. "For the preemies," she said. "Feel how soft." She passed a ball of wool toward Nathan. "My God, those babies are tiny."

He knew his parents' funds had helped build a neonatal ICU at a local hospital, but his mother liked to make things, so she knitted cap after cap. He felt an electric surge of guilt for not having given her grandchildren. That was nothing new. He used to blame her for making him feel guilty, but looking at her now, her legs tucked under her on the sofa, her fashionable reading glasses perched on her nose, raised blue veins showing the age in her manicured hands, he just felt regret for everything that would inevitably pass him by, all of life's promises he could not grab. *Your parents are old*, he reminded himself. *Just enjoy Sabbath dinner with your family.* How many more would there be?

His dad sank down into his favorite wing chair, slipped off his Birkenstocks, and put his feet on the coffee table, his socks worn at the heel. He was the opposite of his stylish wife, who had to make sure he didn't go around in some ratty old sweater and frayed slacks.

"See what I mean?" His mother aimed a needle at her husband's stocking feet. "Those, he gets at the dollar store, too. It's why they don't last."

"You know what else isn't going to last? Me. That's who." Howard groaned for effect, rubbed his hands over his face, the lines there deeper than last year, visible even in the living room's soft light.

"Not the way you're working." Miriam Bernstein's needles clicked.

Nathan swirled his cognac, sensing what was on the horizon, like incoming bombers: the pressure to leave his university career behind and take over his dad's business. What kind of son was he, anyway? Hadn't his uncle pulled him aside at Passover and said, "You want your father to go to an early grave? The man is a heart attack waiting to happen."

"You know what else is not going to last? The wine industry. Not in Napa, not the way it is."

Nathan sat up, leaned forward. This was not what he had been expecting. Maybe his father was going to cash out after all. Hadn't Château Montevista just sold to Coca-Cola? For many, many millions. How did Nathan feel about that, about the possibility of losing the family vineyards, the thing that had felt like a ball and chain all these years? Not good, and after all his complaining about the demeaning aspects of the wine business—the hobnobbing, the wheeling and dealing—that was a surprise. Who had he thought he was? Some Talmudic scholar, too good for the world, as if being in business were somehow beneath him?

"I used to be a winemaker; now I'm a weatherman," Nathan's father continued. "Climate change, global warming, whatever you want to call it—I have to go around checking the weather every day at each vineyard. Napa, Sonoma. Each year is hotter than the last. We had to pull up the pinot grapes, sonny. Just about killed me."

Nathan looked at his mother, who nodded.

"If you were to take over"—Howard raised his hands—"which you're not. I understand, I would tell you no one is putting their money into pinot now. You can forget it—all kinds of new diseases. I've got half the UC Davis viticulture department out there every summer. I'm a science project for them. We've got to pick two to four weeks earlier, and you pray it's just two. And try to get pickers with ICE breathing down everyone's neck." He poured another finger of cognac, swirled it around. "Anybody who knows anything is trying to come up with new varietals."

"I heard someone say that cava is good in these conditions."

"Great." Howard shook his head. "Cheap, fizzy stuff. We'll be making boxed Lambrusco in a couple of years, just to survive. Not that I'm proud. Look, we come from industrial cleansers. Mateus rosé. That's what I'll make. Remember Mateus, Miri?" He smiled at his wife. "Those fancy bottles?"

"Of course I remember. That was what you would buy when you wanted to be romantic."

"I'm still romantic."

"Not with those socks, you're not."

His father reached over and touched the silver candlesticks. "You know why the Jews have survived, sonny? Because we think about the future, not the past."

"Uh, Dad, the whole religion is ancient. It's all about the past, like those candlesticks. How many centuries have families done what we just did, the whole Sabbath ritual?"

"Sure, on the Sabbath we think of what's eternal. But what I want to know is this: How did those Jews know to get out of Spain before it was too late, before the Inquisition was putting out every Jew's eyeballs? How did they know when Prince Henry of Portugal was going to sell them out? How did they know to leave Italy, get out of Constantinople, out of everywhere? Jews even made the maps that got Columbus to the new world. They knew when to get out because they were thinking about the future for at least six days out of the week. Well, this climate-change thing is a whole new world for the wine industry. If I wait until everyone knows it's time to get out, it will be too late."

"So why did Coca-Cola buy Montevista, Pops, if it's all over?"

"A showplace, a hood ornament. Someplace to entertain the big shareholders. They could be shipping all their grapes in from Oregon, for all they care. The vines are just decoration."

His parents were silent for a while, and Nathan watched their worried faces, contemplating their demise, he supposed—the end of the world as they knew it. Nathan wondered how many Jewish sons had seen the same look and had shouldered the burden. All his life, his parents and grandparents had been afraid of another Holocaust. Now, they were facing another kind of catastrophe, Jew and gentile alike. Climate change. And what had he been worried about all these many years, instead of the Holocaust, instead of rising sea levels? His independence. Whom had he been fooling? None of us was independent, when you really thought about it.

"But, Natey"—his mother reached out and patted him on the knee, pulling him out of his thoughts—"your father has a brilliant idea."

"Some grapes actually thrive in heat." Howard leaned forward, looking less aged, more animated. "Penedès, Touriga, Carignan." He said he didn't want to use up valuable Napa acreage with an experiment, but something had come up, the strangest thing.

"Synchronicity," his mother said. "As if the universe knew what he was thinking."

"I'm racking my brain trying to think who I talked to." Howard shook his head. "Oh well—maybe I'm getting senile. I shouldn't have been talking to anyone. I think I'm onto something, sonny, and I don't want anyone else to get wind of it." He leaned close and smiled, tapping his head with his forefinger. "So, maybe not so senile after all, huh?"

Miriam's face lit up, Nathan noticed, as she saw her husband on the trail of a new idea. "Some handsome goyishe lawyer shows up at the vineyard the other day and says he's heard we're looking for land to grow hot-weather grapes. Well, he's selling, or the owner is, and he's there to broker a deal.

"We need to move fast if word is out like this. Someone is selling a citrus farm in the middle of godforsaken nowhere outside of Fresno." Howard stood up, paced the room. "I'm thinking of buying, Nate. What do you say?"

Citrus farm, citrus farm . . . Nathan's heart started to race. Something was off here. What had that woman in Mexico said she was? A citrus farmer. And Jim Fletcher? Didn't he own some orange grove where someone was killed? This had something to do with someone in Mexico—Nathan just knew it in his gut. Someone who made it his business to find out about the Bernsteins. But who? Any one of that weird crowd, really, anyone who was still alive. He should speak to an attorney. Not his father's old attorney, Arnold. Someone a little less antiquated. "Mom, Pop, sometimes synchronicity is not such a good thing. I'd hold off."

His father waved off his concerns. "The land is dirt cheap. I couldn't get ten acres in the Anderson Valley for what they're selling this for. And listen: I don't even have to buy; I can lease to own. So if it all goes south, what am I out? Anyway, I'll have Arnold go over all the papers."

Arnold—*oy*. Arnold had already been old when Nathan was just a kid; he must be ancient by now. "Arnold hasn't retired yet?"

"Nope. He's still on the ball. Good as he ever was."

Then why did Nathan think the handsome *goyishe* lawyer had seen his father as a mark? He pulled out his phone to bring up a map. "Where did you say this was? South of Fresno?" *Not Minsk, not Pinsk—Yiddish for "middle of nowhere."*

"Some burg called Del Rio."

Nathan had to say something, but then his mother looked up, smiling. "Such a perfect Sabbath. I'm so happy to have both my boys together. Just as it should be."

What could he do? That sealed it. He made a mental note to look into this later, see if it had anything to do with the Fletchers. But for now he would wait to tell them about Mexico, the people murdered and dropped on the beach, the weird room in the office building on Sansome Street connected to the Fletchers, all of it. Why spoil his mother's happiness now? What had his grandmother always said?

Some cliché: "You have to take the bitter with the sweet." Maybe that was really how the Jews survived, by savoring the sweet moments like this. He would talk to them later. Sunday, Monday, what difference did it make? Or even in two weeks, after the High Holy Days. After he was certain they were all written once again in the book of life.

14

CALLIE

"**D**id anyone see you?" Nick Lozada asked, peering around the door of Dr. Yee's office and looking over the dirt parking lot toward the VFW hall next door. Once the coast was clear and he seemed certain that any old codgers at the hall were well into their second beer, Fox News blaring from the TV in the corner, he ushered me into Mary Yee's waiting room, where the United Farm Workers leaders and he, their lawyer, were meeting later that evening.

I'd called Nick the week before, after I'd absorbed the fact of Mike's rejection of me—of reality, as I saw it—to let him know that I intended to prosecute pesticide abuse and other violations to the full extent of the law, and that I would welcome the chance to work with him. He seemed wary at first, but I won him over. This was the new Callie, no longer currying favor with the Fletchers and their big-ag buddies to get their endorsements and their funds. I was going to fight them all. And I was going to win.

Nick got back to me a couple of days later and asked me to come to this meeting, said I needed to convince the UFW leaders themselves. So here I was, ready to reassure them. These growers had been getting away with murder, literally, for years. Pesticides accumulated over time, the workers brought the residue home on their clothes, and they contaminated everyone and everything in the house. Time to fight back. It felt good to have found my conscience buried under all my political ambitions, especially after I had gotten so waylaid.

I could hear someone typing away on a computer in the next room. Dr. Yee, I guessed. Nick waved a paper cup my way, lifting a pot of burned-smelling coffee. I needed something to bolster my determination, so I nodded. "Sure."

We were having a middle-of-September heat wave in Del Rio. It had been 104 degrees at 5:00 p.m. when I'd gotten off work and driven past the gypsy camp, taking pictures, jotting down notes. How many weeks ago—a month, maybe—had I promised Juan and the folks at the Flor de Morelia Bakery that I'd get zoning on the gypsy camp, have them clear it out? Not all that long, considering that the Del Rio County zoning department never did anything. That place was the village of the damned, a bunch of overweight zombies who never got out of their chairs, and everyone in town knew it. Juan would forgive me for being slow. Everything was slow around here. Anyway, I'd been otherwise engaged, shall we say, down in Mexico, acting like I was part of Interpol. Callie McCall, aka International Woman of Mystery.

The gypsies' trailers were still there, not a soul stirring outside. I could hear their generators banging away, running the air conditioners at the max.

When I'd run into someone from Zoning chowing down on a double cheeseburger at the Main Street Café, I'd brought up the subject of the gypsy camp. Here's what he told me between mouthfuls: They didn't have regulations on the books that they could use to cite the encampment, which seemed par for the course and also BS. Regulations around here had a way of getting erased. Well, that was about to change, starting now, with the big-ag grower Robert Gerwin's pesticide drift, his flagrant violation of California law. No more spraying on windy days, Gerwin. Those times were over. Time to maintain the 150-foot boundaries *también*. He would soon find out he had to comply with the law, and wouldn't that be a kick in the pants? I wondered how long it would be before I got a call from Mia's campaign—probably from some burner phone so they could say it never happened—demanding that I back off. Sure, not totally legal, but, as they say, that's politics. Oh well. Too bad. Like I said, meet the new Callie.

"Not all the leaders are coming." Nick poured more coffee. "Just a couple of guys and their wives, a few other women with kids. Make it look like a regular Tuesday-night clinic, the ones Mary does on a normal basis."

"Why the top secrecy, Nick?" I shook more powdered creamer into the tarry substance in my cup. "Freedom of assembly and all that."

"Sure. Sounds good in theory. Just not when you're illegal and the cops are moonlighting as anti-labor union goons for the growers. You know how this stuff works down here, Callie. Don't pretend otherwise." He set his cup down on the kiddie table next to some crayons, opened the metal mini-blinds with his thumb, and peered out at the street, which had been pretty dead when I'd driven down it. Nothing much was going on at the VFW. Most vets were up in the foothills, living off the grid. This building used to be a veterinary clinic when I was a kid. In its present incarnation, Dr. Mary Yee, pediatrician, was probably the only thriving establishment on Dinuba Street.

Nick turned away from the window. "Actually, Callie, I'm surprised you're taking this on. Is this the real deal or just window dressing?"

"Real deal, Nick. I'm sick of these growers running roughshod over the law."

"Have you asked for a change of venue?"

"Nope. Keep it all in Del Rio."

"Then it's not the real deal. No judge in this county is going to rule against the growers."

"Jury trial, Nick."

"Ditto. No jury, either."

"We could get some of the pickers on the jury."

He ticked the syllables off on his fingers. "*Il-leg-al.* Anyone who responds to a summons knows he's here by the grace of God and the growers. Anyway, you know anything more about the dead kid over at Fletcher Family Farms? I haven't seen you around since that morning. I'd like to say I'm sorry about your brother-in-law Fletcher dropping dead, but I'd be lying. Couldn't have happened to a nicer guy. I hear it's pretty much chaos in the head office. None of the pickers know if they'll have jobs there. You know anything about that?"

"No and no, Nick."

"Typical for around here. Jesus, I wake up every morning and I feel like shit. Then I go to work, do the best I can for these people, and I still feel like shit at the end of the day. Nothing is enough."

Dr. Yee spoke up from her office. "Stop complaining, Lozada." He shrugged as Mary Yee stepped into the waiting room, dressed in some kind of bright kiddie-doctor lab coat with pictures of kittens and puppies on it. She was carrying a bottle of Lysol wipes in one hand; the other hand, she extended to me. "Hi," she said. "I'm Mary."

"Thanks for doing this," I said, as Mary began using the wipes to swab the table, the Formica chairs, even the box of crayons.

She yanked another wipe out of the container. "These folks who are coming tonight . . . well, you're looking at some real heroes. It's not us, Nick. Not me. Not the DA. I mean, what are you doing after this meeting? Don't get excited. I'm not asking you on a date." She wiped off the doorknobs. "You and I will go relax, have a swim in our pools, watch Rachel Maddow. These folks are heading to a second job, scrubbing the floors of old-age homes, cleaning the freezers of some restaurant. They're doing the same low-paying jobs my great-grandparents used to do." She set the Lysol wipes on the nurses' station counter. "Sometimes I wonder what will happen when this country runs out of slave labor." She sat down on one of the chairs, closed her eyes, and leaned her head back. "There are days when I think I could sleep forever, but the work never ends. How do my patients do it? And no, nothing is enough. You sure you know what you're signing up for, DA McCall?" She raised her head and stared at me.

"I guess I'll find out. This is a good idea, making a meeting look like a normal doctor's visit."

"Enlightened self-interest. I'm sick of seeing small kids with inhalers, babies with neurological damage that could have been prevented."

"That's why I'm here to explain the law."

Nick laughed. "They know the law, Callie. They don't need you to explain it to them. They need you to enforce it. That'll be a new one down here. I think that's what Mary means when she asks if you know what you're signing up for."

Just then, the door buzzed and Nick looked through the peephole. "They're here," he said. "We can get started. Oh, and Callie? File a motion for a change of venue. Then maybe we'll believe you're serious."

Ajit's Valero station and mini-mart was on my way home, but I almost missed it. I was rehashing the meeting, trying to figure out if I'd won over the workers, gained their trust. I supposed I would find out from Nick in a few days. I was pondering how many days I should wait before calling him, when I registered the Valero station just in time to swing a sharp left and pull under the awning next to the pumps. I sat in the car for a while, letting the air conditioner blast my face, and stared at the current outside temp on the car dashboard. A balmy 99 degrees. Well, there was nothing I could do about it. I needed gas, hot weather or no. My tank was almost empty, and getting stuck without gas on these empty roads through the orange groves was never a good idea. I turned off the engine and hopped out, the heat rising up from the pavement, along with the smell of gas fumes, and swiped my card through the reader. After I stuck the nozzle in the gas tank, I looked around for the gypsies. Sure enough, just as Juan had said, there were two girls, dressed in halter tops and cutoffs, their dirty feet visible in sparkly flip-flops, hitting up some farm boy for cash, or so it seemed. He popped the hood of his car, got the oil dipstick, and pretty much ignored them. By the time I'd filled my tank and replaced the nozzle, they were gone. You can't call the cops just because two girls are talking to some guy. That was what I'd tell Juan. I grabbed the window washer out of its grimy tub of cleanser and pulled the sponge across my windshield.

I hadn't eaten since lunch, and Ajit's had a fairly decent selection of things I could throw in the microwave, which was about my energy level at this point in the evening. What little I had of it, I was using to mull over Nick Lozada's taunt about a change of venue. He had to know there was very little cause for a judge to do so. And where would I go? Berkeley? There was no other Central Valley county whose jury pool would be any different. Pesticide drift? The jurors would laugh. *Guy's not responsible if the wind blows the wrong way, is he?* Maybe it *was* just window dressing on my part, a way to make myself feel important and strong again. I hoped not. I hoped I was better than that.

I stood in front of the mini-mart's freezer doors, trying to decide among the delectable offerings of microwavable spaghetti and meatballs, macaroni and cheese, and frozen burritos. I grabbed the mac and cheese. It was vegetarian, I told myself.

"Get out!" Ajit screamed, and I jumped, turned around. Did he mean me? No. He was banging on the bathroom door. "No drugs! No drugs!" he shouted, fumbling with his keys.

With that, the two gypsy girls sauntered out of the bathroom. "Chill, dude," one of them said as she breezed by. I pulled out my phone and took a picture. It was a start, some evidence to get the cops to act. I paid for my mac and cheese, told Ajit I would talk to Chief Karkanian tomorrow, but as I walked to my car, I saw the two gypsy girls sitting on my hood. "Nice ride," the blond one said. "We need a lift home," she added. "We want to go in this car." She stroked the hood. "Sweet."

"Sorry, ladies. I'm not headed your way." I opened the car door, and the dark-haired girl jumped down. The blonde didn't move. I started the engine. She didn't budge, just pulled out her cell phone. I got out and yelled at the dark-haired girl, "Tell your friend to get off the hood." I could see Ajit in the doorway. "Call the cops, Ajit." I walked to the front of my car. "Get off before the cops come. Maybe you don't know it, but I'm the local district attorney, and I can make you pretty miserable."

She slid off the car. "I know who you are. The *rom baro* wants to talk to you. The big man. Here." She shoved her phone toward me. "Talk to him."

I laughed and turned back to the driver's side of the car, but she followed. "The *rom baro* is a friend of Señor Garza. You know? From Mexico. Señor Garza talked to the *rom baro*. He says he needs to tell you something important."

"There." The blond gypsy girl pointed at a '70s-era motor home stationed in the clearing where the gypsies were squatting. A beaten-up Buick had been parked next to it, and a ginger-colored cat lay sleeping underneath, switching its tail to keep away the flies. "He's waiting for you, the *rom baro*. He doesn't like to wait." She opened the door, and the dark-haired girl followed her, running off, catching up with her friend, laughing. She lost one of her flips-flops, turned, retrieved it, and then headed in the direction of the dying almond trees where the other girl had vanished.

I got out of the car, walked around, and noted extension cords running in between trailers, the thrum of the air conditioners they were powering droning in the oppressive heat. This place was a total powder keg. And yes, Del Rio zoning department, there were ordinances that covered fire hazards. I would check on that tomorrow.

"You." The *rom baro* called out from his trailer door, waving his arm like he was pulling me toward him. "Come. Now."

He looked to be between fifty and sixty, a large man, ample but not fat, sunburned, bald on top, the rest of his gray hair close-cropped, his thick brown mustache trimmed. Dressed in a blue short-sleeved shirt, jeans, and work boots, he could have been anybody you might see at Home Depot. If I'd expected an exotic gypsy king, this *rom baro* did not meet my expectations. Only his upright bearing, gruff voice, and barked commands gave him an air of royalty. "What are you waiting for?" He disappeared into his trailer, returning a moment later with a can, which he threw at the cat. "*Bibaxt*," he snorted. "Bad luck. You come now."

Had the girls not mentioned Señor Garza, I wouldn't have been here, but they had. There was no getting away from this. If I hadn't responded to his summons to the gypsy camp, he would have located me someplace else. So I now found myself on the wrong side of the law, connected to a drug lord, and, let's face it, one with deep roots in the valley and most likely in LA as well, considering the way the cartel divided up their plazas. I swallowed hard, desperate for some water, walked up the rickety steps, and entered the motor home. "You know those extension cords running all over the place are a fire hazard," I announced to deaf ears.

The *rom baro* was seated at a yellow Formica built-in table, in front of a computer. He shrugged and continued tapping away at the keyboard. "We have ways to protect ourselves."

"You mean like magic, voodoo, whatever? Tell it to Code Violation," I bluffed, glancing around at the decor, a mix of avocado and yellow plaid carpet, egg-yolk Formica, fake knotty pine, and religious iconography. While I didn't see any crystal balls, a particular velvet cross hanging on the wall jumped out, identical to the one Eva had given me that awful day in the jungle when the planeload of children had landed.

"I know you have the same cross. Eva gave to you. She told me. You will be protected. No worries. Just like no worries about the cords. The laws of magic are strong—something you, like the rest of the *gadje*, the nontravelers, wouldn't understand."

"You know Eva?" I should have been surprised, but this was all so weird, I was beyond that.

The *rom baro* kept typing. "Yes, I know her. She is a traveler, like us."

"I thought she was Mayor Parra's daughter."

"She was, but she ran away. We found her on the streets of LA; we cleaned her up, got her off the drugs. She is now a wise woman, what we call a *phuri dae*. Here, you sit." He slid his bulk from behind the table and pushed me toward his seat. "You know Skype? You Skype with Mr. Garza. Is time now." He walked over to the window air conditioner and flipped the switch to off. "Is easier to hear."

Within minutes, the heat bore down on the metal roof and pushed against the sides of the motor home. I was dizzy from claustrophobia, and that was made only worse when Garza's face appeared on the screen in front of me. "How are you, my dear Ms. McCall?" he asked. Even in my near swoon from heat and fear, and in spite of the blurry picture, I could have recognized Garza from his voice alone, as courtly as ever. What was he going to ask me to do? What corrupt thing would I not be able to reject?

"Fine, I guess. Surprised. Confused."

"Ah, yes. Let me explain. The *rom baro* is an associate of mine. We have certain business interests in common. I needed to know you were in a safe place so we could speak openly. I hope you were not too disturbed by your last day in Mexico. That must have been trying, to say the least. May your brother-in-law rest in peace."

The *rom baro* walked to the refrigerator, and the trailer rocked sideways. I held on to the grubby upholstered seat as he took out a can of beer and popped the top. "I hope" was all I could manage to say about Fletcher. Of course Garza knew about him—he seemed to know everything.

"Well, he had become a liability, a danger to my business," Garza continued. "His activities were disturbing to my dear friend Mr. Chiu, who wanted no problems with his oil transportation business. One does what one must."

"And you?"

He raised his hand, as if to say, *Stop, don't pry*, and I gripped the greasy table, trying to breathe.

"I am a businessman, Ms. McCall. People in the United States have insatiable appetites for many things, which I am more than willing to provide for a profit." His words were not in sync with his face, the motion of his mouth. It was all the more disorienting, as if there were two Garzas: the one who spoke, and the one who eyeballed me as if he could see right into my soul. "I have no need to elaborate on those things. But there is one thing I will not supply, and that is Mexican children for perverse uses. Do you understand me? I'm afraid your brother-in-law did not."

"What about American Transport Solutions? What about them?"

"On occasion, Mr. Chiu has been willing to help desperate families both in China and in the States. He feels that many times it is in the best interest of the children who come from impoverished families, and, of course, financially it is also in his interest."

And it had been in Mike and Fran's interest, as well as Mei-Lin's, their beautiful little jewel, I thought, feeling a stab of grief and loneliness.

"From what I have seen of the Chinese countryside," Garza

continued, "the mines and the fields, frankly, I'm inclined to agree. At any rate, we are in business together, so I'm in no position to disagree. I may have confused you and the delightful Guillermo with my complaints about the oil on the beach. It was *un pretexto*, a cover-up, as you say in English. I wanted to keep an eye on you both." He lifted an index finger, tugged on his lower eyelid, and then winked. "I am certain that you have already started to figure much of this out. Am I correct?"

I looked away from the screen and stared out the sand-pitted windows to the almond trees, feeling as though I had left my body somewhere back in Mary Yee's office, where I had been in control, reassuring, where I had promised to do the right thing and protect everyone from toxic pesticide drift. Where was that Callie now?

"I can see that you are afraid of me." Garza's voice brought me back to the present, to the overheated motor home, the smell of beer, my present dilemma. "That is probably wise. I can be a good friend— just ask the *rom baro*—but I can also be a formidable foe. Remember when I said I was going to ask you to do me a favor?"

Did I remember? How could I forget that garage parking lot in Mexico, the smell of exhaust surrounding Garza's tricked-out SUV, the sound of scotch and ice cubes sloshing in the crystal glass he'd swirled in his hand? How could I forget everything that came afterward? *You help me, I help you. That's the way it works.* Nodding my head, I answered, "I remember."

"Well, that time has come. A loyal employee, a Mr. Nigel Wilson, notified Mr. Chiu that he had been approached by someone we think you know to help arrange the shipment of more children through ATS. Of course, this person was told in the strongest possible way that he had crossed a line—absolutely not going to happen. Mr. Chiu and I had agreed to put a stop to trafficking in people. All in all, too unsavory. This requestor, to use a wonderful word from Victorian novels, misjudged Chiu's intentions, which have for the most part been altruistic. I have reason to believe that this person and another disgruntled employee of mine have turned to my competitors, who were only too willing to oblige. We will have to deal with these people."

I could feel my face covered with sweat and wondered if it was obvious on the screen. I took a deep breath, imagining the kinds of methods Garza might use to "deal with these people."

"Unfortunately, Mr. Wilson passed away very recently, so we were not able to gather more information from him. Heart attack, they say—the usual reason they give under these circumstances. I fear foul play, which only confirms my suspicions about my competitors' being involved."

"Heart attacks do happen." I was grasping at straws.

"Or can be made to look as if they have happened. At any rate, I am certain you know this person, as the name is . . ." Garza flipped through some papers. "Yes, here it is. A Mr. Sam McCall, your former husband. Most unfortunate."

I stared at Garza's face on the screen. Sam McCall. That name, the one I had stupidly taken. I leaned back against the vinyl seat, the sweat on my back sticky and gross. A slap of revulsion made my skin burn. I couldn't believe I had been so desperate not to be left on the shelf that I had grabbed the offer he'd made me. He'd said we'd make a good team, and I'd settled. And now this was the team to which I was so intimately connected. The room started spinning, and I felt like I was going to be sick.

"Please, move closer to the computer, Mrs. McCall. I need to see that you are there."

"This is all a lot to take in, Mr. Garza." I repositioned myself and hoped that would quell the nausea. "I'm not sure what you want me to do."

Garza stared at me for a long while, too long. "I'm sure you'll do what you can to convince your ex-husband of the error of his ways," he said finally. "It would be most helpful. Otherwise, I would have to round up the usual suspects, as Claude Rains said in that wonderful film *Casablanca*. Such a roundup would unfortunately have to include your brother. I think it's best we try to keep him out of this. Wouldn't you agree?"

I searched for something to say that would stop his train of thought, but the words wouldn't come. He repeated the question, and I nodded, almost whispering the words, "Yes, of course. I'll help." And then I recognized what was bothering me. "Excuse me. You seem to know so much. Why don't you use your resources in Mexico to solve this problem? Why me?"

"*Bueno.* Good question. At times I am in need of, shall we say, legitimacy from US law enforcement. Now is one of those times. You can try to convince him to stop the trafficking of children, and, if not, you go to the appropriate authorities, which I cannot do. That makes sense, correct? I know I can count on you. The shipment of children will arrive in San Francisco two weeks from today." He flipped through more papers. "They will arrive on Sansome Street in a large rental truck. Find out who meets that truck, please. It will give me a clue, if nothing else."

I moved away from the screen, still feeling faint, but I heard Garza call out, "*Momento.* One other thing. My former employee will be there, armed and dangerous, as the police say. His name is William Delano. Goes by the name Bud. Very stupid and very violent and, as it turns out, very greedy."

I wanted to get up and run. I was shaking, my legs bouncing up and down, my hands trembling. Adrenaline could do that. It could kill me, too, even before Bud Delano got to me.

"I have some more information to give you, helpful information." Garza's voice pulled me back, kept me from bolting out the door. "You asked about a bracelet, a Huichol bracelet. Well, I, too, have done some investigation. There was a boy at the orphanage who used to sell them on the street. Eva mentioned this place to you, I believe."

I vaguely remembered something about talking to the Mother Superior, but that idea had become unnecessary with Fletcher's death. There would have been no more I could do, or so I'd thought. "One day he didn't return. It happens. Sometimes they just go back to their villages, sometimes not. However, in this case, the Mother Superior at the orphanage has serious concerns. He was diagnosed with tuberculosis and was on medication. She assumes he is no longer getting that medication, which worries her."

I waited.

"His name was José Guzmán. I hope this is of some help to you. Remember, you help me, I help you. *Hasta la proxima*," he said, and the screen went blank.

I moved off the seat and pushed myself up, gripping the side of the table. "Can you turn on the air, please?" I asked. The trailer rocked again as the gypsy king moved toward the window and pushed a button. It wasn't exactly cool, but at least the air started circulating. "Thanks."

The *rom baro* stared at me and then said, "It's your destiny. One can never hide from one's destiny. Now you will see if you have *bahkalo*—good luck, good destiny—or not. We are all tested by destiny. None of us escapes."

"Okay, well, here's your destiny." I tried a little bravado, as I was all out of other ideas. "Keep the girls away from the Valero station. Otherwise, I most certainly will call code violation on this whole camp." I could tell by his smile that he didn't believe me, but I'd scored some points for bravery. I nodded and said, "I can let myself out."

I sat behind the wheel of my car in the now dark grove, shaking too hard to drive away. I thought of that cross Eva had given me for protection. Well, I was going to need all the gypsy magic I could get to save myself from being caught up in Garza's web, to protect Mike, and to free myself at last from Sam McCall. I pushed the ignition, and the car started up. *Gypsy magic better be powerful stuff* was all I could think.

15

NATHAN

Nathan had thought that on a Monday morning, the Berkeley Trader Joe's would be empty, but he couldn't have been more wrong. The store was full of young women dressed in stylish yoga clothes, replenishing the family larders after the weekend, lugging children down the aisles, trying to keep babies from dropping pacifiers on the floor or diving headfirst from the shopping-cart seat. Next time, he reminded himself, he would shop on Friday night with all the other loser bachelors in town.

All he wanted was a few frozen meals, bag salad, fruit, coffee, and some of those roasted pumpkin seeds that he liked, which were what he was attempting to obtain right now. Unfortunately, he found himself behind a woman who was patiently explaining nutrition labels of various snack foods to her thumb-sucking, blanket-clinging offspring. While he hated to interrupt this teachable moment, he had a hot date in the next aisle with a bag of fair-trade coffee that he needed to get to, and this lecture was holding him up from that exciting event. "Excuse me," he said to the woman, reaching over her head for a bag of pumpkin seeds.

"You know those are salted," she informed him.

Nathan pointed to the bag. "Roasted and salted," he agreed.

The woman shook her head, as if to ask how could someone be so cavalier about high sodium amounts. Nathan figured this kind of encounter was just the price of living in Berkeley, the land of the gluten free and the home of the brave sodium police. "Low blood pressure," he found himself assuring a perfect stranger. She beamed, and Nathan attempted what he hoped was a smile. "Thank you for your concern." She told him it was important to care for one another, and Nathan nodded. "I couldn't agree more." Karen would have been proud. Except he didn't have low blood pressure. Frankly, he had no idea what his blood pressure was these days, and for some reason that made him think of that doctor he'd met, Mary Yee. She'd probably be on him to get a checkup. He'd been thinking about her a lot, wanting to see her again, hear her laugh, be around her effervescence. In fact, he was thinking about her now, trying to get the nerve up to call her while he pushed his cart toward the coffee beans.

"Nathan." He heard someone call his name and turned around.

"Nathan, Nathan. Oh my God." It was his neighbor, the doctor's wife, Rebecca, or Bex, as he'd heard her called. She opened a box of animal crackers and handed it to her toddler perched in the kiddie seat. "I've been calling and calling. Don't you check your phone?"

"Oh, sorry," Nathan said, but he really wasn't. He kept his phone off most of the time these days. That way, when there were no calls, he could assume people had tried to get in touch with him but had decided not to leave a message. He felt less lonely that way. He pulled his phone out of his pocket and made a show of turning it on.

"Wow. Okay, so, I just didn't know what to do, and David"—her husband, Nathan knew—"is in surgery, so I couldn't call him." She stopped to catch her breath.

This had to be about more than a neighborhood block party she was organizing. What was the drama? "Call him about what, Bex?"

She gulped air. "There was this guy snooping around your back door. Then, you're not going to believe this, but it was like he was trying to break in. Well, I got a picture, and I sent it to you. Actually, I sent it to the whole block."

Nathan brought up his Gmail and saw the header: "ATTEMPTED BURGLARY ON OUR BLOCK." "I've been trying to call," Bex repeated.

Nathan waited for the attachment to download while she went on with her story. "So, I go out the back door, and I say, 'Hey, what are you doing?' He was not very happy to see me, I can tell you. He said he was a friend of yours, but he looked kind of tough. I mean, not that you're not tough, but you know what I mean."

"Yes, I do, Bex," Nathan said, staring at the picture on his phone of Bud Delano, a picture that reminded him just how not tough he was in comparison with this hulk in a black jacket.

"Do you know this guy?"

"No," Nathan lied. It was too complicated a story, and Bud was too dangerous to try to explain. Besides, it was just Nathan he wanted. Bex and her brood were safe.

"Phew, 'cause I called the cops."

Nathan shoved his phone back into his pocket. "Good job, Bex. Thanks so much."

"It gave me a scare. Broad daylight. Good news is, the cops came pretty quickly. They looked around, checked the doors and windows, and had me send the picture to them. So, there's a police report. Do you want to sleep over at our place tonight? Just in case. I can order pizza."

At the mention of his favorite food, the kid started pounding the cart's handlebar, yelling, "Pizza, pizza, pizza!"

"Oh, no—I've done it now," Bex said. "So, what do you say? We can stream a movie."

Nathan could hear himself mumble all the right words. "Thanks so much. Can't. Going down south to visit a friend." Bex looked into his cart. "Bringing a few treats," he explained. "They don't have a TJ's where they live."

"Well, let us know when you get back." She pushed her cart down the aisle. "And answer your phone."

"I will," Nathan called after her. He waited until she had rounded the corner before he abandoned his cart and headed for his car. He pulled out of the parking lot and onto a side street, just in case Bex should find him sitting in his car, staring into space. All he wanted was to talk to someone who would understand. He called his dad to ask where that property in Del Rio was and told him the same lie, that he was going to visit friends down there, and said he'd check it out since it was on the way. He could hardly call Mary Yee a friend, as much as he might want to. Still, she knew about Jim Fletcher, so she might help him contact the police in her district, help him get to the bottom of this. He started his car and headed toward the 580 freeway.

At a bleak Subway sandwich shop in Chowchilla, he googled Dr. Mary Yee, office in Del Rio. There was no home number or address, just her office, on Dinuba Street. Del Rio was as close to the end of the earth as he could imagine, so Dinuba Street must be one stop before that. And then what? He had no idea, but it would be the last place Bud Delano would think to look for him, and Mary was the only person he could think to confide in. In his mind, she represented some kind of solace, the way she'd taken pity on him, handing him a tissue that day at the China-California event. She hadn't turned away from his sorrow. She knew it herself.

He'd been right about Dinuba Street, a wide, bright, treeless road that ran next to what seemed to be an abandoned rail line. Last stop before the end of the world. On one side, there was a huge feed-and-hay warehouse that appeared closed, a Mexican grocery store, and a Family Dollar store with a few cars parked in front. He slowed, looking for Mary's office, as he drove past a VFW hall with an American flag out front, drooping in the heat, and there it was—a gray clapboard, single-story building with a chalk-blue trim, a sign in front that read DR. MARY YEE. He pulled into the dirt parking lot behind, headed past a huge gardenia bush, its perfume dizzying, and pushed open the door.

Now what? he wondered as he walked to the reception window, but before he could come up with a good reason for being there, the receptionist asked, "You have an appointment?" She peered around the window, probably looking for a child, and when he didn't answer right away, she tried her question in Spanish. *"Tiene usted una cita?"*

"I'd like to see Dr. Mary Yee, please. Nathan Bernstein. A friend. Tell her it's urgent."

The receptionist raised her eyebrows and started to ask a question but hesitated. Instead, she pushed herself away from the desk and disappeared behind a door. A child started whimpering in the waiting area, and Nathan was afraid that if he turned around he would see the alarmed faces of the kid's parents, wondering what the problem was, if they should leave. He almost wondered the same thing himself. Maybe he should just bolt. Mercifully, another door opened and a nurse said, "Please, this way."

She led him into an examining room, and after she'd gone, he sat on a small chair under a window and took in his surroundings. There was a paper-covered examining table, above which a blood pressure cuff hung. There was a sink, a bottle of Phisohex on the rim, a large measuring stick on the wall, a rolling stool. It was pretty bare-bones, he thought, remembering his own Berkeley doctor's office with its upholstered chairs and piles of *National Geographics*.

His heart hammered in his chest. If he'd wanted to appear suave and debonair, promising dating material, he was failing. He attempted to think of some jaunty comment to save the day, was floundering around in his mind, coming up with stupid stuff like *Surprise!*, when the door opened and there she was, wearing a kitty cat–printed lab coat and a hair band with sparkling balls bobbling around. "Makes me look less scary." She laughed as she pulled off the headband.

That laugh. It was as delightful as he remembered, and he felt instant relief.

"You don't look so good, Nathan. What's this about?" Mary scooted herself on the rolling stool toward him, reached for his wrist, and pressed two cool fingers against it. Next, she pulled out a stethoscope, placed it on his chest, and told him, "Breathe in, and now out." She swiped a digital thermometer close to his forehead, looked at it, and put it back in her lab coat.

"You'll live," she said. She stood up, went to the sink, and washed her hands.

"Mary, I met Jim Fletcher. I was supposed to go bird-watching with him in Mexico, but then they—I don't know who killed him, but I'm guessing it was the cartel—dropped his body from a helicopter with two other people. He didn't die of a heart attack."

She turned around and leaned back on the sink, saying nothing, her face impassive.

Nathan babbled as much of the story as he could. After a while, he stopped, as if he'd run out of steam. Did she think he was crazy? He couldn't read her. "Someone connected with the killers tried to break into my house today."

Mary looked at him for a while, as if taking all this in. "You came here because you think I can help?"

"Yes, I thought you could help. You knew about him. That was a start." He didn't say he desperately needed a friend, a confidant, someone to unburden himself to, and that he'd chosen her, which was as much the truth as anything else.

"Okay. Here's what I want you to do." She took his hand and pulled him up. "Lie down on the table. We'll talk later." She cut the light as she left the room but was back in a minute with a blanket and a small pillow. "Sometimes I try to nap. That's what you should do until I close up here. Then we'll talk."

There was a knock on the door. Mary answered and took a small white cup the nurse gave her. "Here." She handed it to Nathan, walked to the sink, pulled a paper cup from the dispenser, and filled it with water.

"What's this?" Nathan took the cup with one pill in it.

"Viagra. Kidding, Nathan, I'm kidding. It's Xanax. You're having a panic attack." She gave him the water.

"Mary, I'm telling you the God's truth. Whoever killed Fletcher is coming after me. The cartel, for God's sake. I swear to you."

"You're having a panic attack, Nathan. Your heart rate is extremely elevated. You have no fever, no arrhythmia, so it's not an infection making you delirious or A-fib cutting off oxygen to your brain. Take the pill. Doctor's orders." She gently pushed him down on the examining table, covered him with the blanket, and propped his head up with the pillow. "You'll be thinking more clearly after you calm down and rest."

A few hours later, Nathan found himself rocking back and forth on a glider in Mary's vegetable garden, breathing in the sharp green smell of tomato vines and holding a basket of just-picked zucchini in his lap. He was exactly where he wanted to be, watching Mary, dressed in short cutoffs and a tank top, picking the garden's abundance for tonight's dinner. A tiny temple chime on an apricot tree behind him clinked in the evening breeze, the perfect soundtrack for his mood, buzzed on anti-anxiety meds.

Every time Mary came close, dropping another squash or eggplant into the basket, he wanted to reach for her hand, pull her to him. It had been a long time since he'd felt this way, consumed by desire's sharp urgency, present even through the haze of Xanax.

All afternoon as he'd lain on the examining table in the darkened room, he'd been vaguely aware of voices and chatter, of Mary opening the door to the room next to him and singing out a greeting—"Hey there, big guy"—to some child, and then the voices had become fewer, softer, until there was nothing. Finally, Mary opened the door and whispered his name. "Nathan, you awake?" He'd mumbled something about being in a dream or some gibberish, the only sounds his mouth managed to form. Mary sat on the stool and rolled toward him so she was at eye level. "You're still loaded, so you're coming home with me. No way am I letting you drive."

And that was how he'd ended up this evening in Mary's vegetable garden, next to a statue of Kuan Yin, who, Mary told him, was the Buddhist goddess of compassion. Clearly, she was a soul sister or devotee or something. The Xanax was scrambling his thoughts.

It was easy in this setting to forget Bud Delano, forget Mexico, just rock back and forth in the warm twilight air, listening to the frogs croaking in a nearby pond, to a pair of doves cooing on the porch rafters. "Nice," he said to Mary when she sat next to him, a white bowl of tomatoes in her lap, a big bunch of fragrant basil on top.

"I don't know if I can ever go back," she said.

"Go back where?"

"To the city. But don't be fooled, Nathan. It might look peaceful here—I try to keep it that way at home—but it's not really. Maybe no place is." She stopped for a minute, lifted the basil to her face, and breathed in the scent. "By the way, I looked up the property your parents want to buy. It's Fletcher Family Farms, all right. I've been hearing rumors from a friend that they were planning on selling. He's a lawyer with the UFW. The workers have been talking."

Nathan stopped rocking.

"And another thing," Mary continued. "There was a murder there recently—that's more than gossip. It's not so unusual around here.

Turf wars, gang revenge, stupid drunken brawls, crimes of passion. Thank God I'm not an ER doc in the valley."

Of course, Nathan thought. Another scamming con artist out there looking to swindle his parents into buying into a bad deal, land his mother would consider to have bad karma. Now that he had some ammo to convince them to back away, he was free to focus on Mary. He wondered if he dared reach for her hand or drape his arm around her shoulder. He hadn't felt this uncertain about what to do since he was fifteen and on his first date with Ruthie Weintraub.

"I used to look at those crosses planted along the roads around here and wonder how anybody could have a car accident on a straightaway with no traffic, until my friend Nick clued me in. They were for guys who'd been murdered, whose bodies had been dumped there."

The lawyer again. His competition had a name: Nick.

"Maybe this Nick guy knows about Bud Delano." Nathan was fishing now. "Maybe I could talk to him." *Get a sense of what I'm up against.*

"Not Nick. He keeps pretty focused on the task at hand, which right now is illegal pesticide spraying. It's how he stays sane."

So now this Nick is sane, as opposed to me, Nathan thought, trying to imagine how he looked to Mary: crazy, driving down here in a panic, needing anti-anxiety drugs. Nathan had no choice but to do battle with Nick, the paragon. "I'm not exactly insane myself, Mary."

He waited, heart in his throat, for some compliment or some assurance, at least, that she didn't see him as a complete reject. But she just rocked back and forth, the glider squeaking underneath them. *Don't look needy,* he told himself. Not that he hadn't already violated that cardinal dating rule a few hours earlier.

Finally, she asked, "How exactly did you think I could help you?" She turned to face him, so close he could see flecks of gold in her dark eyes, a tiny mole on the side of her face, could smell her skin, a whiff of sweat and the Neutrogena soap they used in summer camp. In fact, she was summer and its good memories rolled into one.

"Let's forget all that," he said. "Let's just enjoy the evening. I should never have dragged you into the whole thing. Probably, your friend Nick would be pissed that I had. Not very chivalrous of me." He was hoping she would say something negative about this Nick guy, but she didn't.

After a while, she stood up and said, "Time for me to start cooking. Angel hair pasta with tomatoes and basil and a vegetable antipasto. How does that sound?"

He looked at his watch. It was past midnight. Somewhere down the hall, Mary was sleeping or not sleeping. The fact was, he was not with her. She'd put him in her brother's old room, the one he'd slept in when her parents dropped them off to visit the grandparents in this house that she now lived in. Over dinner she had told him she had to make a decision soon about buying it. She'd said she couldn't imagine leaving her practice, not now, anyway. She'd been pushing her pasta around on her plate. "And just imagine how long I'd have to wait in line at a San Francisco farmers' market for vegetables like these. Consider yourself lucky. I'm going to give you a tart made with my special apricot jam. Are you impressed?" She laughed.

Her laughter pulled him toward her, made him reach out, hold on to her forearm. "Everything about you impresses me, Mary."

"You're on drugs. If this is a seduction, I'll tell you what I want."

"Tell me." He leaned in even closer.

"I want you to help me with the dishes." And with that, she jumped up and handed him a plate. "It's too soon, Nathan. We both have a lot of sad baggage we're carrying around."

He realized, self-centered oaf that he was, he'd never asked her how her husband died.

"Suicide," she answered, when Nathan raised the question. So maybe she wasn't asleep over in her room now. Maybe she was counting all the ways she'd failed her dead husband, as Nathan did with Karen.

Outside, a great horned owl *hoo-hoo*ed—a muffled foghorn sound. He could see how the last thing Mary needed was one more screwed-up guy in her life. He closed his eyes. Mary's first patients started coming at eight in the morning, she had told him before they'd gone to bed. She had some paperwork to do and would like to leave the house by seven fifteen. The owl called again, supposedly a harbinger of death or a symbol of wisdom. For Nathan and Mary, the two things seemed to have arrived together.

The coffee was ready when Nathan came in carrying his sheets the next morning, asking where the washer was.

"Thanks," Mary said, nodding at the bedding, and pointed to a door by the refrigerator. After he'd dropped them in the machine and returned to the kitchen, she poured him a cup and pointed to the milk and sugar. "Black is fine," he said. He wanted to come up with something to say or do, something to make her want to see him again. He thought about agreeing to talk at the Doctors Without Borders event that she'd asked him to participate in, but it felt disloyal to bring up Karen as a lure for another woman, unfaithful to both of them. So he mentioned the owl he'd heard and was relieved when she said she loved that sound. "It's one of the pleasures of the country."

"As opposed to car alarms and the homeless raving outside your window at two in the morning?"

She laughed again. Good—he'd heard women liked a sense of humor, a guy who made them laugh.

"We should go, Nathan," she said. He downed his coffee and said he was ready, all the while knowing he'd be thinking about her on the way up to the Bay Area. Through the desolate moonscape past Los Banos, past all the signs with Pelosi's name in a circle with a bright red slash across it, he'd be scheming about some excuse to get back.

On the way out the door, she stopped and took his hand. "I'm no savior. I'm not a simple woman, not some China doll. That's what white guys always think."

"I've lived long enough, Mary, to know that 'simple' and 'woman' are two words that do not belong together in any sentence in any language in any country." He was hoping she'd laugh again, but his humor had failed.

She looked deadly serious, let go of his hand. "There is one thing I can do for you, though. I can give you some advice. Here it is: Do not go to the Del Rio police."

She repeated that warning as they sat in the parking lot, her car motor humming to keep the air conditioner on. "The police are not always good guys," she reminded him. "And in small towns that are practically owned by people like the Fletchers, the fastest way to get information to them is to go to the cops."

A car pulled in next to Mary's, one of the early patients. His heart sank; he would have to go soon. He wanted to ask her out. Maybe he could show her his family's vineyard or whatever, or get tickets to the theater, anything to impress her. But that wouldn't do it. He knew in his heart of hearts that if he wanted to impress Mary Yee, he was going to have to be a better person, braver, less self-absorbed. That would have to be his task.

"Oh, good," she said, looking out the passenger window. "I texted Nick last night."

Texting Nick at night was not what Nathan considered good.

"He said he had an idea about how to help." She pushed a button and rolled down the passenger window. "Fantastic. You're here," she said, just as the person got out of the car. "Did Nick tell you what this was about?"

Nathan turned in time to see the woman nod her head, hear her say, "He told me enough to get me here, said you'd fill me in." The woman seemed so familiar. He was certain he'd seen her before, and then it hit him. "Oh my God, Mary." He turned to face her. "I know that woman. She was with me in Mexico when Fletcher died. She'll tell you I'm not crazy!" He pushed open the car and said to the woman, "We've met. Remember? This is unbelievable."

16

CALLIE

What had the gypsy king, the *rom baro*, told me, the other night? *You can't escape your destiny.* So, to tell the truth, I was not all that surprised when that guy from Mexico got out of the car, shouting, "I remember you. You were there in Mexico." Shocked, maybe, which is different, which is close to panic. I looked past him over the top of Mary's car, where she stood gawking, first at Nathan, then at me, and I motioned to her to walk around. The last thing I wanted was for our conversation to be overheard. Whatever I could keep private, I would. I had to think fast.

"Remember that guy Bud Delano?" the man from Mary Yee's car bellowed. "Well, he's in San Francisco with Jim Fletcher's wife. The guy who died."

"Wait, wait. Remind me what your name is again? Nathan, right?" Although I knew, remembered it as well as my own, as Jim Fletcher's, as Bud Delano's, I was stalling.

"Yes, Nathan. Nathan Bernstein." He started pacing up and down beside the car.

"Okay, Nathan. First, I'm going to need you to calm down, and second, we need to keep our voices down. We shouldn't even be having this conversation outside." I pointed to the VFW hall, and while it looked closed, the walls had ears, and this was just the kind of juicy tidbit the old-timers would blow up into a nuclear bomb. "Mary, I'm going to have to interview Nathan someplace private."

"What do you mean, interview?" Nathan resumed pacing.

"I'm Callie McCall, district attorney of Del Rio County. I have to interview you. 'Ask questions' is a more informal way of putting it."

"I thought you said you were a citrus farmer."

"And citrus farmer. Or my family was, and I'm trying to keep it going."

He looked at Mary, and she nodded her verification.

"Mary, can Nathan stay at your house until we're both off work and we—I—can figure out what to do next? Nathan, this is something of a shock, and I'm due in court in an hour."

"There's a key under a blue pot in the greenhouse. I'll be home at five."

"You know where the house is?" Nathan asked me.

"It's Del Rio. Everyone knows everything. And I don't want them to know about you. Not yet."

I managed to get out of the office a little early and swung by the pizza place where I'd phoned in an order. Then I drove over to Ajit's for some mini-mart wine, happy to see that the gypsy girls were not there. I arrived at Mary's, bearing these offerings, when Nathan opened the door. "I can't believe this is happening. It's completely surreal," he said, taking the pizza boxes. I put the wine on the counter and the salad in the refrigerator, walked to the sink, and washed my hands. "After a day in court, I need a shower," I said. "But this will have to do."

I grabbed a legal pad and a pen out of my bag and asked Nathan where he'd like to sit. He walked into the living room and sank into the sofa. "Here's the deal," I said. "It's pretty simple. I'm going to ask you questions, and you're going to answer."

"Do I need a lawyer?"

"Depends on what you have to tell me."

"Look, I'm not the bad guy here, Miss . . . Mrs. . . . whatever your name is."

"It's Callie. I know you're not the bad guy, so who do you think is?" I lifted my pen.

Nathan closed his eyes. "Bud Delano, for sure. My neighbor caught him snooping around my house like he was trying to break in."

"And why do you think he would want to break into your house?"

"Because I saw him with Mrs. Fletcher, the dead guy's widow, at an event in San Francisco."

"No crime there."

I was leaving a lot out, I realized, wondering how long I would get away with it, and decided not very long. "Full disclosure here: Mrs. Fletcher is my sister. The dead guy, as you called him, was my brother-in-law."

"You're kidding, right?"

I kept my poker face.

"Oh my God, you're serious. You sure didn't tell me that in Mexico, did you? Wow! That was some act."

I nodded, and when it was clear that was all I was going to do, he shook his head and continued, "Well, I told her, your sister, that her husband didn't die of a heart attack. She didn't believe me, or acted like she didn't believe me. Had you told her? Then I saw her get into a car with Delano. Congo Bud—remember that name?"

I said I hadn't told my sister. "But then, we weren't close. What can I say?"

"Did you know she's hanging around with that thug? Is this old news to you?"

I shook my head. "No, I didn't." Bud knew Jim Fletcher, and from now on, Mia was going to be a sitting duck for the vultures that circled around wealthy widows.

There was a knock at the door; then the doorbell rang twice. Nathan got up, peered through the glass, and opened it quickly. "You guys locked it," Mary said.

"The circumstances seemed to call for it," Nathan told her.

"I brought wine," I announced, anxious for a brief reprieve. I'd been given enough to think about with Bud Delano's arrival and Mia's relationship with him, such as it was. It was possible he was just some limo driver to her, for all I knew, and it was no big deal. "I figured we needed to relax. Red and white. The best Ajit's mini-mart could provide."

"Probably not up to your standards, Nathan," Mary said, "but I'm popping the cork. God, I hate these antivaxxers. It's been one of those days."

"I'll wait until we get through my questions. Probably a good idea for you, too." I nodded at Nathan and looked over my notes.

He'd been hired by Birds of Paradise to lead a corporate bird-watching tour at an exclusive resort in Mexico. Ventana Azul, of course.

"Where are Birds of Paradise's offices?"

Nathan said he didn't know and grabbed his phone to look it up. He pulled up his browser, set his phone down, and continued with his story, said he'd decided to stay in San Benito for a couple of days before the tour, had some personal issues to deal with. His wife had just died. Well, last year, he said. That's why he took the job: to get away. He shook his head. "I got away, all right." The resort sent Bud to pick him up, he continued. "I just thought he was a creep, a jerk. But if he's still alive after . . ." He waved his hand as if to erase Bud. "Then maybe he's the killer. Could be, right?"

"Could be, or not." I shrugged.

"Then the tour was postponed, and then it got canceled. Concha and Marco, the owners of the resort, were like something out of *La Dolce Vita*." He rushed on with his story, as if relieved to get it out. "It was like they were on meth and ecstasy combined." He stopped for a minute, maybe because we both knew where this was going. "And then someone killed them, along with Jim Fletcher, and dropped them from helicopters on the beach."

Mary sat down on the sofa next to Nathan and patted his knee. He gave her a look of such gratitude, I wondered what he would say or do if I weren't there. I might as well help him out. "Mary, what Nathan is telling you is true." They kept staring at me, waiting for more.

"You didn't tell your sister, right?" Nathan asked. "Seems weird."

"It seemed kinder." I told him, deleting the part about how we were pretty much sworn enemies by now. "Nothing I said was going to bring him back, so what was the point?"

"Are you going to do something?"

"What can I do?"

I don't know," Nathan answered. "Prosecute, investigate. You tell me."

"I could use that wine," I said, walking into the kitchen. "Where are the glasses, Mary?" I called out. No one answered. I peered back into the living room just in time to see Mary take Nathan's hand. I waited a few beats, began opening cabinets. "It's wine o'clock. Help me out."

We took our glasses out to the porch and sat under the breeze of the overhead fan.

"To answer your question of am I going to do something, there's nothing I *can* do. Here's why: None of this happened in my district. If you want to pursue it, Nathan, in Berkeley, you can. But realize all you have is a suspected home invasion. The cops will tell you to get an alarm, get a dog, get a gun. Jim Fletcher's murder happened in Mexico. Official-looking papers were signed and stamped, according to my brother, who saw them. Jim Fletcher died of a heart attack, and that's that. Sorry."

"I can't believe this," Nathan said. "These people are murderers."

He tapped on his phone. "I was just looking up the Birds of Paradise offices." He scrolled for a while, waited and then said, "Oh, Jesus. It's on Sansome Street." He showed his phone to Mary. "That office space where we met. Remember?" He turned to me. "Your sister has something to do with it. There are beds and baby cribs in it, like they house children there, like it's some smuggling ring." He pushed his phone across the table to me. "Some kid did that drawing." He pointed to an image on the screen.

I looked long and hard. Sansome Street, Garza had said when we Skyped. Sure enough, the bracelet was almost identical to the one on the cadaver arm. "Can you send this to me, Nathan?"

Mary asked to see it.

"*Yo soy José Guzmán*," she said, reading the name on the drawing. "That was the name of the kid I diagnosed with TB, the one who never came back."

"Are you certain?" I asked. So, Garza had been giving me correct information. Guzmán, from the orphanage.

"Yes. I just looked up the chart again before I came home."

"How did he get to your office? Who brought him?"

"He came alone, he told me. Said a nice lady brought him, but I never saw her. I remember he gave me a fifty-dollar bill that she had given him to pay, and this . . ." Mary walked to her purse and pulled out a velvet-covered cross. "For his 'protection,' he told me. But then he forgot it." She sighed. "Too bad."

Eva. That was who had brought him. "Mary, can you put that in a plastic bag? I don't want my fingerprints on it. I'll take it to the lab, see if we get a match with the body part we have. This might be a start."

"Wow," Nathan said. "Jesus."

I stood up, said I had to go. I wanted to get an early start on this in the morning. "Stick around, Nathan, can you?"

"Of course he can," Mary said. "I'm going to keep him here, where he'll be safe."

—

I got home around eight, fed Vato, let him out, and sat on the back stairs, throwing the ball and mulling over my next steps. Vato seemed to sense my mood; maybe my throws were only halfhearted. He flopped down next to me, panting, as if his close proximity were the comfort I needed. In a certain way, it was, but I knew I needed a few other things. I got up and opened the door, and Vato followed.

I went straight to the gun safe, twisted the knob this way and that, and pulled out my father's handgun, the one he used to keep in a drawer by the bed, saying that was his idea of calling 911. Really, Mike and Mia and I were lucky we survived our childhood. We all had guns; shooting was considered fun. I pressed the button on the side and ejected the magazine, went to my father's desk, got the bullets, loaded the chamber, and pushed it back in until I heard the click. I disengaged the safety and pulled the slide back to chamber a round. If Bud was snooping around Nathan's, he might pay me a visit. I'd be ready.

I made a quick call to Alberto and Rosie, relieved when Berto picked up. I didn't want to get Rosie worried. "Who's on duty tonight, B-Rod? Anyone you know?"

"How come?"

"I have a stalker, or might have. Long story. Just wanted to know if you'd have the guys on duty go by the house a couple of times tonight and tomorrow night."

"Callie, I don't like the sound of this."

"I have my dad's old pistol by the bed. Plus, there's Vato."

"Your dog is no killer, girl. Unless slobber kills, I guess. You want me to sleep over?"

"How would you explain that to Rosie?"

"She'd be glad not to hear me snore."

"I don't think so. She loves you a lot."

"I know. I'm just not the mushy type."

"Maybe you ought to learn to be."

"I probably should. You call me if you need me."

I sat in my dad's old desk chair, staring out the window, listening for the crunch of gravel, tires, footsteps, but I heard nothing, just the creaky chair and a ringing in my ears, under which Nathan's voice, his story, ran. Birds of Paradise, Mia, Sansome Street.

Destiny. There was no other reasonable explanation for Nathan's appearance, or reappearance, in my life. Right now, my destiny and little José Guzmán's had become entwined as well. I wasn't sure if an arm could be tested for TB, but if it could, and it was positive, I had an answer for Garza. I might also get some traction from fingerprint matches from the cadaver and the cross. They might be little José's. After that, we would go to that building where Nathan found the drawing, find out who the landlord was. All of this hinged on a TB test on a cadaver. I shouldn't run ahead of myself.

I thought about Mia's reaction to Nathan's news that her husband had been murdered. If you could indict people for unexpected responses, half the population would be in jail. As far as Mia went, there were a lot of reasons why she might have discounted Nathan. First, she was a snob and didn't talk to people she thought were beneath her. One group she definitely thought was beneath her were Jews. She indulged in the kind of country-club anti-Semitism people like Fletcher and his ilk marinated in. I often wondered whether they disliked Francois because he was gay or because he was Jewish. Mia was such a moral lightweight, nothing more than a Ping-Pong ball for Fletcher, and now Sam McCall, to toss around.

Anyway, I had other things to do besides worry about Mia's snobbery. I was anxious to talk to the medical examiner; he was usually at the morgue early. I'd stop by there first thing. Maybe this case would actually get resolved.

Vato's paws clicked on the hardwood floor down the hall as he came into the office. He put his nose in my lap and stared up at me with true love. Thank God for dogs. "Time for bed, Vato," I said. "Let's go."

I lay in bed, wide awake, listening for car tires on the driveway, the rattle of a window, the creak of a door. Vato had finally stopped grooming himself, and his body sagged reassuringly against mine. Soon he began twitching, chasing something in his dream. The next thing I knew, I was opening my eyes to light coming in from the window.

It was morning. I'd been safe all night.

17

CALLIE

I caught the medical examiner in the hall and asked about a TB test and fingerprints on the cadaver arm. He read me chapter and verse about how unlikely it was for a TB test to reveal anything unless the disease had gone to the bone.

"Just try, okay? And fingerprints." I handed him the plastic bag with the cross.

He shrugged like I was just one more burden to bear and pushed open his door, shaking his head. Whatever.

Back at my office, I rushed up the stairs, hardly feeling my feet in their designer heels or the marble floor beneath, gave Padhma a hug when she passed me in the hall, told her it was a beautiful day. "Almost fall. We survived another summer." I hadn't been this jazzed in forever. Poor Padhma looked confused, like she wondered if I might have just snorted coke. But I was close to closing in on this case, and it was a kind of high.

Next, I texted Mary and asked how our witness was today. She texted back that she'd put him to work weeding the garden to keep his mind off things. And then the rest of the day went by in a blur. Depositions and jury selection for the murder trial of a Sikh truck driver, which I knew we would get a plea on, so I was fairly relaxed.

In fact, I finished up early, had my Prada heels off, and was downing a Diet Coke when Berto charged through my door. "I don't know what's going on, but your brother is here, completely"—he waved his hands as if to say "out to lunch"—"with a baby and his boyfriend, or whatever he is."

"You're kidding," I said, leaping up and running past him just in time to see Mike getting off the elevator. Mei-Lin was bellowing, the sounds echoing down the marble hallway. Francois and Mike looked like they hadn't slept in days. I had never been more overjoyed in my life.

"It's okay, Berto," I said, letting him know he could go. "A little family drama is all."

As soon as he shut the door, Mike threw himself into my arms. "I'm so sorry," he began babbling, but all I could think of was that we were together again.

"Well, just chalk it up to postpartum depression," I said.

Mike didn't laugh. "Someone tried to kill us, Callie."

I pulled back a bit so I could look him in the eye. "Stop it. This is some kind of joke, right?"

"I wish it were," Francois said, setting the crying baby on my office sofa while he unzipped a carry-all and grabbed a bottle. "He's not, and we were all just lucky."

"What do you mean, someone tried to kill you?" I sat back on the edge of my desk, too shocked and confused to stand. Mei-Lin was screaming, and Mike and Fran, their backs turned to me, were pulling things out of the diaper bag and dropping them on the sofa: pacifiers, rattles, you name it. No one was giving me a coherent answer.

"I think she's been poisoned." Mike lifted the baby from the sofa, turned to face me, and walked Mei-Lin back and forth across my office, bouncing her up and down in an attempt to calm her, which did not work. "We should have gone straight to San Francisco General, but the paramedics reassured us that Mei-Lin was okay, and we were panicked, not really thinking. We wanted to get away, so we came here. We just got in the car and drove."

"Poisoned how? Mike, look at me."

He handed the baby back to Francois, rifled around in the diaper bag again, and pulled up a bottle of milk, which he gave to Francois. "We would have been dead if Francois hadn't gotten an earlier flight."

"Francois? Help me here. No one is making any sense." It was hard to think, much less talk, with the baby screaming. I took Mei-Lin and gave her back to Mike. Then I led Francois into the hall and closed the door behind us. "Start from the beginning," I said.

He told me that he'd gotten back from Hong Kong earlier than expected. As soon as he opened his suitcase, he said, the carbon monoxide detector that he always carried went off. "These hotels all over Asia"—he waved his hands, as if to cover the scope of China—"are, you know, very elegant, but people have died." The detector should have woken Mike, but it didn't. Francois said he practically had to drag Mike outside, and then he ran in for Mei-Lin.

He called the police. By now, it was two in the morning. They came and called the EMTs, who checked out Mike and Mei-Lin. Everything seemed okay, or so they said. The neighbors came out because of all the sirens and flashing lights. "Turned out," Francois continued, "the neighbors had a camera that took pictures of people going between the houses in the alley. They hadn't told us because they knew Mike was a lawyer and they were afraid it wasn't legal." Francois, Mike, and the baby sat in the car for what seemed like hours, with the heater running, and then the cops came out of the neighbor's house and asked Francois if he knew the guy in one of the neighbors' surveillance photos. The man seemed to have broken into the house, might have taken the carbon monoxide detectors and screwed up the furnace flue.

"And did you know him?" I asked Francois.

"Yes, and if you were in Mexico, as you told us, so do you."

I leaned against the wall, closed my eyes. "Bud Delano. Am I right?"

"You are right."

"Let's get Mei-Lin to a doctor."

Mary was at home when I called. She told us to swing by, but it wasn't until Nathan stepped out of the door behind her that I put two and two together. He knew Francois from Mexico, from Ventana Azul, of course. Judging by the look on Nathan's face as he walked toward Francois, blinking like he couldn't believe his eyes, his voice lifting as he called out Francois's name, as if the question he was asking were much larger than it appeared—"What are you doing here?"—I knew everything would come out: Francois's involvement, what Mike knew and didn't know. But we had no time for that right now. "We've got a sick baby here, people. Let's have this reunion later, shall we?"

I charged past Mary, grabbed Nathan by the arm, pulled him into the kitchen, and said, "Bring all this up later, and don't do it without me present. I have to know everything firsthand."

Mary took Mei-Lin and her distraught parents into her bedroom and shut the door. Nathan sat down at the kitchen table and motioned for me to join him. "This is too weird. First, Bud Delano tries to break into my house; then it turns out that you live here; now Francois shows up. It's like there was some master plan."

I shrugged and listened to Mei-Lin scream in the next room. "I guess that's a good sign," I said. "At least there's nothing wrong with her lungs." After a while, I told him what the gypsy king had said: "You can't escape your destiny."

"You mean like a palm reader with a crystal ball?"

"You have a better explanation, Nathan, I'm all ears."

Mary came out of her room, a stethoscope still around her neck. "She seems to be fine. The paramedics were right: nothing wrong with her heart or her respiratory system. It's probably something simple, like a headache. Carbon monoxide can cause that." She asked if I would go to CVS and gave me a list: baby Tylenol, Pampers, baby wipes.

"I'm taking Nathan with me. I just told him nobody discusses Mexico, Bud Delano, or any of it without me in the room. Tell my brother, too."

We were loading my trunk with Pampers and assorted baby stuff in the CVS parking lot when Rosie and Alberto appeared, pushing a cart with two cases of Coors Lite. "Coupons." Alberto rolled his eyes. "Rosie can't pass up a bargain, and I've been drinking this like water all summer." He patted his gut, which really wasn't too bad. "You guys planning on starting a family?" He glanced at the Pampers and reached out his hand to shake Nathan's. "Hi, I'm Berto, an old friend of Callie's." Nathan said he was a new friend. Alberto raised his eyebrows and gave me a grin.

"Mike's here with the baby."

Rosie grabbed my arm, was practically jumping up and down. "When can I see her? Oh my God, I have to tell Lupe. We'll have a party. I'll make a *tres leches* cake, *piñatas*, you name it."

"We got the beer." Alberto nodded at the cart.

"Sure," I told them. Maybe by then, we would have put Bud Delano's attempted murder behind us and I'd be ready to celebrate. Maybe. We could hope.

Mary was in the kitchen, layering vegetables into a lasagna, when we pushed open the back door and unloaded our bags onto the counter. "Dinner in an hour." She took the Tylenol drops, said Mei-Lin had finally knocked herself out crying. "But she may wake up fussy again, so thanks. You should go talk to them." She nodded to the living room.

I pulled out a notepad, sat everyone down, turned to Nathan, and said, "You start. We'll take this one at a time, ending with my side. See what we can piece together." By the time we'd gone around the circle, Mary came into the living room, wiping her hands on a dish towel.

"Guys, I've got an idea," she said, nudging Nathan a little and sitting down on the sofa next to him. "My family has this compound up in the national park, one of those inholdings. Why I don't use it more, I'll never know, but it's perfect—locked gate, everything. You'll be safe there. Mike and Francois can hide out in the mountains until they figure something out. They can stay with me until the weekend, · and we can all go up Friday night. How does that sound?"

You could almost feel the collective relief fill the room, like someone had turned on music or a fan and the sound and air had pushed everyone's fears aside. I explained about Alberto and Rosie, how I'd run into them at the CVS and how they wanted to see the baby. "It's kind of a Mexican thing. New babies, new blessings, always a cause for celebration." And Mary, so welcoming, said, "Invite them. Sure. Ask them to bring the banda music, too, when they come," she said, dancing her way back into the kitchen.

I knew I wouldn't have to ask Rosie twice. She was always ready to party. I picked up the phone. "Hey, Berto," I said, "here's an idea."

18

CALLIE

By Saturday morning, thanks to Mary, we had a safe place to hide, a place to heal our family wounds, figure out what next, at her secluded camp in remote Sequoia National Park, where it would be almost impossible for anyone to find us anytime soon, even Bud Delano, our biggest danger. Mary bought us some time, which we desperately needed. On Monday, I would go back to the gypsy camp and try to get a message to Garza: *You help me, I help you.* I'd ask him to get rid of this scumbag Bud. I didn't feel much remorse, no more than asking someone to off a rabid coyote. You do it because you have to.

Enough of this, I said to myself. This weekend, I would just savor the beautiful place we were staying in, let myself walk on the trails by the river and find a small measure of peace.

I stopped on the trail and closed my eyes, turned my face to the sun, promising to come up to the mountains more often, to learn to take better care of myself, get out in nature more. It would probably make me a better person.

I meandered happily by the river, feeling my soul rest. The water flow was calmer in September now that most of the snow had melted off from the high Sierras, but it still rushed by, spray coming off the larger rocks, cooling my face if I stood close. How wonderful to be surrounded by my family, to have them returned to me; to have Mike asking forgiveness; for all of us to be sharing our sides of the story, the combination a more complete picture of the truth, which, now that it had come into focus, could hopefully recede into the past like some strange memory. I felt like I could breathe again and hadn't realized that I'd had such tightness in my chest, as if a band of pain had been wrapped around me. Well, I'd been released—ironically, by Bud Delano. I inhaled the pine scent of the big ponderosas and the sweet, dry smell of September meadow grass while I sat on a log by the river, staring into the clear, emerald-colored water as it passed over the granite on its way to a small beach several yards west.

Mike and Francois were at that beach, and I could see them from where I sat, Mike dipping Mei-Lin's feet into the water. Good-natured Alberto had happily driven Rosie and the kids up to the mountains for the day to meet the baby and have a cookout. Now, he was keeping a watchful eye from his portable lawn chair while Rosie and the children splashed and shrieked in the river nearby. "Be good for them to get out of the bad air down here in the valley," he'd said, thankful for the invitation. That was Berto. His family always came first. I took a moment to feel grateful, too, something I promised myself to do more of, especially now that I knew how bad things could get, how close I could get to losing everything that really mattered: my brother, my niece, their little family.

"Callie." Francois's voice jolted me. I assumed he had left his spot on the beach and the sound of water had drowned out his footsteps. I never heard him approach. "Can we talk?"

I moved over on the log, gave him room to sit.

"This is all my fault," he said.

"True for all of us. You wanted a baby. I wanted to solve a crime and get Fletcher while I was at it. What did Buddha say? Desire is suffering, right?"

"I did not give you the full story the other day." He took off his glasses and began cleaning them with the end of his T-shirt.

This was not what I wanted to hear. His words devoured my mood, swallowed up the light around me. Had a breeze come up, making the ancient trees creak? Was that noise some kind of cosmic warning? "Francois, why? Jesus. Last thing I need is to not know all the facts."

"I don't know this Nathan guy. I didn't want to say everything in front of him. He stumbled into this mess and can get out easily. Mike and I, not so easily." He finished cleaning his glasses, pushed them back onto the bridge of his nose, and then picked up a rock, aiming it at the river. "I'm thinking of moving back to France with Mike and the baby. We can't stay up here forever, hiding out like in some American Western." He turned to face me.

"No," I blurted. I had just gotten them back. They could not leave me.

"Callie, we're not safe." He ran his hand over the fallen log we were sitting on, picked at the bark. "And if Mia wins her campaign, which of course she will, because no one opposes her, am I right? I do not understand American politics. This, to me, seems absurd. . . ."

"Why Mia? What would she do? I think she just wants you and Mike to disappear, not show up at her bridge club."

"Ah, you underestimate your sister. Everyone thinks it was Mike who blackmailed Fletcher, and I let you think that the other night. But he did not." He paused, scrunched his shoulders up to his neck, and then released them with a sigh. "I did, in a manner of speaking."

"What manner of speaking would that be? I'm not following."

He took a deep breath, wrapped his arms around his knees, buried his head in them, and then sat up and turned to look at me, lifting his glasses, squinting, remembering. "I was in Singapore last year at an annual event for my company, which is invested in many companies in Asia, including American Transport Solutions. It was held at the Raffles Hotel, all very dignified and colonial. They invented the Singapore Sling there—did you know that?"

"Go on, Francois." I circled my hands in the air. He needed to get to the point.

"Late one night, I was working in my hotel room when I got a call. Mr. Chiu from ATS wanted to meet with me, and was I available? It was not the kind of summons one says no to. I was told Mr. Chiu would send his assistant, Nigel Wilson, down to take me to his suite."

I wondered if Francois knew Nigel was dead, but I didn't want to go there now.

"I got up to his room, and a group of men, all Chinese, were assembled there. After some conversation, all in Chinese, they left. Only Nigel Wilson, Mr. Chiu, and I remained. Mr. Chiu exchanged some pleasantries, told me the history of the Raffles Hotel and the origin of the Singapore Sling, before he motioned to Nigel, who handed him an envelope. I can't believe I'm telling you all this without a cigarette. At least in Asia you can smoke. Well, except in Singapore. I had to find one of their designated smoking places outside in the heat and humidity after talking with Chiu."

"Go ahead, smoke." Anything to keep him going.

He pulled out his cigarettes, lit one, and took a deep drag like it was his last breath on Earth. "This is where it got scary. Mr. Chiu explained that he was aware that I was now a family member of Mr. Jim Fletcher and, as such, wanted me to give Mr. Fletcher a warning. He explained that Mr. Fletcher had been very cooperative in the past in getting products through customs."

"I take it you mean bribing corrupt officials for ATS."

Francois nodded and dragged deeply on his cigarette. "However, now he was becoming too much trouble. Mr. Chiu handed me the envelope and explained that Mr. Fletcher abused underage children, that the pictures in the envelope were taken in a casino in Macau when Jim Fletcher was Mr. Chiu's guest. He wanted me to deliver the photos to Fletcher and to warn him that this must stop. At that point, I understood I had no choice."

"So you, not Mike, blackmailed Fletcher with the photos."

"*Pas du tout*, Callie. Just wait. Mr. Chiu then said he was aware that my partner and I had been trying to adopt a child and that he sometimes helped American families adopt Chinese babies from the countryside as a charitable service. He would be glad to assist me. In return, I would agree to keep an eye on Fletcher's activities and report back."

"Spy, you mean, and how the hell did he know you were trying to adopt a baby?"

"If the Chinese government wants to know something about you, they can know it, and Chiu would not be such a big operator if he were not close to the government—very, very close. What I don't understand is how Fletcher could have been so stupid as to not know this as well, and how he allowed himself to get caught in flagrante delicto, shall we say."

"Okay, so, that's China. How did you get to Mexico?"

"Ah, yes. Mr. Chiu told me that Nigel Wilson would take care of all the adoption details and that I would be given instructions on what to do next. I made the mistake of telling all this to Mike after I confronted Fletcher, who, of course, denied everything, said it was Photoshopped. But I had fulfilled my end of the bargain, so what did I care what he said?"

"Then why was it a mistake to tell Mike?"

"He xeroxed the photos."

"So, Mike blackmailed Fletcher."

"No, Mike blackmailed Mia."

This was not sinking in. It was like someone was banging a huge gong by my head and all I could hear were the reverberations, drowning out the meaning of Francois's words. "Why would Mike go to Mia?"

"Maybe he knows her better than you do. Mike said she wasn't surprised at all. She just asked him if two hundred and fifty thousand dollars would suffice to keep the story between the two of them. Mike said three hundred thousand, just because, and now we both get tax-free allotments of thirteen thousand dollars per year each, for something like fifteen years, from some private-school-and-college fund. She had Sam McCall draw up the arrangement, which Mike was so happy about."

Sam McCall, again. He was involved in all this. How long had that been going on? While we were married? Could I have been that blind? Uh, yes. Apparently so. What had Garza said? Someone had contacted his competitors? Could Sam have done that? It was possible. He was that greedy—nothing was ever enough. And vain, thinking he was better and smarter than others. Greed, vanity: a deadly combination. He could be dangerous now—to me, to us.

"I eventually received instructions from Wilson. I was to pretend to be working on purchasing hotels in Mexico. It was there that I would pick up the baby. I lied to Mike and told him I was flying to Hong Kong to retrieve the child and handle paperwork. I didn't want any more cats out of bags. But now, I don't think we are safe here. Someone wants us out of the way." He walked to the river, dunked his cigarette butt into the water, and put it in his pocket. "We should get back, but I wanted you to know. I think it explains things. I think this Delano guy is working for whoever wants us out of the way." He reached out a hand to pull me up, and we began walking on a path through the meadow, back to the beach.

"Who do you think wants you out of the way, as you put it, and why? You think it's Sam, right?"

Of course he did. "Callie, we do not know how these people think. I don't even know how Chiu thinks. Mike and I, maybe Nathan, we know things they don't want anyone to know, and now we are a nuisance, the way a mosquito is a nuisance. One kills it just to avoid being bothered."

I would give this information to Garza. He had his ways of resolving these kinds of problems. It would be bye-bye, Bud, and really, who cared? "I'll talk to Mia," I said, stopping on the path. "Get her off your scent and onto mine."

"Your sister is an arrogant fool, like, I hate to say it, many Americans." Francois stopped, stared at the huge granite mountains, shook his head. "Crowds at rallies yelling, 'We're number one!' It's an absurdity. And Jim and Mia Fletcher embody the worst aspects of that kind of American. Do you have any idea," he asked, "how the rest of the world sees you? Uneducated, decadent, vulgar. The Chinese are cleaning America's clock. Guys like Mr. Chiu believe they are fighting an economic war and are their country's patriotic generals. Fletcher's moral failures would be repulsive to a man like Chiu. But Fletcher thought he had all the power. Now, Mia thinks she does as well. That power has probably gone to her head. Who knows how bad she can get? Anyway, I'm trying to convince Mike to immigrate to France, where Mei-Lin will have a better chance."

He made a convincing argument, but I wasn't going to let that happen. "San Francisco is a beautiful city. You and Mike love it there," I chattered as we walked. "I may know someone who can fix the Bud problem." I was practically begging now. "Besides, we have the photos."

Francois turned and looked at me like I was yet another American know-nothing, shook his head. "Photos of what? Fake news, as your president says, enemies out to destroy a good man. All Photoshopped, they could claim. Those photos only worked because Fletcher was afraid of Chiu. No one is afraid of voters in this country anymore, not Fletcher and not Mia."

What could I say? He would laugh at me if I told him about Garza and the gypsies. I would just have to find a way to get rid of Bud and to keep Sam McCall out of our lives. Garza was the man to do it.

Francois stopped a few yards ahead of me, circled back, and put his arm around me. "What is it that they call you? The boss lady? Okay, boss lady, you try. But I need one *leetle* favor."

"Any *leetle* favor, Fran. Just ask."

The favor was simple. I was to pick up the mail and some more frozen breast milk at their house in San Francisco. Easy to do, and the drive would give me time to think.

I left our mountain hideout at around 7:00 a.m. and got to San Francisco at noon. Martha Bittner, their lawyer, the one I'd met at that fateful baby shower, opened the door and threw her arms around me. "Oh my God, what a nightmare." She ran through all she had done in Mike and Francois's absence: contacted the furnace people, who'd checked everything out; gotten the alarm company to set up a system with a panic button that would go straight to the police. "What else?" she asked. "Oh, here." She handed me a pile of mail in a plastic bag, the mail Francois had requested I get, in addition to the containers of frozen breast milk from that company Mother's Is Best. They were running out, and Mike wouldn't even hear of formula.

Martha headed into the kitchen and spooned coffee into the filter. "This whole situation requires copious amounts of caffeine washed back with wine. You want some?"

"Sure," I said, opening the freezer, where I found around a hundred plastic bags filled with milk.

"They fit right into the bottles," Martha told me. "Next thing you know, rich parents will be hiring wet nurses. Skip the whole bottle business. That's what income inequality looks like—the seventeenth century." She poured me a big mug of coffee and led me back to the living room. "Put your feet up," she said. "Mike's going to have to lighten up. Helicopter parenting is one thing; he's practically a B-52 bomber, ready to obliterate any problem in Mei-Lin's path."

"You should have seen his reaction when I suggested baby formula."

"I can only imagine. Did he give you his whole spiel about high-fructose corn syrup?"

"Yeah, it's poison, plus everything horrible about Nestlé that he could remember, which was quite a bit. Anyway, Fran wanted his mail. Work, he told me, but I'm afraid it's visa applications for Mike and Mei-Lin. He says he wants to move back to Paris."

"Did he? I'm not surprised." She sipped the coffee. "He does that about every two months."

"Really?" I was almost giddy with relief.

"Yeah. If the foie gras in some fancy restaurant in San Francisco is not up to his standards, he wants to move back to France. If the wine on a tour up in Napa is too jammy, bam! Time to go back to France. If some vulgar American at a party has the temerity to ask what he does for a living, something you would never do in France—*mon Dieu*, so rude—time to move to Paris. He'll get over it. He always does. Although this whole attempted-murder thing puts leaving the country in a new light."

My spirits, which had been lifted so swiftly, sank once more. Martha was right. This was different. This just might drive them away.

"You have any ideas about what to do?" she asked.

As a matter of fact, I did. I'd had hours to think about it during the drive up 280. "Do you know any PIs? People who do family law usually do."

"Sure. I use them—divorces, parents with teens who have drug problems. Why?"

"I need someone to do some footwork. I could talk to the SFPD, and they'd add my request to the pile. You know how long that would take."

"Right—lifetimes." Martha nodded.

"I think the perp who attempted to kill Mike and Fran tried the same thing in Berkeley." Martha started to ask a question, but I held up my hand to stop her. "Long story—let's save it for later—but the Berkeley police have a picture of the guy, and Mike's neighbor has a picture of the guy, so thank God for nosy neighbors. I'm sure the man in both photos is one and the same. Like I said, long story."

Martha got up, retrieved the coffeepot from the kitchen, and refilled our cups. "You want to illuminate me on why someone would want to get Mike, Fran, and Mei-Lin out of the way?"

"Well, because even if Mike and Fran's adoption papers look legal, someone knows they're onto a human-trafficking ring."

"The baby trade. Jesus. I thought those guys were smarter than that."

"Can your PI also get surveillance pictures from a garage on Sansome Street?"

"I can't see why not, if they're there."

"If they are, we go to the cops. Until then, Mike and Fran stay with me."

"Wait. Paris versus Del Rio—let me think."

"Yeah, well, I have a dog, a gun, and a good friend who's a cop."

Martha patted my knee. "Well, aren't you a regular little Annie Oakley?" She paused, got up, and looked out at the bay from the sliding glass doors. "Don't you ever miss it?"

"Miss what?"

"San Francisco. I mean, you're down there in the hinterland. How do you do it?"

"I had a plan, but it didn't work out. I was going to run for my brother-in-law's state senate seat. He died, and now my sister is campaigning in his place. She will win."

"You can't fight her?"

"It's not a priority anymore. I have to help Mike."

"I hear your farm is worth a fortune. Why don't you sell and invest the money, and you can all move to Paris? I'll join you."

"I can't just sell. You know who's buying in the valley? The Saudis. They plant almonds or alfalfa and then ship the crops back to the mother country. Somehow, selling the Central Valley's precious water, which is what I'd be doing, goes against my principles."

"Uh-oh." Martha turned away from the view.

"Uh-oh what?"

"You're a do-gooder, just like your twin brother. That's a dangerous thing to be."

I finished up my coffee and checked my phone. Mary Yee had texted a list of things Mike wanted. Since they didn't have cell phone service up in the mountains, she'd contacted me from home. "Martha, check this out," I said, as she put the plastic containers in a cooler with dry ice. "Mike wants Mei-Lin's music box, the one that plays Mozart." We grabbed a paper bag from under the kitchen sink and headed into the nursery, where we pulled the cords on several music boxes until we heard the tinny, version of Eine Kleine Nachtmusik coming from one.

Martha hummed along and then said, "He thinks Mozart will help her math skills. Seriously, I hope they're saving up for this kid's therapy."

I dropped the music box into the bag, along with a stuffed dog, a rattle, and a really soft blanket. Then I grabbed some onesies from the drawer, just in case. Martha stood at the closet. "Would you look at this?" She held up a tiny, sparkly dress. "Adorable. Einstein plus prom queen. But hey, no pressure."

I laughed, gave her a hug, and said I'd talk to Mike, tell him he needed to throttle back the helicopter stuff.

Martha said not to bother. They had enough on their plates, and she was only half serious anyway. "They really are the most loving parents. Mei-Lin is a lucky little girl."

—

Vato bolted out the door, barking and leaping, as soon as I opened it, running joyous circles around me as I carried the cooler into the house and went back for the bags of mail and baby things. I dropped everything on the counter, put the milk in the freezer, and grabbed a beer. Vato and I headed out to the backyard, where he did his ranch-dog work, chasing ground squirrels, digging up their warrens. I'd let him run it off. He'd been inside all day, and it was dark by the time I finally got him into the house by using the magic power of a can opener.

It was getting dark sooner these days, I realized, standing at the door, calling Vato, banging the can with a fork. Maybe it was the cooler air, maybe the weekend in the mountains, maybe Martha Bittner's sense of humor, maybe knowing Mike and Fran and the baby were safe, but I was starting to think we were all going to survive this. Mia would win the election, and Fran was right about the fake-news line—she would figure we couldn't really hurt her. Garza might very well deal with Bud and whoever was employing him. I hated to be so coldhearted, but I was a ranch girl. I shot rattlesnakes before they bit the dogs, blew ground squirrels away before they ruined my garden. Bud was on the bottom level of the bardo, or whatever it was—the great chain of being. Low.

In my mind, I ran through all the things I had to do the next day—gypsy camp, work, drive to the mountains—and began getting ready. I grabbed Mei-Lin's things and the mail, thinking the best idea was just to put them in the trunk. That way, I wouldn't forget them in the morning rush. I put the letters one by one in Mei-Lin's bag, and I did feel like I was snooping, looking through the mail, which I was, hoping not to see anything from the French consulate or wherever people went for visas. There were a few thick letters from ATS. I hoped they weren't transferring him. As I slipped the envelopes into the bag, one return address caught my eye. It read, "ATTN: Nigel Wilson." I looked at the postage date. It had been mailed two weeks earlier, from Hong Kong. I took a screenshot—it was something Garza might be interested in—and then I wrestled with myself about opening it, until I gave in.

Pictures. More blackmail, I guessed. I took a closer look. The first photo was of a parking garage, address visible. Sansome Street. I sat down at the kitchen table, feeling weak, dizzy. My ears started to ring. There were images of Mia, and Sam McCall, standing next to a U-Haul van with no windows, and, of course, Bud Delano. There was one of people, some of them children, being led out of that van. I tried to get a shot of the license plate and succeeded. I had them now. This was pure gold.

There was a third and final picture: a man getting out of the van with the trafficking victims. I looked and looked again. I started to shake. I was going to be sick.

Alberto. The man was Alberto Rodriguez.

My heart started pounding, beating out the facts. Alberto knew where Mike and Fran and Mei-Lin were. He knew the alarm code for the gate. He knew everything.

I went upstairs, got the gun from next to my bed, walked out in the black night, started my car. The only plan I had was to get to the mountains, get my family to safety. The gun lay in my bag like a time bomb. If Alberto was there and I needed to use it, so be it. And if he wasn't, which was my fervent hope, we'd be long gone by morning.

19

CALLIE

I pressed my foot hard on the gas pedal and raced up Highway 180 into the foothills, my headlights swiping the dry, overgrazed grass and the stalks of desiccated sunflowers lining the road. Every so often, I glanced at the speedometer; by now, the needle was wavering on seventy-five, twenty miles over the limit. I could push it another five miles per hour, more or less safely, I figured, and stepped harder on the pedal, swerving right, then left, rushing past the dormant buckeye and blue oak, looming skeletal in the headlights. At a half-boarded-up summer community, I found a mini-mart with a neon sign saying PUMPS OPEN ALL NITE, pulled over, filled up, and did what I should have done before I left the valley: called Berto's cell phone. It was too late to call the house landline. Rosie turned off the ringer once the kids were in bed. Needless to say, when I got his voice mail, I didn't leave a message. True, they could be watching a movie, they could be in bed—or he could be up at the cabin.

Doing what, Callie? I asked myself, as I lifted the nozzle and twisted the gas tank cap. What was it I was afraid of? That he was there to finish the job Bud Delano had failed to do in San Francisco when he'd tried to kill Mike, Fran, and the baby by tampering with their furnace. But "afraid" was not the word I was searching for, was not the feeling that made me squeeze the nozzle trigger hard just to keep my hands from shaking, my arms, my whole body. The fuel hummed from the pump, and I tried to merge three images in my head: Berto was an old friend, he'd been one of Fletcher's victims, and he was a child-trafficking criminal capable of anything. The latter eclipsed everything else, and I couldn't see past it. Panic tunneled my vision—everything looked like a long, dark passageway I had to crawl through—and whatever my friendship with Berto had meant up to that point, I knew I could not count on it now. He had gone dirty, as cops say, and his first priority would be to save himself, not my brother, Francois, and the baby. Or me.

I slid into the car, opened my bag, lifted the gun, unfastened the safety, and set it on the passenger seat. In less than two seconds, I'd be able to grab it and shoot, and that was all the security I was going to have. *Pull the trigger, Callie; think later.* Taking a few deep breaths, I started the car and drove up the road into the dark mountains, toward the ponderosa pines, half of them destroyed by beetle kill, the other half huge and foreboding in the moonless night. A wave of nausea swept over me, but I couldn't stop, I couldn't turn back. I had gotten my brother into this nightmare, and I had no choice but to battle whatever waited ahead and get him out.

Past the sign that said ELEVATION: 6,650 FT., I knew I was getting close. I slowed and found Mary's gate. It was closed. Maybe that was a good sign, maybe not a sign at all. Berto knew the code, after all. I'd given it to him. As soon as I found some roadside parking, I turned around and retraced my path, this time cutting the headlights off so no one would notice my car if they were pulling out of the gate. I turned into Mary's drive and shut off the overhead light so it wouldn't go on when I got out of the car, grabbed my gun and my bag.

I didn't want to use the light from my cell phone to see the gate code keypad, nothing that might call attention to me, so it took me a few tries to punch in the right numbers. Eventually, I hit on the combination and the gate creaked open, a sound so loud, it was almost a shriek. I ducked into a clump of wild azalea in case anyone heard and decided to investigate, reminding myself that the temperature up here at night was too cold for rattlesnakes to be hunting. Still, I listened for the telltale buzz, relieved when there was nothing, not a rattlesnake, not footsteps. Hunkered down there, I waited until my eyes adjusted to the blackness around me. Finally, certain no one was coming, I stood and followed the dirt driveway's gray path, with only starlight to guide me. *So many stars*, I thought, looking up, as if some wild beast had clawed and punctured the inky-black roof of the sky.

A bat whooshed by, and I jumped. The night seemed suddenly full of sound, distant owls, animal movement in the grass—a brown bear, maybe, pulling on a tree branch, or a deer running, since it was breeding season. I kept the gun pointed in front of me, both hands locked around it, and I was so absorbed in the night sounds, in watching my footsteps along the road in the tin-colored starlight, that when I came upon the cabin, I was surprised by the bright warmth coming from the windows, by their orange, homey glow. Only a second or so later, I saw what I'd known I'd find all along: Alberto's white truck, parked in the shadows, huge and threatening, like a tumor the doctor points out on a light board. I headed toward it without much of a plan. *Shoot first, think later.* And then I saw the other vehicle parked on the right side of the cabin, a black SUV. There was someone else there. One woman and one gun were not going to do this job. I would have to bring in the police, which meant going to Grant Grove, where there was cell reception. And how long would it take to get someone up here? I crouched along the side of the SUV; backed around it, still in a crouch; and headed to the road, staying down until I was out of sight of the cabin. Then I started jogging to the car, the blood rushing through my ears so fast I hardly heard the owls, the deer, the bears.

Or the footsteps behind me.

A huge body grabbed me, its hands covering my mouth and nose. "Gotcha," the voice hissed, its hot breath the last thing I remembered before something hit my head, before a searing pain kicked my knees out from under me, before everything went blurry and was gone.

When I came to, I was on the floor, facedown. In front of me, under the table, I saw several Scrabble tiles. *That explains it*, I thought. I'd fallen out of my chair. It was Saturday; I'd challenged Mike to a game. I'd just racked up a triple word score using the letters "XYLO" next to the word "phone." How had I dropped them? Somewhere, I heard a dog wailing. Was it Vato? No, not a dog, but something was howling, some terrified animal. The rug smelled like old, wet sweater, dirty shoes, dust. I wanted to get up, but there was this weight on my back.

"See what happens when you get nosy, Callie?"

A familiar voice, one that made my skin crawl, but whose? All I wanted to do was sleep, but I needed to stay awake, needed to know who was talking to me, what he was going to do. I forced my eyes open, looked at the Scrabble tiles, tried to spell "xylophone."

"Get her up, Rodriguez," the voice said. Berto's hands went under my waist and pulled me up. I got only a brief glimpse of his face, his expression like one of those Aztec death masks, like a man whose soul had already left his body. Then he spun me around and I was staring into the face of a monster, a giant snake, its head swaying back and forth, ready to strike. I tried to scream, but I couldn't. I had no voice. Finally, the monster spoke. "You look like shit," he said. Sam McCall came into focus, his eyes as reptilian as I had pictured. He pointed my own gun at me. "Till death do us part, Callie. I guess this is the way it has to be. Throw her on the sofa, Rodriguez, and somebody shut that goddamn brat the fuck up," he yelled up the stairs. "Delano!" I heard footsteps pounding down the wooden risers.

"Cuff her like you did the other two, Rodriguez. Don't just stand there," Bud Delano said, not looking at me before he turned and ran back up the stairs.

Berto pulled a PlastiCuff from his back pocket and tied up my wrists. "You bastard," I whispered. He looked at the window above my head as if I weren't really there, his eyes as flat and black as the glass. But he was sweating; I could smell him. He was scared. It was me or him now. Not a chance I would win that round. McCall was certain to kill me. "Where's Mike? Where's my brother?" No one answered. Oh my God, I couldn't breathe. They were already dead. The room started to spin again, but then I heard Mike scream the word "no." A long, low, howling vowel. He was alive. "Mike," I yelled. "Mike!" But he just kept screaming. Then I heard Bud's footsteps again. He was carrying the baby car seat.

"We're late," Delano said. "This bitch cost us some time. Berto, do your job. McCall, the transport at the Flying J is going to be waiting for the cargo that's going to Arkansas. I gotta go now. I'm throwing this one in with the rest that I'm taking to Frisco. Mia says she's reselling the brat. She got another fifty-G bid for it. You and Rodriguez follow. Just get rid of her and the other two." The door slammed, his truck revved, the tires ground into the dirt, and then his engine's whine disappeared into the night.

I heard no sound for a long time besides my own rapid breathing. Eventually, the refrigerator started up with a whir and Sam's chair scraped the floor when he stood. I stared at the Scrabble tiles again, at the board still on the table, remembering how happy we had been, how safe we had felt in this fairy-tale cabin in the woods, like clumsy bears welcomed out of the storm, and how, like the ungainly bears, we had thought would be restored to our princely and powerful selves. I could feel the wet tears streaming down my face. I did not want to die.

"Do what we paid you to do, Rodriguez. We're running out of

time. I'll be outside." Sam didn't even look at me as he walked to the door.

I heard Berto unholster his weapon, saw his reflection in the window, the gun raised, aimed at my temple. I closed my eyes. "The Lord is my shepherd," I mumbled, and waited.

Soon enough would come the explosion, the head-shattering sound. Soon enough, there would be nothing.

20

CALLIE

A blast erupted. My head jerked back and my eyes flew open, and when they did, I saw McCall sprawled on the floor in front of me, blood oozing from underneath him, as if he had fallen and overturned a bucket of paint. I smelled the rusty, meaty odor of blood and something else, like shit. I was not sure what had happened, just that McCall was dead, and the sound from the gun still echoed in my ears, and Berto was cutting the PlastiCuffs off me. I remembered seconds earlier, over my prayers, having heard Berto's voice saying, "Wait, McCall. You've got her gun. You do it. She's all yours." Then the blast, the thud of a body. A body that was not mine. No, I was still alive, sitting in a pool of water, slowly realizing that I was saved and also that I'd pissed all over myself.

"Stay there!" Berto screamed at me. "Don't touch anything." He turned and ran up the stairs, and I could hear Mike screaming, "Where's my baby?" over and over as Berto led him down, Francois following.

"Get up!" Berto yelled at me again. "Get in the truck!"

"I'm not going anywhere with you!" Mike shouted.

"Get in the fucking truck, *cabron*, before they send your girl to God knows where."

"How much time do we have?" I asked, coming to my senses.

Berto tapped his phone. "They're supposed to move the cargo," he said, waving his hand frantically. "The kids, the girls, the labor for the chicken plants, all of them—whatever they got. The shipment's going out at two a.m. We have one hour."

I held out my hand. "Give me the keys, Berto. Give me your gun. No one trusts you. No one is going anywhere with you, like Mike said."

Berto dropped his keys into my palm, turned over his gun. "What the fuck ever. Please, I am begging you to get in the truck."

I kept the gun aimed on him as Francois helped Mike into the backseat, kept it aimed on him as he got in the passenger seat and fastened the seat belt, and then I climbed in and started the engine. "Where are we going, you son of a bitch?"

"Mandarina." He gave me the address. "The stash house those undercover guys told you about. It's a transit point. Hurry, Callie. We got less than an hour now They're waiting for McCall and me, but they won't wait forever. Drive this motherfucker like you stole it."

Past the boarded-up town, Rodriguez checked his cell service, and once he determined he had it, he was barking orders, punching in more numbers, and then shouting at Karkanian, saying "get the tactical guys," saying "a bunch of kids," saying "U-Haul panel truck" and "license number ZAH-something." "Zero two hours," he yelled. "But tell the tacticals I'm going in first."

I caught Mike's eyes in the rearview mirror, tears streaming down his face, felt his hands gripping the back of the seat, shaking it wildly. "We'll get her, Mike, I promise."

"How much time now?" I asked. We were dropping down a thousand feet toward the valley floor, toward its clusters of lights, the wide, white splash of the Walmart distribution center's sodium lamps. I told myself, *This is what hell must look like as you fall.*

"Thirty-five minutes," Berto said. "Take Valley Hills Road. It's coming up in about ten minutes, goes off to the left. It's a shortcut."

"Guess you traffickers know all the back roads, right, Berto?"

He rolled down the window, turned his face to the wind, and then rolled it up again. "Okay, what happened back there was self-defense, just so we're all clear. McCall turned around, pointed his gun at me. I'm a cop, trained to shoot when that happens. That's how it went down."

"You're telling me how it went down? Anything else I ought to know from a dirty cop before I bring charges and send your ass to San Quentin, you lying piece of shit?" I was screaming. "You brought them to the cabin. What the fuck?"

"What's your version, Callie? It was your gun. Had your prints all over it. You're lucky I got him to turn around, or else someone could say you shot a defenseless man in the back." He punched the side of the door. "Ain't nobody got time for this. Drive faster."

I stepped on the gas, the headlights blasting a path into the horrible darkness in front of me.

"There's a turnoff. See the green sign? It's sharp, so go slow, and then it's curvy. In about two, three miles, the road straightens. When it does, you let this thing fly right to Orange Grove. And no, Callie, I didn't bring McCall into this—you did. You married him. Why'd you do a dumbass thing like that? He married up. What did you do?"

Berto was right. Sam was the son of a bus driver. He used to ridicule his dad, said his old man thought he really had it made when he got promoted to driving the Geary bus. Up and down the same street every damn day. Sam swore he was going to be somebody. He used to say "by any means necessary." I thought it was a joke. It wasn't. He wanted to get to Fletcher, get close to the movers and the shakers, he used to say, close to power. Jim Fletcher wouldn't have given a social climber like Sam the time of day without his being family. I was the "any means necessary."

Berto wasn't done. "Then you came down here like you were some savior, going to show all the rubes and brown folks how to live, right? You don't know shit about what it takes to survive here, Callie. You were *la princesa* in your father's castle. We were the ones who knew things, knew what needed to be done, what could be done to us if we didn't play the game. So you can get off your pedestal. I shot a man in self-defense, and I saved your fucking life. No one in town will doubt me. They know your family, and all that shit is going to run downhill on you."

We were getting close to Mandarina. I was shaking so hard I could barely hold on to the wheel. We'd come to the straightaway, and I was pushing ninety miles per hour. *Please, God, don't let there be a stray cow, a fallen board, on the road.* But what hit just as hard was what Berto was saying. It was true. I'd come down here intending to plunder this place to get what I wanted just as ruthlessly as any grower. It had been all about me, hadn't it? Until now. Now, it was about us. How we were going to live through the next hour, and all the rest of our hours, together.

Just then, the sign ENTERING MANDARINA COUNTY appeared in the windshield. "What now?"

"Pull over into the school parking lot and let me drive. They're expecting me. All of you get down and stay down. When we get there, I'm going in. The guys stay hidden, but, Callie, I'll need you."

I did what he said, pulled over at the high school, put the car in park, waited for Berto to get out of the truck. He didn't move.

"I was one of those kids. Fletcher's kids. Fourteen. At first I thought he was joking when he said what he wanted to do." He passed his hands over his face. "Sex things guys do to each other."

I kept quiet, didn't let him know that Rosie had told me about Fletcher abusing him and that his confession wasn't news to me. He needed to get this off his chest. I looked at Mike in the backseat, but he didn't seem to be listening. He was past that. His expression was just one of frozen horror and pain.

Berto continued, "His family, him, well, they were like kings or gods to us Mexicans back then. What did I know? You think my parents talked to me about blow jobs and guys doing stuff to guys? They didn't even talk about guys doing stuff to girls. Anyway, I didn't stop him the first time, and after that he told me he would tell all my friends it was my idea, that I was a *maricon*. I was a fourteen-year-old kid, and I would rather have died than let that get spread around town. It went on for two years like that. Somehow, my dad found out, nearly killed him, and sent me away, was happy when I knocked up some village girl, happy I was *todo normal*. He was even happier when he heard the baby was a boy, that I'd had a son named Guillermo, like it was just another sign of my masculinity. So I figured Fletcher owed me. That's what I told him. That's what happens when a stupid guy thinks he's smart. But he let me know how disposable I was. Just the son of a wetback. Hell, I had Rosie and the kids to think about. Asked me if I wouldn't rather be a rich man than a dead man. Said he'd make it worth my while." He turned to face me. "Look, at first I thought it was just your basic labor-contracting fraud. And then when the kids started coming in, Fletcher told me they were going to some Christian charity to be adopted out to rich families, that it was all good. But I knew if Rosie found out what I was doing and that I had gone along with Fletcher for the money, she would hate me if I didn't fix this. She would hate me for thinking that being desperate for money was some kind of excuse for being a child-trafficking piece of shit. She wouldn't stay married to me, Callie. If I wanted to keep my family, I was going to have to do something to make things right. It wasn't enough just to go to confession or pray." Berto rubbed his hands hard against his face. "I thought when Fletcher was gone I'd be free, but . . ." His voice drifted off, and then he opened the door and got out of the car, and we switched sides.

—

Berto drove to the stash house, made a call to Karkanian, told him to give him ten minutes and then come in like the wrath of God—lights, sirens, everything. He looked down at me where I was crouched next to the passenger seat. "There's a .357 in the glove compartment. I'm going in there; I'll tell Mia Sam's still up at the cabin, that he's wounded and I had to leave him. They'll be in a hurry, so they won't have time for a big explanation. I'm going to give that Bud dude time to get the kids out of the cellar. That's where you come in." He told me what I had to do. "Go around to the back and wait for Bud to put the kids in the van. After that, you're on your own. Do what you need to do, but that truck doesn't leave the drive."

"Why don't you just have the tactical team charge in?"

"Why? Because there's a crap ton of gasoline in open containers in that cellar. All Bud has to do is throw a match, and those kids are ghosts. That's their plan after this goes down: just burn the place to the ground. Got it? It's up to you to stop that from happening. Now, take the gun and get out."

I ran, ducking behind the few cars parked on the side of the road, for about half a block and then circled back, watched as Berto knocked on the door, as Mia opened it. I had a few seconds while they digested whatever Berto told them, and I ran for it, diving under an oleander bush. I undid the Magnum's safety and waited, trying to stop my violent shaking. I had to get a grip. I conjured up an image of Mei-Lin and Mike, and a bolt of rage steadied my hand.

Just as Berto had said, Bud came out of the back door with a flashlight, lifted the wooden doors to the root cellar, and disappeared down the steps. I took my chance and ran to the side of the truck opposite the root-cellar door, flattened myself on the dirt and gravel.

Soon I heard shuffling, heard Bud bark, "*Apurense, cabrones*"— hurry up, bastards—saw small brown feet, some of them in worn rubber sandals, saw the white box of Mei-Lin's car seat. She should be crying. What had they done to her? But I couldn't think about that now.

The neighbors would just chalk up the fire to another meth lab, Mia would say how hard it was to find good tenants, and the cops wouldn't sift through the debris for pieces of bone, believe me. All you had to do was be rich and white, and everyone took your word for things. Well, not anymore, *cabrones*. The truck wobbled as the kids climbed in. I moved around to the front of it, crouched behind the left tire, and waited.

The truck door slammed, and Bud's heavy boots pounded toward the driver's side. *Now,* I told myself. *Now.*

I jumped up. "You sick fuck!" I screamed into Bud's startled face, and the gun went right into his carotid artery, just as I'd planned. I didn't even hear it go off, though there must have been a blast. I felt the gun kick and jumped to the left just in time. Bud fell toward me, blood gushing from his neck like a hydrant.

The sirens were blaring now, filling up the night with their high-pitched wails, and the squad cars' blue lights flashed like strobes, swirling in the darkness around me. I ran to the truck and climbed in, all the kids screaming, their little mouths shaped in terrified circles, as they watched a blood-covered *gringa* grab the car seat, back out of the truck with a baby, and run.

21

CALLIE

About a month after I got out of the hospital and after I recovered from what turned out to be a pretty serious head wound from where Bud had clobbered me, I launched my campaign for the state senate at a kickoff held in the Del Rio High School gym. It was a big event. Well, big for Del Rio. The school put up my name in large black letters on the marquee where the football game was usually advertised; someone's American history class spent the afternoon hanging red, white, and blue streamers; and the Del Rio newspaper gave a couple of journalism students laminated cards bearing the word PRESS on lanyards to wear around their necks. It even paid them to cover my campaign event. The owner of the Main Street Café lent us a big urn for coffee, some local Mennonite women supplied the cookies, and the Flor de Morelia Bakery made seventy-five sweet and savory tamales. So, yeah, pretty much, it was a Del Rio gala.

Mia was no longer running for office. She had really fallen off the face of the earth, as far as the media was concerned, and after a few short news articles, which didn't even mention Bud Delano or Sam McCall, the whole thing evaporated. It wasn't like the *LA Times* or the *San Francisco Chronicle* really cared about what happened down here in what Martha Bittner had called the hinterland.

In the end, Mia had simply followed the advice of an expensive and famous California attorney who had skillfully used the abused-wife defense, which tended to work well in the cases of rich white women. Others, not so much. She convinced the judge that she knew nothing, was found not guilty, and then headed off to Betty Ford for her drinking problem, leaving Berto out of the story. He'd paid his dues, as far as I was concerned, and if Mia could get off, Berto should get a Purple freaking Heart. Needless to say, he was relieved that his name didn't get mentioned in connection with the trafficking. Still, he said Mia's story was unbelievable bullshit. "She knew everything Sam McCall was doing." Rosie just rolled her eyes. "*Se acabo*," she said. It's over.

As a state senate candidate, I now had no serious competition, just some Orange County carpetbagger the conservatives put up to keep a seat warm in the state assembly. He could forget it. I was a local hero, no longer known around town as DA McBitch, or if I was, it was meant in a good way. After all the bad press, the town needed a celebration, and I hoped to give it one.

I remembered very little at first about what had happened after I'd grabbed Mei-Lin's car seat and raced toward the police, shouting, "I've got her. She's safe." Only that Mike ran toward me and took the car seat out of my hands just before I dropped to my knees in the middle of the road, unable to go any farther. I remembered an ambulance ride, sirens fading in and out of my consciousness, an oxygen mask over my face, the bright lights of the emergency room, the gurney speeding down the hall. Recently, more memories had begun to come back to me every day, and I was flooded with both terror and relief each time one surfaced.

"*Tuviste mucho suerte*," Rosie told me in the hospital. I was lucky that Berto had been there and that, *gracias a Dios*, he'd had a bad feeling that night and decided to check on Mike in the cabin. I left it at that, because I *had* been lucky, after all, and didn't want to push it.

I had a friend who was willing to get rid of my enemy to keep me and my family safe. How many people can say that? Whatever else he'd done before he shot Sam McCall was so much water under the bridge, as far as I was concerned.

Sometimes at night in the hospital, I would wake, disoriented, screaming, the room dark, and be back on the floor in the cabin with Sam's foot on my spine, ready to crack it. Then a young nurse would appear, swab my face with a cloth, insert something into my IV, and hold my hand until the drug took effect and I was safe, floating in some kind of golden ether. So many angels of mercy in the world, in spite of the Fletchers, the Sam McCalls, the Bud Delanos.

Recently, I was starting to remember my visitors, too—Mary and Nathan bringing flowers, telling me I was famous. "Not just Del Rio famous, Callie," Mary said, showing me the *San Francisco Chronicle*, the *LA Times*. "California famous." I knew the attention wouldn't last long, but it was nice while it did.

Nathan pulled his chair close to my bed and told me that, in a way, I'd saved his life, as well as the life of those kids. "I'd been barely hanging on," he said, "but now I'm going to be taking over my family's vineyards, dry-farm the grapes down here. Watch me raise the minimum wage for farmworkers, too, Callie, because that's what I plan to do. It's a whole new beginning." I saw Mary put her hand on his shoulder. "We'll be a great team," she said, "the three of us. You'll be helping us in Sacramento, Nathan's going to turn us into the next Napa—okay, maybe Lodi, but still—and I'm going to get everyone to ban pesticides with your help in the assembly. Paradise on Earth, right?"

I lay back on the pillow and felt love all around me, like the first orange blossoms scenting the air in May. Corny, right? But I was on drugs, and the two of them were beaming.

Even Chief Karkanian showed up, bringing a bunch of store-bought mums wrapped in cellophane, saying, "I got the damn attorney general's office calling thanks to you, McCall." In spite of trying to appear unimpressed with any phone call from Sacramento, he couldn't hide that he was proud of me. He shifted in his seat, the plastic rattling around the flower stems, and gossiped for a while about how the undercover guys couldn't stop talking about the city girl in high heels who'd taken out a trafficker. He asked me about Rodriguez, and I held my breath, wondering what he wanted to know. Berto had given notice. Had I heard? "Says he's got PTSD. He's going to work over at Dusty Barkin's big-ag PI firm. Truth is, they pay better, 401(k) and Delta Dental thrown in. Maybe I should get some doctor to say I've got a stress disorder," he joked, just as one of the nurses came in and gave him a sign. "They told me not to overstay my welcome." He got up and, hesitating for a minute in the doorway, nodded at me. "Just so you know, you got my vote, Callie. You'll do Del Rio proud."

In the emptiness of my hospital room later, I worried about that expectation, because, of course, I had it, too. *Would* I do Del Rio proud? How? Well, I would have to figure it out, I guessed, the way I'd figured out everything else.

They let me out after three days, and a week or so after that, I put Vato in the car and took a little drive past Fletcher Family Farms, which Nathan's family had picked up for a song, and over to the gypsy camp. I wanted to find out if Garza knew what had happened.

Just past the dying almond orchard where they'd set up their trailers, I slowed and had to do a double take. Everything was gone. Well, not everything. There were black plastic Hefty bags strewn around, some of them already broken into by dogs, coyotes, or raccoons. Tire tracks pressed down the dry grass, and I saw dirt-shaped rectangles, the dead areas where the trailers had parked. I walked over to where the *rom baro*'s trailer had been and kicked around in the dust, hoping to find something they'd left behind. No luck.

I doubted Zoning had gotten to them, because that office worked at a glacial pace. It could have simply been time for the gypsies, the travelers, to head south. The weather would soon start to turn colder at night, and the tule fog would settle in the valley in the mornings. I'd drive over to Ajit's mini-mart later and ask when he'd last seen the gypsies, but I couldn't stop the feeling that their recent departure had something to do with *el evento*, which was what Rosie called that horrible night in the cabin. I wondered if Garza had told the *rom baro* his work here was done. Or maybe it was just a coincidence.

I looked up, and above me, thirty thousand feet in the air, a northbound jet's contrails marked the sky with a chalky white line. I figured all the passengers had probably opened their laptops and were looking at their screens by now. But if any of them had left their shade open, had pushed their forehead against the window, they would be looking down on the forgotten part of California, the great Central Valley, a huge, flat patchwork of plowed dirt, fruit and nut trees, dairy farms and raisin vines, alfalfa and cotton, that stretched for 450 miles, roughly the same distance as from Miami to South Carolina, a quarter of the eastern seaboard. What once had been a vast inland sea until massive shifts, earthquakes, created the great rivers—the Kings, the Kaweah, the Merced, and the San Joaquin—was now a valley lined with wide concrete canals, the rivers dammed up, their water pumped south to Los Angeles.

Around the small town of Wasco, just east of the Grapevine, one grower's huge holdings of almonds and pomegranates, 180,000 acres, used almost as much water in a day as the city of Los Angeles. To the passenger on his way north, what might have looked like boring farmland was anything but. The valley was a battlefield and had been ever since the arrival of the white man. To the victor belonged the water and the profits.

It had been said that when the Yokuts roamed this part of California, it was possible to traverse the whole length of the valley on a network of inland waterways, and that Native women fished in lakes and vernal pools by simply scooping the fish out of the water, using the reed baskets they made from rushes growing on the riverbanks. Herons and geese once filled the sky, and herds of tule elk grazed in the endless grassland. All that was gone now. Tulare Lake, in the south, was drained to grow cotton, the cotton sprayed with Paraquat, the vast herds of elk hunted to extinction.

I shook myself and began to call for Vato, who'd taken off running once he'd been released from the car. Last I'd seen him, he'd been heading through the almond grove in the same direction the two gypsy girls had gone that evening not so many days earlier, though it felt like a lifetime ago. I followed his path into the trees, calling and getting more alarmed when he didn't come. Finally, I spotted him a few yards from where I was. "Come on," I called. "Come on, Vato." But he wouldn't move. He pawed at the ground and then rolled in the dirt, stood up, and pawed the ground again. As I got closer, I heard him whimpering. I stopped in my tracks and held my breath. Vato was no cadaver dog, but all dogs, and ranch dogs especially, could smell a dead animal, a dead anything, and that was what he was acting like. I didn't need to wonder what he'd found. In all likelihood, it was José Guzmán's original grave. Someone had carried part of the body to Fletcher's farm, someone who wanted Fletcher caught. I remembered saying something to Berto that day we'd been called to the scene, something about talking to the gypsies. I should have followed up on my hunch. But I wondered if the gypsies would have told me anything back then if I'd asked. Maybe I'd had to prove myself first. Maybe all of this had been part of my destiny and could not have happened any other way.

I walked over to Vato, who was pawing and whimpering even more. He'd managed to dig up something. At first glance, it looked like a bit of purple cloth, until I saw the silver medallions and the shape of a cross. Then I saw the decomposed body and turned away. The gypsies had probably buried it there on instructions from Garza.

I was just guessing, but it seemed the most logical explanation. Still, how had Garza found out? Eva or the *rom baro* or both. The cross was Eva's calling card. She knew about the body the same way Rosie knew things I didn't know. What had Rosie told me that first night I'd seen the pictures of Fletcher with the little boy in the casino in Macau? *All the Mexicans know about Fletcher.* There would be a look, a raised eyebrow, a cryptic comment from one picker to another amid the clanking of ladders in the groves, a whispered *"Has oido?* Have you heard?" And Eva, on some nighttime Flecha Amarilla bus that left from the parking lot of the Vallarta Market at midnight, the local cops paid to look the other way and not check for papers, would have carried the message south to Garza like the messenger of the gods bearing the wishes of mortals to Mount Olympus, setting off the chain of events that now shaped my life.

I supposed I would never know how they'd buried the body, or who had carried the arm to Fletcher's orange groves, or what ritual cleansing the gypsies had performed after dismembering the dead. Still, Eva or the *rom baro* must have been the ones who had called the dispatcher or seen to it that someone else had called on a burner phone later tossed into a canal. I was willing to bet my last nickel. What had she said the day at that terrible airstrip in Mexico? *Who knows what happens to these kids? They die of infection, dehydration. They collapse on the floor of some chicken factory in Arkansas, drop dead in the orange groves. They become a liability for the traffickers. They get hacked up, tossed in a Walmart Dumpster, buried in shallow graves if they're lucky.* Was this what we used for fertilizer? The lives of other human beings? Small children? It had to stop. *How can you not see what's going on around you?* she'd asked me. Well, I was blind no more.

I pulled out my phone and called Chief Karkanian. And then I waited.

In the end, the cadaver Vato found was not a boy's, not José

Guzmán's. The mutilated body belonged to a girl, about thirteen. It didn't bear thinking what had happened to her—raped, beaten, hacked to death. You get the picture. As far as I knew, José Guzmán had simply disappeared, like so many before him, swallowed up by the need for cheap labor all over the country—the meatpacking plants in Nebraska, the oil fields of the Dakotas. So much slaughter—the earth, the rivers, the animals, and the poor. What were the boy's chances? And, since I benefited from so many José Guzmáns' cheap labor, what did I owe them? Plenty. We all did.

A few days later, as Rosie, Berto, and I drove to the high school gym where I was to give my first campaign speech, I couldn't stop thinking about that debt I owed to the laborers and the small farmers, to the Okies and the immigrants, and to Rosie and Berto, who were now ferrying me to my campaign kickoff. I'd been too nervous to drive.

"I can't believe you're scared to talk to a bunch of farmers after everything you've been through." Rosie shook her head, turned around in the front seat, and blew me a kiss. "You're going to be fantastic. *No te preocupes.*"

It was one of the still, warm nights of early autumn, and as I moved through the overheated high school gym toward the make-shift stage, I heard a group of persimmon farmers saying they just hoped the weather would hold, that there wouldn't be some early freeze. I thought about all the fears and worries farmers had, and when I took a seat, I told myself Rosie was right. What did I really have to fear? These men had to farm; all I had to do tonight was talk.

Finally, the fire chief said we were at capacity, he was closing the door, and the local parish priest stood up and quieted the crowd. He led us in prayer and then asked that we stand for the Pledge of Allegiance. Next up was Chief Karkanian, who lumbered to the podium and spoke about Alberto Rodriguez's courage and mine and how the crowd ought to just listen to me—only he called me "the gal"—and give me a chance to say my piece. He pointed to Bill Veeman, who owned the local firearms store and was sporting his MAGA hat, and said, "That means you, Veeman. Nobody's taking your durn guns, and besides, she's a better shot than you'll ever be." It was the perfect warm-up—everyone laughed—and with that, he handed me the mic.

I started to speak, and the noise reverberated through the large hall. "Sorry," I said, holding the mic away from me, my hands still shaking. "There. That's better. I'll try that again." I laughed, grateful I'd found my trial-lawyer voice, relieved that my words weren't shrill and shaky. "I'm sure you all know the recent events that led to my standing up here." I saw heads nodding and shaking, because while the *Chronicle* and the *LA Times* might have forgotten the murder and the trafficked children, Del Rio hadn't and never would. "I'm not going to remind you of my family's history in the valley; some of the folks in this gym know it better than I do." That got a few laughs. "I'm going to go farther back into the past first, so we can make a leap into the future."

I painted the same picture that I'd conjured up while standing in the abandoned gypsy camp as the plane flew overhead: a picture of the valley a few hundred years ago; of the geese, the fish, the vernal pools. "Look," I said, "we've done incredible things by shaping the rivers to our will, by growing the huge amounts of crops we grow here, by feeding the nation and the world, but we've done great harm as well." I had only to mention the fate of the Westside farmers, whose oversalinated, overfertilized land was now as bare as the moon. "The Westside is a cautionary tale to all of us. It's a place good for only Superfund sites. I think it's safe to assume that's not what we want here in Del Rio." That got a few murmurs from the crowd. I wasn't sure they were all happy with where my speech was headed, but I soldiered on. "We can no longer brutalize the land, and we can no longer brutalize the people who work the land. We are going to have to change, but we're going to need help." I knew help from outside was often beneath a farmer's dignity, so I reassured them with the following: "It's not because we are weak in Del Rio; it's because we deserve better."

I rattled off my ideas about a Marshall Plan for the valley, heard the flimsy folding chairs creak as folks in the audience shifted in their seats, and I paused, watching, as they looked at each other, not sure they liked what they were hearing, even if it came from a native daughter, one who'd held her own family to account. It sounded liberal, sounded like environmental regulations and taxes. "God knows," I went on, "the life of a farmer is hard enough without more taxes and more regulations, but we're going to have to have some more of those if we don't want to end up being a place where the government dumps its toxic waste." A few people got up and left, a handful coughed, and I heard more murmurs, but I didn't stop there. "We have to have better enforcement of labor laws, and we have to stop brutalizing children, stop turning a blind eye to child labor. I know you, I grew up with you, and you and I are better than that." After what I'd just done, they would have a hard time arguing with me.

I was hitting my stride. I could feel it. "I want to end this speech tonight," I told my audience, "by quoting a great Central Valley farmer, César Chávez." I heard a gasp or two, even a few groans from the older farmers who had never forgiven him for the grape boycott and would carry their resentment to their graves. But we were a new generation, and the farmworkers had been on the right side of history. I looked at my notes, cleared my throat, and started to read Chavez's words: "We cannot seek achievement for ourselves and forget about progress and prosperity for our community. Our ambitions must be broad enough to include the aspirations and needs of others for their sake and for our own."

I stopped and waited, letting that sink in, because really, I was talking to myself as well. When I'd come up with my plan to run for state assembly, I'd been just as ready to exploit this place as others before me. I had changed, and others could, too.

The squirming stopped, and the gym filled with a deep silence. I was certain at that moment that I'd lost them to the Orange County carpetbagger, with his message of hate and greed. It took a minute for me to understand that the noise I was hearing was applause. A few people got up from their seats, and then a few more. I looked out at the now standing crowd, and I saw Karkanian and Mary Yee, Nathan and Berto and Rosie. I saw my father's old friends, one guy with an oxygen tank, his lungs shot from breathing in too much dust or from bouts of valley fever.

I felt almost dizzy, sensing the trust they were willing to extend to me and because of the huge responsibility I was asking to take on. Even though they were clapping, some calling out my name, I knew it was not about me. I was only a mirror for their better angels, and I had to deliver on their best hopes. I took a deep breath and glanced at the gym doors in the back. Was I thinking I could make a run for it? Maybe, but that was when I saw her, as if I'd conjured a woman from Mexico, from that terrible airstrip in the middle of the jungle, and she had appeared. Eva was leaning against the back wall, with a young boy by her side. Once she saw that I recognized her, she raised her chin in a subtle greeting, leaned over, and whispered something to the kid.

He listened, nodded, and, after a few seconds, lifted his arm and waved at me, flashing the bright beads on his Mexican bracelet as he did.

ACKNOWLEDGMENTS

I am so grateful to the brilliant, visionary team at She Writes Press: publisher Brooke Warner, project manager Shannon Green, and proofreader Elisabeth Kauffman. A million thanks for helping me bring *Del Rio* into the world. Your work on behalf of women writers is inspired, and I am honored to be a She Writes novelist.

I am thrilled with the cover Julie Metz, an incredibly talented cover designer, created for my book. Julie, thank you for capturing the feeling of *Del Rio* so perfectly in color and composition.

This book would not be what it is if it were not for my amazing book coach, developmental editor and copyeditor Annie Tucker. Annie, one of the most fortunate days of my life was when you agreed to take on this project. Our Monday afternoon editing sessions were the highlight of my week. I loved watching my draft take shape, my characters spring to life, and my plot and setting come into sharper focus and clarity under your insightful guidance. Thank you from the bottom of my heart. I will be eternally indebted.

To the organizers and teachers at the annual San Miguel Writers' Conference and Literary Festival—Director Susan Page, the outstanding writer and teacher David Corbett, and the agent April

Eberhardt, who first told me about She Writes Press and introduced me to the gifted Annie Tucker—my heartfelt thanks.

To all of the writers and organizers at Women's Fiction Writers Association: Your online friendship, support, and guidance has meant the world to me over the past five years. The annual WFWA retreat in Albuquerque was one of the best events of my year. I can't wait until we can gather again.

To my wonderful publicity team at BookSparks: Crystal Patriarche, CEO; Tabitha Bailey, Senior Publicist; Paige Herbert, Publicist. Thank you for supporting my book and my writing life.

To my marketing team at Caroff Communications—Michael, Jacqui, and Tara—thank you for helping this shy, introverted writer go out into the world. You've been fantastic.

A huge thanks to all the people who shared my ranch life with me for over a decade and a half. I am so grateful for your strength, sense of adventure, sense of humor, and commitment to the Sierras and to the Central Valley. To the Save Jesse Morrow Mountain team, the Monday night Lodge gatherers, the Friday afternoon book group, the Wednesday afternoon ladies of the mountain lunches (AKA the Pinkies), the Hole in the Sky Salon event attendees, the Saturday Wine Tasters, the Stone House Artist Residencies, the Kings Canyon Indivisibles, and the Woolsey Family—thank you for helping shape such an important part of my life.

Finally, to David and Anna, you are the loves of my life.

ABOUT THE AUTHOR

© Gabriella Marks

Jane Rosenthal studied creative writing at San Francisco State University. She worked for NPR and California Public Radio before teaching radio production and English in public high schools in Oakland, California. For fifteen years, before relocating to Santa Fe, New Mexico, Jane lived on a ranch in the Sierra Nevada mountains complete with horses and cattle, fulfilling her dream of being a western cowgirl. Now, she can be found exploring the many cultural offerings of her new home in New Mexico or traveling to her favorite *pueblos mágicos* in old Mexico when she's not in her office with a window overlooking the Georgia O'Keeffe landscape around her and writing those novels that have been kicking around in her head all these many years.

SELECTED TITLES FROM SHE WRITES PRESS

She Writes Press is an independent publishing company founded to serve women writers everywhere. Visit us at www.shewritespress.com.

Cut by Amy S. Peele 978-1-63152-184-3
Can you buy your way up to the top of the waiting list? In their quest to find out, transplant nurse Sarah Golden and her best friend, Jackie, end up on a sometimes fun, sometimes dangerous roller coaster ride through Miami, San Francisco, and Chicago—one from which they barely escape with their lives.

Glass Shatters by Michelle Meyers $16.95, 978-1-63152-018-1
Following the mysterious disappearance of his wife and daughter, scientist Charles Lang goes to desperate lengths to escape his past and reinvent himself.

The Tolling of Mercedes Bell by Jennifer Dwight $18.95, 978-1-63152-070-9
When she meets a magnetic lawyer at her work, recently widowed Mercedes Bell unwittingly drinks a noxious cocktail of grief, legal intrigue, desire, and deception—but when she realizes that her life and her daughter's safety hang in the balance, she is jolted into action.

True Stories at the Smoky View by Jill McCroskey Coupe
$16.95, 978-1-63152-051-8
The lives of a librarian and a ten-year-old boy are changed forever when they become stranded by a blizzard in a Tennessee motel and join forces in a very personal search for justice.

Water On the Moon by Jean P. Moore $16.95, 978-1-938314-61-2
When her home is destroyed in a freak accident, Lidia Raven, a divorced mother of two, is plunged into a mystery that involves her entire family.

The Wiregrass by Pam Webber $16.95, 978-1-63152-943-6
A story about a summer of discontent, change, and dangerous mysteries in a small Southern Wiregrass town.